# Jennifer – The Shackleford Legacies Book One

## Beverley Watts

BaR Publishing

# Contents

| | |
|---|---|
| Title Page | |
| Chapter One | 1 |
| Chapter Two | 10 |
| Chapter Three | 19 |
| Chapter Four | 27 |
| Chapter Five | 37 |
| Chapter Six | 45 |
| Chapter Seven | 53 |
| Chapter Eight | 64 |
| Chapter Nine | 74 |
| Chapter Ten | 82 |
| Chapter Eleven | 94 |
| Chapter Twelve | 105 |
| Chapter Thirteen | 113 |
| Chapter Fourteen | 121 |
| Chapter Fifteen | 133 |
| Chapter Sixteen | 143 |
| Chapter Seventeen | 152 |
| Chapter Eighteen | 162 |
| Chapter Nineteen | 171 |

| | |
|---|---|
| Chapter Twenty | 182 |
| Chapter Twenty-One | 191 |
| Chapter Twenty-Two | 201 |
| Chapter Twenty-Three | 210 |
| Chapter Twenty-Four | 218 |
| Author's Notes | 220 |
| Keeping in Touch | 223 |
| Claiming Victory | 224 |
| Books available on Amazon | 231 |
| About The Author | 233 |

# Chapter One

'In truth, I cannot see what the problem is.' Jennifer Sinclair put her hands on her hips and favoured her father with a frustrated glare. 'To stand in the way of progress simply because one dislikes change is quite simply preposterous.'

Such was her annoyance, that the fact she had dared speak so to her father concerning such an emotive subject in polite company went entirely over her head. Not to mention the fact that the person expressing such distaste was a fellow member of the Lords.

Unfortunately the scandalous indrawn breaths of those watching told another story altogether. Nicholas Sinclair gave an inward sigh, recognising that ever more exaggerated tales of his daughter's wilfulness would undoubtedly be circling around the *ton* within minutes of his guests' leave taking.

Knowing it was expected, his eyes turned wintery cold. Seeing their flinty depths, Jennifer flinched, finally realising her faux pas. His low, 'Go to your room, Jennifer,' was uttered in a tone she'd never heard from him before. Swallowing, she gave a low curtsy, bowed her head and hurried from the room.

As she ran up the stairs, she caught sight of Anthony's wife through the open door and couldn't help stifling a chuckle. Georgiana's horrified expression was a cross between concern for her friend and overwhelming relief that she hadn't been the one to make a cake of herself in public.

On entering her bedchamber, Jennifer seated herself on the window seat and waited for the summons that would inevitably come. She wasn't overly worried, although her father's steely expression didn't bode well. Still, he'd never yet tossed her over his knee, and she didn't think that at one and twenty, he was likely to start now. Lifting her feet up onto the seat, she hugged her raised knees.

Jennifer was well aware that she would have tried the patience of a saint over the last eighteen months. She was into her second London season and despite the surfeit of gentlemen vying for her attention, she'd yet to find one who so much as piqued her interest. Sighing, she rested her head on her knees. Her parents had promised not to force her into wedlock. But that didn't mean they would stand idly by while she blithely turned away suitor after suitor.

It wasn't that she didn't want to be married. The problem was, she wanted a marriage like the one her parents had. And most of the titled gentlemen she'd been introduced to were no more than unlocked cubs. So far up their own nether regions that they had no idea what to do with a woman who actually possessed opinions of her own. She knew that the offers were dwindling - despite her being the daughter of the powerful Duke of Blackmore. She'd even heard mutterings of, *'what does one expect of the offspring of a vicar's daughter.'*

And now, all she'd done with her outspokenness was make matters worse. For her father, her mother and most definitely herself. Groaning, she dropped her feet to the floor and went to ready herself for bed. Evidently the summons was being postponed until the morrow.

She thought back to her father's stony expression. Mayhap she did have cause to be worried after all…

∞∞∞

'I cannot allow her behaviour to go entirely unpunished,' Nicholas declared wearily after the last of their guests had departed. 'At the very least, she will have to return to Blackmore for the remainder of the season.'

'I know.' Grace gave a tired sigh of her own. 'In many ways, we only have ourselves to blame. She has grown up in an uncommon household. But Jennifer will never bow to a man, and in truth, I would not wish her to have to.'

'Then she will remain unwed,' Nicholas retorted.

'I have seven sisters who share the same characteristics as our daughter, and they have succeeded in finding men who value their independence,' Grace responded tartly.

'Well, naturally she gets her wayward traits from her aunts,' Nicholas countered drily, 'since her mother has always been the epitome of a dutiful wife.'

Grace chuckled. 'I may have been in awe of your bad temper when we first wed, but I soon realised you are eminently persuadable given the correct encouragement.'

'I'll have you know my temper is legendary amongst my peers.' Nicholas gave a low groan as his wife settled herself on his lap.

'They don't know you like I do,' she murmured, bending down to kiss him.

'My counsel is valued above most others.'

'Unquestionably.' She nuzzled into his neck.

'My statesmanship is universally acknowledged by all who know me.' His voice had turned a little hoarse.

'Stiff-rumped,' she agreed, blowing gently into his ear.

A sudden loud knock had them both springing apart like guilty adolescents. Grace hurriedly climbed to her feet just as the door began to open. Seconds later, their eldest son, Peter stuck his head through the gap. 'Am I interrupting anything?' he grinned.

At three and twenty, Peter was fast becoming his father's double, and as he stepped through the door, Grace caught her breath. It was like looking at her husband over twenty years earlier. Without the scowl admittedly.

'When did you get here, dearest?' she asked as Peter raised her hand to his lips.

'About half an hour ago and from the gossip below stairs, it seems my arrival is not a moment too soon.'

'You know it's not necessary to listen to kitchen gossip to discover the latest catastrophe,' Nicholas commented drily. 'You could simply ask us. We keep no secrets.'

'And where would the fun in that be?' Peter retorted, giving his father a low bow. Nicholas shook his head and chuckled. Then stepping forward, he enfolded his eldest son in a tight hug.

'Steady on, father, I can't even begin to tell you how long it took me to get my cravat exactly so.' Peter complained. 'Truly, it would save me hours if you allowed me my own valet.'

Nicholas simply raised his eyebrows. 'How long did it take him this time?' he quizzed Grace.

'I think it might be a record,' she responded with a tinkling laugh. 'I don't think we actually reached the minute mark.'

'It's alright for you,' Peter grumbled, throwing himself into a chair. 'You're old and crochety and nobody cares whether your cravat is straight or your shirt collar sufficiently starched. I have a reputation to maintain.'

'It's a good thing I'm sending you to Scotland then,' was his father's unsympathetic response.

Peter gave a theatrical sigh. 'I'm simply a pawn in your ongoing machinations.'

Nicholas gave a snort. 'You make me sound positively Machiavellian. Caerlaverock will be yours one day, and it's important to make clear you will be no absentee landlord.'

'Will I not?' Peter sighed. 'It takes nigh on a week to travel so far, and I'm certain Gifford has everything in hand.'

'Gifford is getting old,' Nicholas countered. 'He's written that he has a replacement in mind. We cannot afford to be deemed good-for-nothing Sassenachs. Culloden was barely a hundred years ago, and the Scots have long memories.'

Peter nodded. In truth he was looking forward to inspecting the Blackmore estates near to Loch Lomond. It had been far too long since his last visit. And this time he would be doing it without the Duke looking over his shoulder.

Despite his joking, Peter was well aware of the responsibilities that came with being the heir apparent and was gratified his father trusted him enough to deal with their prickly tenants over the border.

'How are Tempy and Adam? Is Jamie back from Eton?' Grace asked seating herself with a sigh.

'He's all ready for Oxford apparently. Aunt Tempy says she has no idea where he gets his intellect from,' Peter grinned. 'Uncle Adam chased her into the rose garden for her impertinence, while Lily declared she'd never seen any evidence that her brother had anything between his ears other than fresh air.' He shook his head and laughed. In other words, Ravenstone is in wild disarray as usual.'

Before either of his parents could answer, a knock at the door signified the housekeeper bringing in a tray of hot chocolate. 'Mrs. Jenks, you're a lifesaver,' Grace breathed with a grateful smile.

'There's no sense in you fretting without a bit of sugar in you, your grace.' The housekeeper did not pretend ignorance of the latest calamity to befall the Sinclair household.

Grace grimaced in response. 'It seems that lurching from one catastrophe to another is the Sinclair lot...' She paused and gave a rueful grin. 'Actually I think mayhap it's more of a *Shackleford* issue. My poor husband simply keeps getting caught in the way.' Taking a grateful sip of her chocolate, she smiled at the housekeeper. 'It's late Mrs. Jenks and high time you took to your bed. Thank you so much for your thoughtfulness.'

'Is there anything else I can get for your graces?'

Nicholas shook his head before adding ruefully, 'Get some rest, Mrs. Jenks. I suspect my daughter's behaviour is going to be on the lips of every household this side of the Thames, and we're relying on you to keep us informed.'

'So what exactly has Jennifer done to warrant all the scandalmongering?' Peter asked as the housekeeper closed the door behind her.

'Your father was soothing ruffled feathers over Parliament passing the bill giving permission for the new railway,' Grace answered, warming her hands on the cup of chocolate.

'Jenny's support for such new innovations might well be admirable, but she has yet to master the art of diplomacy. Would you care for a brandy?' At Peter's nod, Nicholas climbed to his feet and went over to the sideboard. 'Of course that's without even considering the fact that in Society's opinion, ladies in general should not harbour such radical opinions.'

'Or any opinion at all, really,' Peter added drily.

'Quite so.' Nicholas handed his son the snifter of brandy. 'I have no wish to clip Jennifer's wings. And even if I wanted to, I don't think I'd succeed.' He shrugged and gave a weary chuckle. 'I love that she has her own views and ideals – she reminds me of her mother.' Sitting back down he tossed a wry glance over at his wife who favoured him with a small unrepentant wink.

'That said, I have no choice but to do *something* to appease the stuffed shirts. They're afraid of change and will do everything in their power to maintain the status quo.' He shook his head. 'Innovation will not be stifled, and in truth I'm of the same opinion as Jennifer. But if such change is to take place without the resistance of those in power, it must needs be coaxed along, however frustrating that may be to those who wish to change the world overnight.'

'So Jenny must be reprimanded to appease the blockheads.'

Nicholas grimaced. 'If you wish to put it that way. I will continue to use my influence to encourage change, but being dismissed as a radical will not help me win the so-called *blockheads* over. But in regard to Jenny, I was thinking more of the old adage, *out of sight, out of mind.*'

'Why don't you send her to Scotland with me?' Peter leaned forward, his eyes alight. 'It's an age since we've spent any amount of time together.'

Grace and Nicholas looked at each other. 'She would not be able to go without a chaperone,' the Duchess insisted.

'Malcolm is accompanying Peter...' Nicholas began.

'...And Jennifer's presence would give Felicity an excellent excuse to go with him,' Grace concluded with a wide smile. 'Do you think Jenny's likely to put up much of an objection?'

'I think she'll be delighted,' Peter answered. 'How long is it since she made the journey that far north?'

'It was before Nicholas was born I think,' Grace responded. 'She's certain to know we are banishing her.'

'She's hardly being locked away with only bread and water,' Peter scoffed.

'Jennifer might be impulsive, but she's astute enough to know why we're sending her away. And I think Peter's right – she'll relish the idea of an adventure away from the gossipmongers.'

'I never thought I'd hear myself say this, but I'm concerned she'll miss nearly the whole of her second season...' Grace let her voice trail off.

'That will be the chief reason she agrees to go,' countered Peter with a short laugh.

His mother sighed and nodded 'You're right. She has no time for Society's current crop of popinjays, but I do so want her to make a good match. And by a good match, I mean someone who will love her for *her* and care nothing about her outspokenness.'

'She is very unlikely to find such a man by participating in a London season.' Nicholas placed a comforting hand on Grace's shoulder. 'You've always known that darling. Mayhap we are doing her a favour by broadening her horizons. By next season, the gossips will have moved on to the next unfortunate. If Jenny is still not betrothed by then, perhaps we will consider allowing her more freedom to choose her own suitor – within limits of course.'

Grace placed her hand over that of her husband. She was well aware of the huge compromise Nicholas was making. It was quite one thing to watch his sisters-in-law make complete cakes of themselves while choosing their own suitors, but giving his own daughter the same licence was an entirely different matter altogether.

## Chapter Two

'I'm to accompany Peter to our estates in Scotland.'

Both Mercedes and Victoria stared at Jennifer wordlessly for a second. 'And Aunt Grace has agreed?' Mercy whispered at length.

Jennifer nodded. 'If I'm being entirely honest, I have no objections. This season has so far been unbearably tedious with not one gentleman even worth dropping one's kerchief for. And I know you both agree.'

'Don't you wish to be wed?' Victoria questioned.

Jennifer gave an inelegant snort. 'Who would have me? Especially as I'm now so out of favour.'

'You're still the Duke of Blackmore's daughter,' Mercy argued.

'But I don't wish to be married simply because of whose offspring I am.'

'Well, I'm entirely certain that by next season they will have forgotten about your faux pas entirely,' Victoria added, leaning forward to give her friend a warm hug.

'If they haven't, perhaps it will separate the wheat from the chaff.'

'No, it will simply mean that those who court you despite your ruinous reputation will be either purse-pinched or ambitious.'

In contrast to Victoria's kind-hearted approach, Mercy's was matter of fact and unembroidered.'

'Mercy!' Victoria protested, 'I don't believe that's the case at all.'

'I hope you're right,' Mercy responded, 'but I do not believe sugarcoating the situation will help Jenny at all in the long run.'

'Oh for goodness' sake, I only disagreed with my father,' Jennifer declared. 'I do that all the time.'

'But not in front of…' Mercy paused, counting in her head, 'Three Earls, two Marquesses and a Viscount.'

Jennifer scoffed. 'Nearly all of them are actually my uncles by marriage, and by default are entirely accustomed to outspoken females.'

'But unfortunately the one you were indirectly insulting is not.' Mercy gave an unrepentant grin. 'I wish I'd been there to see it.'

Jennifer sighed. 'You are a destroyer of hope, Mercedes Stanhope. I have no idea why I call you a friend.'

'I think you deserve better than the current crop of peacocks strutting around London's drawing rooms,' Mercy retorted. 'And so do your mother and father, else they wouldn't be sending you away.'

'And you might meet a wonderful man who falls head over heels in love with you knowing nothing of your father's title,' Victoria added.

Jennifer shook her head and chuckled. 'Truly, I don't know what I'd do without you both.'

They were interrupted by a knock on the bedchamber door. Seconds later, Victoria's twin sister, Georgiana stuck her head round the door. Jennifer beckoned her to come in. 'You've heard then?'

George nodded, seating herself on the other side of the bed. 'Anthony said you could come and stay with us, but your father wasn't havin' none of it.' She gave a sudden grin. 'I told Tony I reckoned you'd rather be adventurin' in Scotland than stuck in the middle of nowhere with me in the family way.'

'*With child*, George,' Jennifer corrected her with a chuckle. Having been dragged up in the slums of Exeter, Georgiana Shackleford was finally learning to speak in the manner befitting her station, but she still had a long way to go.

'That's what I said,' George answered, waving her hand in a *whatever* gesture.

'How are you feeling sweet?' Victoria asked, taking her twin sister's hand.

'Fit as a butcher's dog,' George answered with a wink. 'So, I don't need a nursemaid.'

'I don't object to indulging you,' Victoria protested.

'You're not coming to Bovey just to run around after the likes of me,' George retorted.

'London is going to be intolerably dull without all of you in it,' Mercy sighed. 'I shall be glad to be spending the summer in Cottesmore Hall.'

'How are Aunt Chastity and the twins?'

'Oh, Olivia and Catherine are growing like weeds. They're nearly ten now and poor Kit has no respite from them at all. The last time I saw her, Stepmama was looking particularly fatigued.'

'Poor Chastity, the twins are a bit of a handful,' Victoria commiserated.

Mercy laughed. 'Rather pity my poor father. I don't think he knows what's hit him.'

'Cottesmore's not that far from Bovey. Why don't you all come and visit. Anthony would love it.'

Mercy gave a chuckle. 'Oh, I'm certain he'd be over the moon,' she commented drily.

'We can spend the time in the garden,' George declared, excitedly. 'Now it's been cleared, there's a delightful … err, thingumajig … that's perfect for reading.'

'Arbour,' supplied Victoria. 'How *is* your reading coming along?'

'I finished *Frankenstein* last week,' Georgiana confessed. 'I know it's considered unsuitable for *ladies*, but Prudence lent it to me.'

'*Frankenstein* – isn't that about some kind of hideous monster?' Jennifer raised her eyebrows. 'It does sound typical of Aunt Prudence.'

'Scared me half to death,' George admitted cheerfully. 'I'm sure Pru will allow me to lend it to you.' She threw Jennifer a mischievous look before adding, 'Scotland's a long way to travel without something to take your mind off your arse…'

∞∞∞

'The thing is Percy lad, I'm not as young as I used to be. Getting up the steps to the pulpit is beginning to take me longer than actually reading the deuced sermon.'

Percy made the appropriate sympathetic noises. In truth, Reverend Shackleford hadn't actually read a sermon since accidentally stepping on his eyeglasses the Christmas before.

The two men were seated in the Reverend's study enjoying a memorial glass of brandy. The Reverend had declared it only right and proper since they'd just conducted old Willie's funeral. Unfortunately nobody could remember Willie's last name or how old he was – that knowledge had long been lost to the annals of time. Much like the date of his last wash. On the plus side it had been decided to conduct the service with a closed casket...

But as the Reverend declared solemnly, old Willy had been living in Blackmore since before Nelson cut his first tooth, and the least they could do was drink him on his way upstairs. At least Reverend Shackleford hoped that was the direction the old tatterdemalion was headed.

'I think I could do with a change of scenery, Percy,' Augustus Shackleford was musing. 'What do you think Agnes would say to a spot of missionary work in West Africa?'

Percy, who'd been taking a sip of his brandy at the time, promptly spat it out over Flossy's head. The little dog had been snoozing on the curate's knee but as a bead of brandy dripped onto her nose, she enthusiastically licked it off and wagged her tail.

'Oh you can't take Agnes away from civilisation, Sir. She wouldn't last three months. You know how she is. She'd likely kill someone with one of her potions and end up being the main course in the funeral banquet.'

The Reverend hmphed, still obviously deep in thought.

'And who would look after Flossy?' Percy added desperately. While he and Agnes hadn't always seen eye to eye, he didn't relish the thought of her ending up in somebody's pot.

'You're right, Percy lad,' the Reverend sighed at length. 'My self-sacrificing nature gets the better of me sometimes.' Much to Flossy's chagrin, the curate was no longer holding his brandy glass above the little dog's head, so she contented herself by licking the drops off his waistcoat instead.

'I understand Miss Jennifer is returning to Blackmore ahead of the season's end,' Percy commented thinking it best to change the subject.

The Reverend tutted. 'Made a bit of a cake of herself by all accounts.' He shook his head. 'Taking after her mother and aunts I'm afraid. Chit's a Shackleford in all but deuced name.'

'Oh I don't think she's quite as bad as all that,' Percy chuckled. 'Do you know what the Duke and Duchess intend to do about her misconduct?'

'Sending her up to Scotland with Peter according to the note I received from Grace.'

'Well, there you are, Sir,' the curate exclaimed slapping the arm of his chair. 'Why don't you accompany her north? She is your granddaughter after all and I've no doubt she would benefit from your ... err ... *wisdom*.'

The Reverend frowned and took a sip of his brandy. 'It's a deuced long way,' he declared pensively at length.

*Not as far as West Africa,* was on the tip of Percy's tongue, but concerned his superior would think him flippant, he said instead, 'Just think, you'll have her undivided attention for the whole journey. What an opportunity that would be to gently direct her feet back onto the path of righteousness.'

The Reverend grunted. 'I never managed to do it with the rest of 'em. And anyway, how the deuce would you manage without me?'

Percy was entirely sure he would manage perfectly well with his wife Lizzy's assistance. However, he really didn't want to hurt the Reverend's feelings, and knowing the clergyman wasn't quite ready to hang up his cassock for good, Percy was more than happy to spend the summer looking after parish affairs without Augustus Shackleford's oft ill-timed interference.

'I will do my best, of course, Sir,' he answered with an

exaggerated sigh, 'though I cannot help but think this is an opportunity that may never present itself again. Miss Jennifer is at a very impressionable age…' he paused and gave a small self-conscious cough, stifling the sentiment that Jennifer Sinclair's pliable years had been and gone, if they'd ever existed at all… 'and I feel certain she would benefit from your guidance.' In truth, he'd never been less certain of anything in his life. He couldn't name one of the Reverend's offspring who'd actually reaped any benefit at all from their father's guidance. Guilt swamped him.

Unaware of his curate's internal spiritual battle, Augustus Shackleford nodded his head thoughtfully. 'I can't argue with you there, Percy,' he murmured. 'But I doubt Agnes would agree to travel all the way to Scotland.'

Percy was entirely certain that Agnes would chain herself to her chaise longue before climbing into a carriage heading in the direction of the heathens on the other side of the border, but naturally he didn't vocalise such an opinion. 'Mayhap she would be perfectly content to remain in Blackmore with myself and Lizzy here to offer succour,' he suggested carefully.

The Reverend narrowed his eyes and steepled his fingers, making a show of considering Percy's words. As a man of the cloth, Augustus Shackleford would never deliberately eschew the Almighty's work, however onerous it might be.

That being said, if he could do it with his wife at the other end of the country…

∞∞∞

'Absolutely not, I forbid it!' Grace immediately bristled at Nicholas's highhanded words. Unfortunately, he hadn't yet finished. 'How you can possibly think foisting your father onto Malcolm and Felicity while they are five hundred miles away and *safeguarding our children* is even a remotely good idea is beyond me.'

In actual fact, Grace herself was of entirely the same opinion. However, her husband's imperiousness brought out the worst in her, and she heard herself retorting in a tone just as highhanded, 'Well then, if you think it such a bad idea *your grace*, perhaps I should accompany them myself.'

Nicholas took a deep breath and counted to ten. 'It's not that I think Augustus is not to be trusted,' he began carefully.

'Do you not?' Truly, it had been a long time since Nicholas had seen his wife so up in the boughs, and he knew he'd handled things badly. Unfortunately, her words had caught him completely unawares. He was not to know that his wife's anger was in the main because she completely agreed with his assessment of the situation.

They'd been in Blackmore a mere two days when her father paid her a visit. That should have been warning enough, but unfortunately she'd been so taken aback at his request to accompany Jennifer and Peter to Scotland that she'd found herself entirely bereft of tried and tested excuses. In truth, most of her anger was directed at herself.

'Why does he want to go?' Nicholas's question abruptly averted their burgeoning quarrel.

Grace sighed and sat down on the drawing room window seat. 'Truthfully, I think he's bored,' she answered with a grimace. 'Percy does most of the day to day running of the parish, and I think my father feels at rather a loose end. He mentioned he hadn't had occasion to spend much time with his grandchildren as they were growing up.'

'Thank God!' Nicholas's comment was heartfelt, earning him another glare.

'I think perhaps we should discuss his request with Malcolm and Felicity,' she answered, making an effort to swallow her ire.

Nicholas nodded. 'Peter too will need to have a say. If we are to trust him to make decisions concerning Caerlaverock, then we cannot burden him with the Reverend if he is unwilling.'

'I'm certain he will be delighted to spend time with his grandfather,' Grace retorted indignantly. Then she looked at her husband's incredulous expression and burst out laughing.

# Chapter Three

Brendon Galbraith stared at his father in exasperation. 'Ah ken ye're not best happy wi' the situation,' he growled, 'but if we're to have a say in the matter o' the land hereabouts, it'll be best done workin' wi' the laird, not agin him.'

Dougal Galbraith drained his whisky. 'I'll nae be workin' wi' no bloody Sassenachs,' he muttered.

'Nobody's askin' ye tae, Da. But like it or no, the Sinclair's own this land. And they have done since well before Culloden, however much ye might want tae pretend otherwise. An' it were your great, great, grandfather who bloody sold it to 'em.'

'Aye, well, I dinnae hae tae like it,' Dougal muttered, pouring himself another drink. 'Ahh ye takin' a wee dram afore ye go tae grovel tae the likes o' Gifford?'

'Ah'll nae be grovellin' as well ye know,' Brendon grated in frustration, snatching the whisky bottle from his father's hand. 'An' if ye spent less time wi' yer head in this bottle, ye might see the truth o' the matter. Gifford has spoken wi' the laird and his son's gaunae meet wi' me. An' if ye cannae haud yer weesht, ah'll thank ye to bide here.'

Brendon shook his head and strode out of his father's small sitting room and out into the draughty hall. 'Ah'll nae be bowin to no Sassanach either,' his father yelled after him. 'So dinnae ask.'

Brendon gritted his teeth but didn't reply. In truth, if he'd stayed one more minute he might have actually been tempted to wring the old bampot's scrawny neck. Instead, he whistled to Fergus, his Irish wolfhound and strode outside the crumbling keep. He loved his da, but there were times he could bloody swing for the dafty.

The weather outside was warm and dry. On the one hand, it made a nice change from the wet chilly weather early June usually brought, but on the other, it meant the midges would be out in force. Glancing up at the sky, he reckoned he had about two hours until the sun started to lower, and the little bastards came out for blood. Enough time to walk up to Caerlaverock and speak with Gifford before he needed to be back and inside.

Fergus came up beside him and nudged at his hand. In spite of his fearsome appearance, the wolfhound was a complete bairn. Soft as butter and twice as daft. Brendon picked up a stick and threw it as hard as he could. With a loud bark, Fergus loped after it. In the distance, he could see the shores of Loch Lomond, and on a large bluff beside it, Caerlaverock, the Duke of Blackmore's seat in Scotland.

It had been an age since the Duke himself had travelled the five hundred miles from Blackmore. Brendon couldn't blame him – it was a hell of a journey. He thought back to the last time Nicholas Sinclair had honoured them with a visit. It was nearly four years ago. He'd brought his wife and his eldest son and heir with him then. Peter Sinclair had been nigh on a man, though possessed of the recklessness that gripped most boys on the verge of manhood. Brendon wondered what changes the intervening years had wrought.

The Scot doubted if he'd ever possessed such foolhardiness. His ma's death had robbed him of his childhood well before he was ready, and as the only son, the only oats he'd ever sown were in the ground while his da lost himself in the bottom of a whisky bottle.

Sighing, he brought himself back to the present. Like it or no, Dougal was his responsibility and the possibility of becoming steward to Caerlaverock was no small thing. It would provide a previously undreamt-of security for both him and his da. And if it meant locking the old bampot up for the whole of Peter Sinclair's visit, then so be it.

In truth, though, financial security wasn't the main reason he was desperate for an audience with the Viscount. The terrible incident he'd witnessed at the MacFarlane's mine three months earlier had been keeping him awake at night, and he urgently needed Sinclair's help. He'd been in the process of writing a letter to Blackmore requesting aid when he heard about the impending Ducal visit and decided that a face-to-face meeting would be much more beneficial.

In retrospect, he should have sent the missive anyway, but until only a few days ago, he'd been under the impression that Nicholas Sinclair himself would be making the journey. However, after speaking with Gifford, his hopes had been dashed. The Duke was sending his son and heir in his place.

Since it was far too late now to send a request for help to his grace, the young Viscount would have to do.

∞∞∞

'Well, I cannae say I'm overjoyed at the prospect of keeping an eye on the Reverend for the next month, but if it's yer wish he travel with us lad...' Malcolm gave a philosophical shrug.

'Believe me, the last thing I want is to saddle you with my father-in-law,' Nicholas retorted. 'If you feel it's too much for you and Felicity, simply say the word, and I'll make an excuse.'

'Aye, I know ye would, lad. But it might turn out to be a blessing in disguise. Augustus is nae as young as he used to be. It's an open secret that Percy's dealing wi' most everything now. Taking the Reverend away from Blackmore will let ye know whether the lad can step into Augustus's shoes when the time comes.'

Nicholas frowned, then gave a short laugh. 'Trust you to focus on the practical my friend. I must confess the thought of Augustus retiring has been on my mind recently. We both know he won't take it well. And you're right, this could be an excellent opportunity to encourage him to step back. Do you think Felicity will be able to tolerate a month with the old rascal?'

Malcolm gave a pained wince. 'I dinnae doubt she'll have something to say about it, but hopefully, she'll get o'er her Friday face afore we're all confined together in the carriage.'

'Don't worry, I'll send you with two carriages,' Nicholas chuckled. 'That way you can take it in turns…'

'Have ye told Peter and Jennifer?'

Nicholas winced. 'Not yet. I thought I'd save that for the night before you leave.'

Malcolm laughed out loud and slapped his thigh. 'Now that I cannae wait to witness,' he chuckled.

'Then perhaps you and Felicity had better join us for dinner,' Nicholas responded dryly.

'I would'nae miss it fer the world, lad, would'nae miss it fer the world…'

∞∞∞

Pulling on her gloves, Jennifer took a last look around her

bedchamber. Her luggage had already been taken out to the carriage. Stifling a sudden excitement, she pulled open the door and made her way down the large staircase. This trip was going to be the first real adventure of her life - not least due to the fact she'd have no lady's maid to assist her during the weeklong journey.

And then there would be the presence of her grandfather. Chuckling, she thought back to dinner the evening before. Peter had definitely not been happy to discover the Reverend would be accompanying them. In fact, in a rare show of pique, he'd stomped from the table at one point, only to return sheepishly half an hour later. Her brother was generally easygoing, sometimes even impetuous, but he was no sulker. Deep inside he possessed their father's serious nature though he mostly went to great lengths to hide it – especially from his Corinthian friends.

Reaching the bottom of the stairs, Jennifer smothered a grin. Undoubtedly, the time away from the table had given him time to think. Plus of course, he hadn't yet had pudding...

The carriages were waiting near the main entrance at the foot of the steps. She'd already said her goodbyes to her mother and father, but that didn't stop the fierce hugs and last list of instructions pushed into her hand. Malcolm, Felicity and Peter were already in the first carriage. Jennifer had elected to join the Reverend in the second carriage for the first part of the journey. In truth, she was quite looking forward to it. Her grandfather could be very entertaining when he put his mind to it.

They were to pick the Reverend up from the vicarage en route, and as Jennifer climbed into the carriage, she made sure to be facing the front. Despite the clement weather, she was furnished with a hot brick in case her feet became chilled, and a blanket should she decide to take a nap. As the carriage door was shut, she cast a last look at her mother's anxious face and leaned out of the open window. 'I will only be away for a month, Mama,' she laughed. 'You need not look as though you're never going to see me again.'

'Please do not tempt fate,' Grace countered, gripping her daughter's hand.

'Truly, we are well protected,' Jennifer protested, leaning out to give her mother one last kiss.

In fact, the main reason they were travelling without servants was the Duke's conclusion that the provision of sufficient protection was more important than someone adept in the use of curling irons. Especially since there would be a full complement at Caerlaverock.

In addition to the four coach drivers, there were six *footmen*. In reality, the men were all retired sailors whom the Duke had personally trained to provide added protection for his family. On arrival at Caerlaverock, they would be accommodated in the nearby village of Banalan under the watchful eye of Chapman, their leader.

As well as the bogus footmen, both Malcolm and Peter were more than proficient swordsmen and marksmen and Jennifer herself was sufficiently skilled to hit a moving target. The drivers had been instructed to keep to the busy main roads and under no circumstances to travel outside of daylight hours.

In all honesty, as Peter muttered to Malcolm, the biggest danger to their health was sharing a carriage with the Reverend for five hundred miles...

'Give Nicholas a hug from me when he gets back from Eton,' Jennifer called out as the carriage pulled away. She watched in the small rear window as her parents grew ever smaller until the carriage turned a bend, and they were finally out of sight. Swivelling forward, Jennifer unexpectedly found herself blinking back tears. And they hadn't even left Blackmore land yet.

Taking a kerchief from her reticule, she firmly dried her eyes, determined not to behave like a foolish little girl. In a few minutes, her grandfather would be joining her in the carriage, and she was entirely certain he'd waste no time before swiftly coaxing her out of her blue devils.

∞∞∞

Sitting on his trunk, watching the Blackmore carriages coming down the lane, the Reverend had the uncomfortable feeling that his life was about to change forever. Despite his bluff manner, Augustus Shackleford was no fool. He was well aware that the Duke of Blackmore would be watching Percy carefully during his absence.

He knew also that the time was fast approaching when he'd have to hang up his cassock for good. He didn't know which was worse – the thought of spending all day every day with only Agnes for company or being consigned to the family pew for every service with no opportunity for a quick nap halfway through the sermon.

He could hear the faint sound of chanting coming from the church. They were halfway through the week of Whitsuntide and one or two of the faithful would be in the church every day. It meant that Percy wasn't able to see him off. In some ways, the Reverend was relieved. He was only going away for a month after all, and the curate had already promised faithfully to keep him informed via a weekly letter.

Agnes of course had not yet risen from her bed, which just left Flossy.

He looked down at the little dog who wagged her tail encouragingly, reminding him that it wouldn't *just* be him and Agnes... As the carriages approached, he bent down to pick her up, shrugging off his mawkish reverie. All was well. He'd already had a quick word with the Almighty and despite his feelings of disquiet, the Reverend was confident he was taking the right path.

Leaving his trunk to two of the burly footmen, he climbed through the open door of the second carriage, seating himself opposite the only other occupant.

'Good morning, Grandfather,' Jennifer murmured, with a small polite bend of her head.

As the carriage moved off, the Reverend regarded her with a pained sigh. 'Tare an' hounds, lass, it's going to be a deuced long journey as it is without you sitting the whole way with a poker up your arse.' And with that, he relinquished a wriggling Flossy who promptly threw herself ecstatically into his granddaughter's arms.

With Flossy clambering all over her, Jennifer abandoned her attempts at graciousness and after finally managing to settle the little dog on her lap, gave a wicked grin. 'Can you remember when you let slip about old Queen Charlotte's mishap with the duck pond at Aunt Hope's wedding?' she recalled. 'You said you'd tell me the truth of what happened when I became old enough.'

She arched an eyebrow. 'Well, dearest Grandpapa, I think that time has finally come. However, feel free to take your time, after all, we have five hundred miles together. I can wait...'

# Chapter Four

By the time the two carriages finally reached the shores of Loch Lomond over a sennight later, tempers were most definitely beginning to fray. The journey had been largely uneventful though slow as they'd sacrificed speed to retain the same horses throughout the journey. Jennifer had had no idea how difficult it was to simply pin one's hair up. Truly she was beginning to resemble the scarecrow in Mrs. Higgins's raspberry patch. And all her cajoling and pleading with her grandfather concerning Queen Charlotte's mishap with the duck pond had been for nought. She could never have imagined the Reverend actually had it in him to be so closemouthed.

More worrying, however, was the fact that throughout the journey, he'd seemed determined to lecture her on various passages of the bible - mainly on the wages of debauchery, avarice, wrath and ... what was the other one? Oh, sloth, that was it.

In truth, debauchery was a subject that had never really come up in their previous dealings. Jennifer thought for a second and came to the conclusion that neither had avarice, wrath or sloth. True, her grandfather most definitely enjoyed the finer things in life, had always relished a good sparring match and she could certainly vouch for the fact that he'd never had a particular problem with inactivity, aside from the times he was in a meddling mood.

But such was his zeal at the beginning of the journey, she couldn't help wondering if he was becoming a little dicked in the nob. Fortunately, the further north they got, the more his enthusiasm for pointing her towards the light appeared to wane. Indeed, Jennifer noticed he seemed to be having an internal battle in particular with wrath - severely testing even Felicity's legendary aplomb when he crossly declared the matron to be notoriously picksome and stomped off to get himself a third tankard of ale.

Of course, his action could also have been an indication he was losing his internal battle with debauchery...

After that, conversation between the five of them had gradually dwindled to monosyllables.

As Loch Lomond came into sight, Jennifer felt she'd never been so glad to see a body of water in her life. Excitedly she peered through the window trying to get a glimpse of Caerlaverock. She was sharing the carriage with Felicity as the matron had suggested they might wish to assist one another in repairing their toilette, declaring it would not do for them to arrive at their destination looking like tag-rag and bobtail.

Consequently, Jennifer's hair was now adequately coiffured, and her dress still damp from the cloth Felicity used to remove the dust. As they turned a bend, the young woman gave a squeal and turned to her companion. 'Is that Caerlaverock?' she breathed, pointing to a large house standing on a craggy outcrop overlooking the loch.

Felicity leaned forward and gave a relieved nod. While she'd only visited Caerlaverock on one previous occasion, the memory of her visit had stayed with her ever since. It was seeing Malcolm's sheer joy at being back in the home of his birth that had reaffirmed her feelings for the Scot.

She experienced a sudden lightening of her heart. She knew it was her husband's dearest wish to one day retire close to his birthplace, though he would never abandon the Duke while he believed Nicholas had need of him. But perhaps one day, they would come here and live openly as man and wife.

The carriages turned onto the road bordering Loch Lomond, and Jennifer gazed in wonderment at the majestic scenery surrounding it. Truly, she could never have imagined anywhere quite so beautiful. It was late afternoon, but this far north the sun was still high in the sky casting moving cloud shaped shadows on the purple covered hills rising steeply on the other side of the loch. In awe, her eyes rested on the huge mountain, dark and mysterious towering above the water in the distance.

'Ben Lomond,' Felicity clarified, pointing at the moody peak. 'The word *Ben* is from the Gaelic *bheinn*. It means mountain or hill.'

Jennifer threw Felicity an arch look. 'You sound like Malcolm,' she grinned before turning back to the window and watching avidly as they approached the peninsula on which Caerlaverock was situated. Finally, the carriages turned off the road and a few minutes later approached a set of large wrought iron gates.

After a couple of minutes waiting, a large, gruff man came out of a tiny cottage situated to one side of the entrance. Without speaking, he quickly doffed his cap, then set to, unlocking, then dragging the gates open. The narrow drive beyond was a gentle climb towards the top of the bluff, taxing the skills of their coach drivers as they made sure to keep the horses moving at a pace that would keep their hooves from slipping on the cobbles but wouldn't tax them too much at the end of such a long journey.

Finally, the road levelled out and bent to the right to follow a high wall - clearly, the boundary of the formal gardens though the house wasn't yet visible. Eventually the road curved back to the left, and the loch suddenly appeared through a copse of trees in the distance. Still following the line of the wall, the carriages slowed as they came upon a large gate. Seconds later, they clattered through a high archway and out into a large courtyard.

As the carriages finally drew up outside the wooden doors, Jennifer suppressed a gasp. She'd had no idea that Caerlaverock was so considerable. Before leaving Blackmore, her father had given her an impromptu history lesson, so she was already aware that the house was Jacobean. Climbing thankfully down from the carriage, Flossy in her arms, she spied an older man with a shock of white hair bowing to her brother.

'Welcome tae Caerlaverock, ma lord,' he beamed, clearly delighted to have visitors. 'May ah be so bold as tae say you're a wee taller since last ah saw ye.'

Peter laughed and shook the elderly steward's hand. Clearly, this was Gifford. Smiling, Jennifer stepped forward.

'Ma lady, tis a pleasure tae welcome ye. For a wee minute there, ah thought ah was lookin' at her grace.'

'It's very good to see you too, Gifford,' she responded with a small curtsy before putting Flossy on the ground. The little dog promptly stood on her hind legs and wagged her tail.

'She loves an audience,' Jennifer laughed. 'Her name's Flossy.'

'It's guid tae meet yer, Flossy,' the steward smiled, bending down to give her a quick fuss. 'Ah dinnae ken what auld Fergus'll make o' ye.'

Straightening up again, his smile broadened. 'Malcolm Mackenzie, as I live and breathe, yer nae lookin' a day older than the last time ye were here.'

'Clearly my wife is taking good care of me,' Malcolm beamed, stepping forward and holding out his hand. Both Jennifer and Felicity looked at him in surprise.

'Ah didnae ken you'd wed, ma auld friend, that be guid news indeed.' The old steward took Malcolm's proffered hand in a firm grip, and the two men shook hands, clearly well acquainted.

Then, taking hold of his wife's hand, Malcolm pulled her towards him and made the introductions. 'This is Felicity Mackenzie. My wife. She's made me the happiest man alive.'

'It's an honour tae meet ye, Mrs. Mackenzie. A braw woman was well o'er due to keep this auld ne'er-dae-weel in line.'

This was the first time Felicity had ever been introduced as Malcolm's wife, and the matron found herself fighting back tears, but before she could respond, a loud snore erupted from behind them. 'Grandfather!' Jennifer gasped, turning and hurrying back towards the carriage, Flossy in tow.

Gifford blinked and looked towards Peter who offered a rueful grin. 'Another unexpected addition to our party, I'm afraid.'

'LET US PRAY,' a voice bellowed abruptly from inside the carriage. There was a pause, then, seconds later, 'Thunder an' turf, Jennifer, you nearly gave me a deuced apoplexy. Are we nearly there yet?'

∞∞∞

The inside of Caerlaverock was a testament to the Scotland of a bygone age. Wood panelling, high, intricately decorated ceiling and colourful tapestries decorated the entrance hall, though the large square room was dominated by a huge ornate staircase that put Blackmore's to shame. Jennifer gazed around her in wonder as they were shown into a cosy sitting room where a cheerful fire burned to ward off the late afternoon chill.

'Ah ken ye must be nigh on exhausted, and yer bedchambers'll be aired and ready within the hour. Until then, can ah offer ye a wee dram tae gae along wi' yer tea?'

Naturally Peter, Malcolm and the Reverend acquiesced eagerly. Jennifer and Felicity however, decided on a large slab of the delicious homemade shortbread ready and waiting on the sideboard.

'So who is the fellow you'd like to put forward as the new steward?' Peter asked, taking a cautious sip of his whisky. From the first eye watering swallow, he sensed the fiery liquid would put him on his back if he was foolish enough to overindulge – especially on an empty stomach.

'His name be Brendon Galbraith. His clan were the original landowners hereabouts.'

'Dougal's son?' Malcolm queried with a frown.

'Aye. Tae be fair, old Dougal might hae been a tad fiery when he was a lad, but he's nae likely tae be causing trouble fer his son.'

'The Dougal I remember would cause trouble just fer the hell of it,' Malcolm retorted. 'What makes you think he'll bide his tongue this time?'

'Fer his son's sake I hope. Brendon's a guid lad. He was steward tae the MacFarlane up tae three months back. Ah dinnae ken exactly what happened, an' Brendon willnae speak o' it, but ah dae ken Alastair MacFarlane's no the full shillin.'

'I hope he'll tell me the truth of what transpired,' Peter interrupted with a worried frown. 'If he refuses to speak of it, I cannot risk putting my father's estate into his hands.'

'Aye, ah ken,' Gifford sighed. 'But ah reckon the lad'll come clean wi ye. The Gilbraiths need the coin. That place o' theirs'll be roond their ears come winter. But ah've told the lad the Duke values honesty above all things.'

'Amen to that,' declared the Reverend, brandishing his empty whisky glass. Jennifer smothered a grin. Evidently, her grandfather had put aside his internal battle with debauchery for the moment.

Shortly afterwards, they were shown to their respective bedchambers. Jennifer's turned out to be a large airy room with the same highly decorated ceiling as downstairs. The polished wooden floor was covered with thick rugs and in the middle of the room stood an enormous fourposter bed. Her belongings had already been unpacked and a fire crackled cheerfully in the hearth of an exquisitely carved fireplace. But best of all, in front of it stood a large tin bath full of steaming hot water.

Without further ado, Jennifer shrugged off her stained travel clothes and dipped a toe into the water. Still deliciously hot. With a groan, she stepped in and sank to her haunches. Truly, it was bliss. Halfway through, a cheery lady's maid knocked and entered with a bale of towels in her arms.

'Guid tae meet yer ma lady, ah'm Jenet,' she beamed with a quick curtsy. 'Will ye be wantin' yer hair washin' noo?'

Jennifer gave a delighted sigh and nodded. Then she tuned out the maid's excited chatter and gave herself up to the simple enjoyment of being pampered. Forty-five minutes later, she was wrapped in a gigantic towel in front of the fire while Jenet brushed her hair to help it dry.

'I think I may go for a walk before dinner,' Jennifer mused as the maid bade her turn the back of her head towards the fire.

'Och, ye dinnae want tae be oot noo wi the midges, m'lady,' Jenet proclaimed in horror. 'The wee beasties'll gie ye more'n a nasty bite.'

'My mother mentioned the midges,' Jennifer answered. 'I'd forgotten all about them. She says they're worst at dawn and dusk.'

'Aye, her grace has the right o' it. Dae ye wait 'til the mornin' when the wee beasties be abed an' ye'll nae end up lookin' like ye been skelped.'

Jennifer smiled at the maid, though she had no idea what *skelped* meant, she understood enough to recognise it wasn't something she'd relish.

'Ah'll be back tae gae ye a hand in dressin' fer dinner,' Jenet continued, helping her into a robe and picking up the travelworn clothing. 'Will ye rest until then ma lady?'

Wrapping the robe around her, Jennifer nodded her thanks. 'I confess I'm done to a cow's thumb, and the bed looks wonderfully inviting.'

As Jenet departed, she climbed to her feet, intending to get into bed, but the orange and pink hues splashing across the sky like an artist's palate drew her to the window. Below her was the large courtyard they'd first arrived at. There was no sign of the carriages, and Jennifer guessed the horses would be getting a well-deserved pampering.

Beyond the courtyard, the ground sloped gently towards a copse of trees, and beyond them, the loch spread out in all its glory. The bluff on which the house stood was not so high, but enough to see a goodly way in both directions.

Resting her head against the mullioned pane, Jennifer drank in the scenery, wondering how her father could have stayed away for so long. The wild beauty of the land called to her in a way she couldn't even begin to explain. Already, she was dreading the thought of having to return to the mayhem that was London.

∞∞∞

Reverend Shackleford sat by the fire and brooded. This was

so unlike him, he found himself actually brooding about his brooding. In truth, he couldn't put his finger on exactly what was wrong. The dinner had been more than edible and the company excellent. Flossy had clearly settled in very quickly if her deuced snoring was anything to go by - she was currently lying as close to the hearth as she could without actually setting her coat alight.

Mayhap he was simply tired. It had been a long time since he'd travelled so far, and his nether regions were currently taking it in turns to complain. A good night's sleep and he'd no doubt be corky. But despite his certainty that a few hours in the arms of Morpheus would cure all his ills, the Reverend wasn't yet ready to retire to his bed.

He thought back to the journey and his clumsy attempts to guide his granddaughter back towards the path of righteousness. In truth, he'd likely strayed further from the deuced path than she had. Sighing, the Reverend shook his head. He wasn't sure he was really suited to missionary work, and since their arrival at Caerlaverock he'd felt like a fish out of water. Scotland was so far from Blackmore it might as well have been deuced Africa. Especially since he couldn't understand a word of what they were saying. Abruptly, he was overwhelmed by a feeling of homesickness so acute, he even found himself missing Agnes's snoring.

He wondered what Percy was up to. Would Blackmore be running like clockwork *despite* the absence of its vicar or *because* of it?

Never had Augustus Shackleford felt so uncertain - so *unneeded*. Had the Almighty abandoned him? Allowed him to take a wrong turn? Of course he might also have had too much cheese at dinner.

Whatever the reason, this would not do. Wallowing in self-pity was for lesser men. There was a reason God had sent him here.

He just had to hold fast to that. All would be revealed in good time – the same as always. He'd never been one to abandon ship and there were almost certainly a fair few skirt wearing heathens who'd appreciate his guidance.

The Reverend felt a little better, but he still wasn't yet ready for his bed. Perhaps he'd write a letter to Percy. That would keep the curate on his toes, just in case he started having ideas above his station. It wouldn't hurt to remind him that Blackmore's vicar hadn't yet abandoned this mortal coil for tea and toast with the Almighty.

# Chapter Five

The next morning dawned cloudy and damp. This, Gifford assured Jennifer was much more usual than the sunny, breezy weather they'd experienced of late. Breakfast was a hearty affair with such outlandish items such as *tattie scones* which were apparently made from potato, and *white pudding*, which to her uneducated eye looked exactly the colour of Peter on the mornings after he'd dipped in too deep at his club.

As she perused the huge choice on offer, Jennifer realised she was famished. Her weariness the night before meant she'd only picked at her dinner and retired almost immediately afterwards. Piling her plate high, she took it over to the table where Peter and Malcolm were chatting with the steward.

'Ah ken ye're eager tae meet wi' Brendon, so ah asked him tae come by this **efternuin**, if that suits ye m'lord? This mornin' I thought mebbe ye'd like tae inspect the hoose.'

Peter gave a smiling nod. 'That sounds like an excellent plan, Gifford.' Clearly he was relishing the opportunity to fulfil his role of heir apparent without the Duke looking over his shoulder.

Before Jennifer had the chance to ask Gifford to tell her a little more about the house, the Reverend arrived with Flossy capering around his ankles.

'How did you sleep, Grandpapa?' she asked, bending down to slip

Flossy a furtive piece of white pudding.

'Like a babe,' he responded cheerfully. Jennifer had been a little worried about her grandfather's uncustomary quiet after their arrival yesterday, especially since his singular behaviour during their journey, but clearly all he'd needed was a good night's sleep – the same as the rest of them.

'Will Felicity be coming down for breakfast?' Jennifer asked Malcolm. 'I was wondering if she'd be amenable to taking a stroll around the grounds …' She glanced out of the window at the ominous clouds and added, 'before it starts raining.'

'Och, it'll nae rain, jus' a wee spot o' mizzle,' Gifford explained.

'A cross between drizzle and mist,' chuckled Peter when he saw Jennifer's puzzled frown. 'What about you, Grandfather. Are you up for inspecting the house, or a constitutional with the ladies?'

Although the Reverend had already decided to spend the morning having a snoop around the house, he certainly hadn't bargained doing it in company – where the deuce was the fun in that? Tucking into his ham and eggs, he thought quickly. 'Well, I've a mind to spend the morning in conversation with the Almighty,' he answered at length. He wasn't shamming it - he was entirely capable of talking and snooping at the same time. Come to think of it, it was a perfect opportunity to have a bit of a chat with any heathens he happened to come across.

'Still,' he went on slyly, 'I reckon Flossy might appreciate a turn around the grounds after being stuck in the carriage for so long.'

'I'm not sure Felicity will be joining ye,' Malcolm interjected. 'I think she plans to stay abed today to recover from the journey.'

'Is she ill?' Jennifer asked anxiously.

'I think it's more that she wishes to keep her own company with a good book. As the good Reverend stated, we've all been cheek by jowl fer ower a sennight.' He gave a grin. 'Dinnae ye fret. By the morn, she'll be more than ready to talk the hind leg off a horse again.'

Jennifer gave a relieved nod and rose to her feet. 'I shall gather my things and wait for Flossy in the small sitting room we were in yesterday, Grandpapa. Please don't trouble yourself to hurry. Like Felicity, I have a good book.' She refrained from mentioning that her novel was about a doctor who created an artificial man from bits and pieces of corpses. It was hardly reading matter for a man of God – *or the granddaughter of one*, she thought guiltily. Truly, her Aunt Prudence had a peculiar taste in fiction. Nonetheless, Jennifer had to admit the story was both riveting and terrifying.

∞∞∞

After listening to his da describe the Duke as the spawn o' Satan for the fifth time in as many minutes, Brendon had finally had enough. 'I cannae sit here listenin' to ye blatherin' fer one second more,' he growled, pushing away his breakfast plate and climbing to his feet. 'Yer backside's oot the bloody windae.' With that, he stalked from the room and made his way outside. One of these days he'd actually manage a civil leave-taking from his only surviving parent. The old bampot spent too much time remembering the old days. To hear him tell it, William Wallace died no more than twenty years back.

Brendon shook his head. He'd yet to give Dougal an accounting of what happened with the MacFarlane and the worry of what his da would do if he found out that the clan chief was ill-using wee bairns as young as five or six... Brendon shook his head, a sick feeling in the pit of his stomach.

What he'd discovered had to be brought out into the open, but without allies, Brendon had had no chance of bringing down MacFarlane. The Duke of Blackmore was the only one with enough influence to put a stop to the bastard's practise of using young children to work a gold mine that everyone believed had been abandoned at least two years earlier.

He fully intended to tell Peter Sinclair the whole of what he'd discovered, but as far as Brendon was aware, the Viscount was still untried. Gifford had hinted that Malcolm Mackenzie would be accompanying his lordship. Brendon could only pray that was the truth. MacKenzie had been the Duke's right-hand man for many years and could be relied upon not to allow the young Viscount to simply take matters into his own hands and jump out of the bloody frying pan into the fire.

Brendon was also painfully aware that had the Duke known what Caerlaverock's neighbour was involved in, his grace would never have sent his son and heir into such a conflation.

Confessing all might risk his chance of becoming Caerlaverock's next steward, but in truth, it didn't matter. It was far more important to save the children still living from the same fate as those poor wee bairns he'd discovered by accident three months ago.

With difficulty he swallowed his anxious thoughts and concentrated on his next step. He'd been instructed to go to Caelaverock at two p.m. He was already wearing his Sunday best tweed and had no intention of returning anywhere near his cantankerous father until well after his interview was finished.

Tucking his cap into his pocket, Brendon took the track towards the loch shore, Fergus trotting happily beside him. The walk was nigh on an hour, but it would help clear his mind and hopefully calm his ire. Going into the meeting at Caerlaverock with an uneven temper would serve no one.

Directly in front of him, in the middle of the loch, the tiny island of Inchgalbraith rose eerily out of the mist. It was once a stronghold of the Galbraith Clan, and to his da, it still was.

Brendon had no doubt the daftie would cheerfully live like some tattyboggle in the ruins of the castle his ancestors had built there.

Though Dougal refused to acknowledge it, the truth was that Clan Galbraith had ceased to exist over two hundred years ago. The penalty for being on the wrong side of yet another rebellion. Most of the worthwhile land had been sold to the then Duke of Blackmore who'd promptly built a house right on the shores of Loch Lomond. According to his da, the position of the building had been deliberate – simply to rub what was left of Clan Galbraith's noses in the dirt.

While Brendon doubted the reason had anything to do with a desire to provoke the sad remnants of a disgraced Clan, they unquestionably had a wonderful view of the magnificent mansion from the rundown tower that was all that remained of his great, great, great grandda's home.

∞∞∞

Jennifer was glad she'd elected to put on her warmest pelisse and bonnet. In truth, she'd never expected to wear either of them, and had only packed them on her mother's insistence. Evidently the vagaries of the Scottish weather had remained engrained in the Duchess's mind.

Exiting the courtyard through a small gate in the wall to the left of the main entrance, Jennifer stepped onto a path that appeared to weave down through the trees towards the edge of the loch. Letting Flossy off her lead, she smiled as she watched the little dog dash backwards and forwards, nose to the ground, clearly lured by the multitude of exciting smells.

Carefully picking her way along the stony track, Jennifer felt a sudden easing in her chest as though something heavy had just been lifted. Out here, there was no one to disapprove. No one to instruct her to be someone she wasn't. She knew that both her parents were beyond proud of the woman she'd become. They had always allowed her the freedom of her own opinions. But, though they had little time for the ridiculous dictates of society and balked against them whenever they could, even a powerful force such as the Duke of Blackmore was forced to at least pay them lip service.

And society said that women did as they were told and did it quietly, without complaint.

Truthfully, Jennifer didn't know where she would possibly find a man prepared to allow her the freedom she'd known growing up. Until now, she hadn't realised that the worry of it was weighing so heavily. Like all young women of good families, she was expected to marry – and marry well. While she couldn't imagine her father forcing her into wedlock with someone she despised, Jennifer knew that even his legendary patience would only stretch so far.

*What would her parents say if she declared her wish to remain unwed?*

And that was the crux of the matter. Since her come out, Jennifer had gradually become more and more disenchanted with the whole marriage mart. She hadn't shared her feelings with her closest two friends, aside from the conversation in her bedchamber, but she guessed that Mercy at least shared her disillusionment. It was difficult to know what Tory thought. George's twin sister still kept her innermost thoughts very much to herself.

She knew there were men out there with the same progressive point of view as her father – indeed, in addition to the Duke, there were ten of them in her family. Both Peter and her Uncle Anthony were about as far from pompous as it was possible to get, and despite the lurid tales she'd been told of her aunts tying their collective garters in public, they had all found husbands able to look past their supposed shocking behaviour and see their true worth. Indeed, in every case, the men in question had not only recognised, but actively encouraged their wives' free spirits.

So Jennifer knew it was possible. But where to find such a man? There had certainly been no evidence of any tolerance in any of the stuffed shirts she'd come into contact with since her come out.

She was so lost in reverie that she wasn't paying attention to the closeness of the loch as she finally broke free of the copse of trees. Only a sudden shout, made her stop and turn in surprise. 'Stop, lest ye hae a mind for a swim.'

Frowning, Jennifer looked back down at the ground and nearly yelped in surprise. Her feet were inches from the edge. Her preoccupation with her thoughts and the green covering of algae had nearly ended with a dunking. Heart in her mouth, she hurriedly stepped away from the edge, and turned to see a man running towards her. Behind him was the biggest dog she'd ever seen.

In shock, she instinctively retreated, felt the ground beneath her foot give way, and promptly fell backwards into the freezing cold loch.

∞∞∞

Dougal Galbraith didn't need his son to tell him he was being an old bampot, but like always, his mouth ran away with him. As he watched Brendon storm out for the second time in as many days, a sudden thought hit him. What if his foolish comments aboot the Sinclair family got back tae the Duke and actually cost Brendon the job? The job they both sorely needed him tae get if they were tae survive another winter.

Sighing Dougal poured himself another whisky. In truth, he would'nae blame the lad if he did'nae come back. Things were away tae hell in a handcart. If they did'nae dae the plantin soon, it'd be too late. And here he was – gettin' pished like always. It was enough tae make even a sober man weep. He took a deep swallow and poured another.

'Bloody Sassenachs,' he muttered, this time to himself. Hoo dare they turn away a Galbraith? Well, if Sinclair haed the bloody gall tae send his son packin', Dougal Galbraith'd have somethin' tae say aboot it. In fact, he'd do better than that. He'd gae an' have a chat wi' the cub himself. Right noo.

Tossing back the last of his whisky, Dougal climbed unsteadily to his feet and shrugged on his coat. He'd show them bloody guid fer nothin' Sassenachs the wrath o' a true son o' Caledonia.

The feardie would nae even *think* aboot nae makin' Brendon steward once the Galbraith haed finished wi' 'im.

# Chapter Six

'Dear God, woman, are ye a complete eejit? What dae ye think ye be doin?'

Jennifer surfaced spluttering as a hand unceremoniously grabbed hold of her arm and dragged her clear of the murky water. For a second, she was actually dangling in mid-air, then before she could protest, the man hoicked her up to his shoulder and she was enveloped in strong arms, one of which was supporting her in the most scandalous position. She could scarce take in the fact that he was striding along the side of the loch, conveying her who knew where. Awareness dimmed until her whole being was focused on the cold which was swiftly seeping into her very bones. Right now he could have been taking her to hell itself and she would not have complained provided it was warm.

Minutes or it could have been seconds later, she had no idea of the passage of time, she heard him swear softly and felt the vibration of his boot kick against something hard. Abruptly they were inside. She heard the soft lapping of water, then felt him climb something, only to jump down again. Seconds later she was put down surprisingly gently and several blankets draped over her shoulders. Her eyes tightly shut, she snuggled down into their fetid warmth gratefully.

'Ye'll need tae take off yer wet claes if ye dinnae want tae catch yer death.' The deep masculine voice was matter of fact, and harsh reality began to encroach into her hazy dreamlike state. Nevertheless, Jennifer determinedly buried her head in the blankets until suddenly a small bark intruded. *Flossy*!

Her eyes flew open, and she flung off the blankets, jumping to her feet, only to stumble as the sodden mass of her skirt wrapped itself around her ankles. Gazing round wildly, she abruptly realised that she was on a *boat*. Reeling in shock, she sank back down again with a whispered, 'What have you done with my dog?'

'Dinnae worry, she be here.' Jennifer watched as the man leaned to the side and plucked the little dog from where she was nestled in between the front paws of an Irish wolfhound. Had the beast been about to have her for dinner? With a gasp, Jennifer snatched Flossy out of the stranger's hands and cuddling her close, glared at her erstwhile rescuer.

'Where are you taking me?' she demanded, frustrated to hear the wobble in her voice. The stranger raised his eyebrows at her tone.

'Home, ah hope, once ye've stripped off all yer wet claes.'

'If by claes, you mean clothes, I will certainly not remove anything in front of you.' Jennifer was proud that this time there was no wobble in her voice. 'It is ungentlemanly of you to even ask, sir.'

'They be drookin – soaking wet,' Brendon pointed out wearily. 'An if ye insist on sittin' in 'em, you'll likely be deid o' an ague wi'in a week.' He shrugged. 'Still, it be your funeral.'

Jennifer opened her mouth to utter a scathing retort, but could think of nothing at all, so closed it again. Embarrassingly, her teeth clattered together noisily. And to make matters worse, Flossy, clearly not enjoying being pressed against wet clothing, wriggled out of her arms and promptly seated herself back with the man's brute of a dog.

Swallowing, Jennifer hugged the blankets closer to her and took a good look at her companion for the first time. Slowly her face suffused with colour. He was by far the most arresting man she'd ever seen. His eyes were a startling cerulean blue in an almost harshly beautiful face. His nose was slightly crooked as though he'd broken it once upon a time and his face bronzed from too much time outdoors. Full lips and wavy midnight black hair worn longer than was the fashion amongst the dandies of London completed the picture. Shockingly, she found herself wondering what it would be like to be kissed by those full lips.

'So are ye gaunnae take off yer claes or stay starin' at me as though ye're expectin' ma heid tae fall off?'

Jennifer pursed her lips at his brusque tone. 'I thank you for your assistance, but I think I'm perfectly capable of walking back up to the house without any more help.'

'Ah ken ye'll not get ten yards wi' the weight o' that skirt flappin' round yer ankles,' he responded bluntly. 'That's why ah brought ye here since you was too heavy fer me tae carry all the way up tae the hoose.'

How dare he insinuate she was too heavy to carry. Why, she had the tiniest waist span of all her acquaintances. Vexingly, Jennifer felt tears gather in the back of her eyes. Furiously, she blinked them away, refusing to give him the impression she was nothing but a ninnyhammer.

'Would you please turn your back,' she managed at length, her voice husky with unshed tears. Unexpected sympathy shone briefly in his eyes, before he obligingly swivelled to face the other way. His sudden compassion was nearly her undoing, and she found herself sniffing as she cast off the blankets.

As she fumbled with the buttons of her pelisse, her hands began to shake with the cold. Indeed, her whole body felt as though it was caked in ice. Clumsily, she tossed the cloak onto the floor and started on the buttons of her blouse. Thank goodness she'd decided against wearing a dress. To have had to ask him to undo the buttons down the back would have been too humiliating.

By the time she'd stripped off her skirt and petticoat, she was simply too cold to even think, and she could have wept in gratitude when he passed a dry blanket back to her as she sat shivering in her chemise. How he'd known she'd finished undressing, Jennifer had no idea.

Two more blankets followed and finally she uttered a small, 'You can turn round now.'

He turned back and eyed the mound of clothes on the bottom of the boat.

'Fer cryin' oot lood, it's nae wonder it were like carryin' a coo wi' all that coverin' ye,' he commented, shaking his head. 'We'll nae be able tae dry it in a month o' Sundays. Ah'll have tae carry ye up.'

Jennifer reddened in mortification, assuming by coo he meant cow. 'I wouldn't wish you to strain anything,' she declared stiffly. 'After all, a man of your advancing years must take extra care when indulging in any kind of physical labour.'

She was satisfied to see his eyes narrow but, 'Ah reckon ye'll be as light as a feather wi'oot that ton o' claes ower yer,' was all he said.

Feeling somewhat mollified, Jennifer hunched down into her blankets. 'Let me ken when ye're guid an' warm and we'll start back up tae the hoose,' he added.

'Would it be acceptable for me to ask your name?' Jennifer asked after a moment.

'Ah dinnae ken – would it?' he grinned at her, and her stomach did a sudden flip. His smile was truly devastating. Just as she was thinking how to reply to such a flippant response, he waved his hand and shrugged. 'Dinnae fret, ah'm teasin' yer. Brendon

Galbraith at yer service, ma lady.' He stood up and bowed with a flourish.

'You're the one applying for the position of Caerlaverock's steward?' Jennifer questioned in surprise.

'Aye,' he answered, sitting back down. 'Well, I was. I dinnae ken whether turnin' up wi' the daughter o' the Duke naur naked is gaunnae help wi' it.'

'How do you know I'm the Duke's daughter?' Jennifer quizzed, ignoring the bit about her being nearly naked.

'Yer a Sassenach,' he shrugged. 'Ah dinnae ken who else ye can be.'

Jennifer frowned. Now he mentioned it, it wasn't only his reputation at risk, but hers too. Even if it was his deuced fault for startling her in the first place. Biting her lip, she thought quickly. 'Gifford said he was expecting you at two this afternoon. Do you have any idea what the time is now?'

'There's nae sun, but ah reckon it's nae yet twalhoures.' He saw Jennifer's puzzled frown and added, 'midday.'

'So you still have at least two hours before you're expected up at the house?' Jennifer clarified. He nodded cautiously.

'Then I suggest you take Flossy and walk up to the house. Once there you can ask whether anyone knows who she belongs to. Make sure you speak with my brother or my grandfather...'

'Yer grandda's here too?'

Jennifer frowned at the interruption. 'Flossy belongs to him,' she explained. 'Please don't interrupt.' She thought for a second before continuing, 'Tell them you found her wandering on her own.

'Obviously they know Flossy came out with me this morning. Once they realise I'm missing, they'll send out a search party.'

She paused and tapped her fingers on the gunwale pensively. 'I'll say I slipped into the loch, managed to climb out, and realising I could not traverse the distance back to Caerlaverock while soaking wet, I discovered this boathouse, found it unlocked and came inside to remove my wet clothing and wait to be rescued. All eminently sensible.

'Nobody will know we've been alone together, and you will be lauded a hero for drawing attention to my plight.' She gave a satisfied chuckle. 'Likely you'll be offered the post of steward on the spot.'

'Ah dinnae think ah can leave ye here alone,' Brendon protested with a frown.

'I'll be perfectly fine,' she answered firmly. 'It will not take long for you to reach the house, and I'm entirely certain they'll send a search party for me immediately.'

'But ye'll be here alone,' he repeated patiently as if to a child.

'I will be perfectly safe,' she reiterated in the same slow tone. 'Nobody but you knows I'm here.'

He stared at her in silence for a second, his face impassive. Then, 'Are ye always this buckle-horned?'

She stared back, her lips quirking. 'I've never heard the term buckle-horned, but I've been described as shockingly loose in the haft and I'm guessing that means the same thing.'

∞∞∞

Reverend Shackleford popped the last piece of shortbread into his mouth and chewed appreciatively. Whatever other oddities there were in Highland cooking, the shortbread was truly manna from Heaven. Then he finished off his dish of tea and climbed to his feet. Time for a bit of exploring. He'd given his grandson a goodly head start, so providing he was careful, it was a big enough house to ensure they didn't cross paths. Not that he was up to anything havey-cavey. He just preferred to do his nosing around with Percy, but as the curate sadly wasn't present, alone.

He thought mayhap he'd start at the top of the house and work his way down. If it was anything like Blackmore, the servants' quarters would be located under the roof. While he suspected most of the domestics would be hard at work, there might just be an opportune moment to have a quick chat about the good book – if nothing else, it was always a good excuse for being where he shouldn't. And that reminded him – no point in talking about the Bible if he hadn't got the deuced thing with him.

With a chuckle and quick muttered apology upstairs for the expletive, the Reverend returned to his bedchamber and picked up his well-used copy of the Bible – King James Edition, naturally. He assumed that the Godly amongst the servants would be familiar with the text.

So, he'd have a good look around and if he bumped into any unfortunates who'd strayed from the path, he would simply offer a gentle reminder. Not that he could blame them for straying - being forced to live with the deuced midges up here would turn anybody into an atheist. Of all God's creatures, the little beasties as Gifford referred to them had to be the most unpleasant. Why some of the locals wore skirts, he had no idea. Likely they were possessed of either a deeply troubled nature or baubles like leather. Still, he could definitely help with the former.

Armed with his bible, Reverend Shackleford went in search of the back stairs…

∞∞∞

As Dougal came closer to Caerlaverock, his steps slowed. The fresh air had helped to clear his whisky addled head and what had seemed like a good idea an hour ago, now seemed nothing more than flumgummery. He sat down on a convenient rock and pulled out his flask. Then he scratched his chin and looked towards Caerlaverock while he sipped on the fiery liquid.

Gradually his ire returned as his thoughts regurgitated old grievances. By rights that hoose should ah belonged tae the Galbraiths (sip). No matter which way ye looked at it, the bloody Sinclairs were naethin but thievin' peratts (sip). It wa' high time the laithsome sassenach maggots gaed back tae England (sip). And what's more, Dougal Galbraith was aboot tae tell 'em so.

He tossed back the last of the whisky, then pushed the stopper back in and wobbled to his feet. There was a small gate in the wall surrounding Caerlaverock he knew Gifford kept unlocked. Dougal guessed it was to save the old steward's legs when he left of an evening since he lived in Banalan and the gate being where it was almost halved the distance. He himself only knew about it after watching the old bampot come and go a few times.

Determinedly the old Scot weaved his way towards the gate which he knew was positioned in a slight fold in the hill to hide it from prying eyes. While he walked, he tried to assemble his scattered thoughts, but in the end, all he kept muttering to himself was, 'The bastarts'll nae mak a bawheid o' ma son.' Ten minutes later, he let himself through the veiled gate and followed the footpath towards the house.

# Chapter Seven

As the Reverend listened to yet another string of completely incomprehensible words come out of the servant's mouth, he actually began to panic a little. Indeed, he couldn't help wondering at what point the family would realise he was missing. He might not be discovered until supper. Or longer. They might even discover his remains on the same chair, shrivelled and wrinkled like those deuced mummy things from Egypt.

Truly, Augustus Shackleford had never met such a boring, wearisome, *longwinded* individual. It was taking the chucklehead twenty words for what could be said in three. Or so he assumed, since he couldn't actually understand a word the fellow was saying. How the devil had he managed to pick on the saintliest servant in the house? The Reverend was beginning to think the fellow could well be in the process of quoting the whole of the Bible ad verbatim. Either that or he was talking about the weather.

Nodding benevolently at the impassioned servant for the umpteenth time, Reverend Shackleford happened to glance out of the window and gave a slight frown. An unsavoury individual seemed to be making his way up a narrow path at the very edge of the formal gardens. The man was weaving this way and that, so much so that the Reverend wondered if he might actually be more than a trifle foxed – a sorry state of affairs since it wasn't yet lunchtime. Here indeed was an individual sorely in need of God's benediction. Just what he needed to get him out of his current dire predicament.

Turning back to the gabster who didn't appear to have noticed his audience's attention had wandered, Reverend Shackleford took a deep breath, leaned forward and slapped his right hand on the man's head. Startled, the servant spluttered to a halt. With one eye on the window, the Reverend muttered a quick blessing then clambered to his feet, crossing himself hurriedly as he did so. Then yelling, 'AMEN,' he tucked the Bible under one arm, lifted his cassock off the floor with the other and bolted.

∞∞∞

By the time Dougal got as far as the house, he'd almost entirely forgotten what he was actually doing there. Bemused, he stared at the inconspicuous door in front of him, then rummaged around in his pocket for his flask, absently removing the stopper and putting the opening to his mouth. It was the realisation that he'd finished its contents some time ago that helped clarify things a little.

He was here tae tell them thievin' bastart Sassenachs ... err ... what? Dougal frowned in concentration. Somethin aboot his son. Aye, that was it. Somethin' aboot Brendon ...

Certain it would come to him eventually, the old Scot tried the door. To his befuddled delight, it was open. With only the slightest hesitation, he stepped through and found himself in a long corridor, black as the Earl o' Hell's waistcoat.

Leaving the door slightly open to let in some light and, of course, on the off chance he needed a hasty escape, Dougal began feeling his way along the narrow passage. Thankfully after a few seconds, the darkness began to retreat until he could see his own hand. Breathing a sigh of relief, he tiptoed further until finally, he could see lights at the end of the passage. Whilst his ideas of what he would do when he got there were vague at best, they did involve refusing to move until he'd had an audience with the Maister o' the hoose.

As he got closer to what looked to be a large hall, Dougal began rehearsing in his mind what he was going to say. A little more sober now, he recognised that accusing the Duke's son of being a thievin' bastart would not only get him thrown out, but likely land him in jail. 'Noo, haud on a wee minent, Dougal,' he muttered to himself, his footsteps slowing, 'Ye dinnae ken who yer gaunnie meet.'

Hesitating at the entrance to the large square hall, he scratched his head and tried to sort out his muddled thoughts.

'Can I help you, my son?' A sudden loud voice behind him had Dougal almost jumping out of his skin. Spinning round, he stared in abject terror as a large black garbed apparition loomed out of the darkness. Lord save him, it was a bogle. Abruptly convinced he was about to be dragged all the way to hell itself, Dougal gave a strangled battle cry and yelled, 'Ye'll nae be taikin a Galbraith wi'oot a fight, yer devil.' Then with another, even louder whoop, he launched himself at the spectre which appeared on their first connection to be surprisingly solid.

'Thunder an' turf, what the...' Dougal had time to note that the apparition's voice didn't sound much like a bogle either, before the demon staggered forward into the large hall while the Scot hung limpet like around its neck shouting, 'Ah'm nae feart o' ye bawcan. Ah'll gie ye a skelpin ye'll nae forget.' They did an almost credible waltz around the room, then just as Dougal was attempting to swing his leg around the demon's neck in an effort to climb onto its shoulders, the doorbell rang. For a few vital seconds, Dougal paused, and a muffled cry for help came from under his elbow. He looked down in surprise, thinking it strange that the denizen of hell should have such a convincing English accent, before the bogle blundered into a large marble pedestal and began to topple backwards. They both crashed slowly to the floor just as the butler, MacNee, staunchly ignoring the fracas, opened the door.

On the threshold stood Brendon Galbraith carrying a small shivering dog in his arms.

Being on the top of the pile of two, Dougal looked up with a frown, rubbed his eyes and commented, 'What the bloody hell have ye done wi' Fergus?'

∞∞∞

Shivering, Jennifer tucked her knees up onto the bench she was sitting on and covered them with her blankets. To her estimation the would-be steward had been gone at least twenty minutes. Surely she wouldn't have to wait much longer.

With nothing else to occupy her thoughts, she found herself reliving the last half an hour since Brendon Galbraith had fished her out of the loch. Although she'd been barely conscious at the time, she remembered the feel of his strong arms around her and the solid warmth of his chest. She shivered again, this time for a different reason. He truly was a handsome man. Was he married? Engaged? She found it hard to believe that there wasn't a line of willing females camped outside his door.

She remembered what Gifford had said that morning about Galbraith leaving employment with another clan. She frowned trying to remember. *MacFarlane*, that was it. Had Galbraith been dismissed? Clearly he was trustworthy – well at least he hadn't tried to take advantage of her - though she supposed that didn't mean he wasn't light fingered. But somehow she doubted it. There was something honourable about the Scot. Every action he'd taken since fishing her out of the freezing water had been congruent with someone who had an inherently compassionate nature. And that didn't match her image of a thief or worse. And besides, Gifford had declared the Clan chief dicked in the nob.

Resting her head on her knees, she sighed. Despite her abundance of blankets, the cold was beginning to creep back in. How long had it been now?

Abruptly a small sound caught her attention. She swallowed in sudden fear. Were there rats onboard? She'd heard tales of rodents the size of cats eating people's toes and fingers. Granted, the unfortunates having their extremities removed were dead at the time, but still...

The noise came again, and Jennifer frowned. It sounded like someone sniffing.

'Who's there?' she called, not entirely able to keep the panic out of her voice. 'I ... I have a weapon,' she lied, while casting desperately around for something she could use to defend herself.

The sniff came again, and this time it sounded suspiciously like a sob. Frowning, she gingerly put her bare feet back onto the deck and stood up. Peering down the stairs into the blackness of the little boat's cabin, she eventually made out a small form, curled up on the floor. It had to be a child. With a slight gasp, she stepped forward, only to watch the shape scuttle backwards into the farthest reaches of the cabin.

∞∞∞

'Da, what the devil dae ye think yer daein?' Brendon roared, putting Flossy on the floor and hurrying over to drag his father off the prone clergyman. 'Are ye daft? Can ye nae see, ye be giein a skelpin tae a man o' God?'

Dangling in mid-air on the end of his son's vice like grip, Dougal frowned and looked down at the groaning figure below him. In broad daylight, what had looked to be a shroud was clearly a cassock. 'Hoo was ah tae ken? The eejit didnae annoonce himself.'

Sighing, Brendon stood his father back onto the floor and bent down to help the Reverend onto his feet. 'Tare an' hounds, the chawbacon's addled,' Augustus Shackleford muttered, checking that all his extremities remained intact.

'Ye should ken better, tae sneak up thatwey.'

'I was not sneaking,' the Reverend retorted, his ire well and truly roused. 'As I recall, it was you who attacked me, you … you *heathen*.'

'Ah'll gae ye heathen, ye toom-heidit Sassen…'

'What the blazes is going on?' Peter's voice cut into the mêlée, and all three men immediately fell silent.

Brendon stepped forward and bent his head. 'Ah hope ye'll forgive ma intrusion and that o' ma foolish da, ma lord…'

'… An' jus who dae ye think ye be callin foolish?' Dougal interrupted.

Brendon gritted his teeth and glared over at his father. 'Haud yer wheesht,' he growled. 'If ye open yer mouth agin, ah'll be gaggin' ye.' Unthinkingly, Dougal opened his mouth to argue, then thought better of it and subsided with a scowl.

'Ma lord, ye can dae as ye wish wi' ma da, but first - ah foond this wee dog wanderin' near the loch.' He gestured towards Flossy, now happily ensconced in her master's arms. 'Ah'm thinkin' ye ken her?' When his audience continued to stare at him blankly, he added desperately, *'She wernae wi' anyone.'*

'Didn't she go out with Jenny?' Peter asked, abruptly grasping what the Scot was trying to say.

'Aye,' Malcolm confirmed. 'Did ye see a lady wi' the dog?' he asked Brendon.

With an internal sigh of relief, Brendon shook his head. 'There were no lady wi' her.'

'Thunder an' turf, she could have fallen into the deuced loch.' Reverend Shackleford's face turned pale. Grace would never forgive him if anything happened to her only daughter.

Peter raked his hand through his hair in agitation. 'Will you show me where you found the dog?' he asked Brendon.

'Aye, gladly,' the Scot responded. 'Shall we be takin' a horse for fear the lady may be injured?'

Peter nodded. 'Excellent idea. Gifford, can you have a horse saddled immediately?'

'Ah'll wait fer the horse. Ye and the lad get ye gone.' Malcolm waved Peter towards the door.

'Here, take Flossy. She might help. There's a bit of Freddy in her yet.' The Reverend gave the little dog a quick fuss and handed her back to Brendon.

'Can you ask Mrs Darroch to have a hot bath taken to my sister's room, Grandpapa?' Peter looked over at his white-faced grandfather. 'We'll find her. If she's fallen into the loch, she's an excellent swimmer.'

The Reverend gave a worried nod before glaring at his erstwhile opponent who was busy muttering, 'Tatties ower the side an' nae mistak.

∞∞∞

'I won't hurt you,' she called, this time as gently as she could.

The almost inaudible sniffing continued unabated. Hesitantly Jennifer put a foot down on the first step. 'Will you let me help you?' she asked, scrutinising the gloom below her and taking another step down.

'Gonnae no' dae that,' a small voice responded, surprisingly firmly.

'You want me to stay here?' No response. 'Please, I want to help you.'

'Ye gat anythin' tae eat Maistres?'

'My brother will be here very soon. If you're hungry, I can take you to my home. They'll give you lots to eat there.' Jennifer hoped it was true. She'd certainly have some explaining to do returning half naked with an urchin in tow.

'Ah'm nae gaun anywhere wi' ye,' the voice returned promptly.

Before she could take another step, there was the sound of footsteps and the door to the boat shed abruptly opened and a voice shouted, *Jennifer?*'

Sighing with relief, Jennifer hurriedly pulled the blankets tight around her and stepped back up into the small cockpit. 'I'm here,' she returned fighting tears of her own.

'Thank God.' Peter's head appeared and behind him was Brendon Galbraith. Absurdly, Jennifer felt her face suffuse with warmth for the second time in as many hours. She was almost alarmed by the feeling of excitement that rushed through her at the sight of the large Scot. Was she imagining the heat of his stare behind her brother's back? An excited bark brought her back to her predicament.

'Yer dog led us here,' Brendon explained gruffly, clearly uncomfortable with the statement - a half-truth at best.

Peter blinked as he took in her state of undress. 'I fell into the loch and had to take off my wet clothes as you can see,' Jennifer commented in her most matter-of-fact manner. 'To avoid catching an ague, naturally.'

Peter sighed and glanced back at Brendon. 'It's fortunate I listened to your advice about a horse, Galbraith,' he declared ruefully. Jennifer thought she was the only one who caught the wince in Brendon's answering shrug.

'I take it you're not injured in any way?' Peter continued, turning back towards the boat. Jennifer shook her head. 'Do you think you can ride and maintain your modesty?' he added drily.

'I'm certain I can,' she answered determinedly, clutching her blankets. 'But before we go, there's a slight problem.'

'I assume we're no longer talking about the problem of getting my naked sister back to the house with no one the wiser aside from the previously unmet gentleman standing beside me?' He clicked his fingers and added, 'Or of course, controlling a horse whilst holding on to the vast number of garments you appear to have removed?'

Jennifer gave a slight frown, then shrugged and nodded. 'There's a child in the cabin,' she declared bluntly, ignoring the small cry of protest coming from down the stairs behind her. 'I think whoever it is has been hiding there for some time, and he or she is very hungry.'

While Peter stared at her as if she'd lost her wits, Brendon frowned and immediately stepped onto the boat. 'Ah'm thinkin' ye should be takin' yer sister ma lord while I look tae the bairn,' he suggested over his shoulder.

Many members of England's upper echelons might well have bristled at the Scot's authoritative tone, but like his father, Peter didn't have an egotistical bone in his body. He also possessed the Duke's practical streak, so he merely nodded and stepped forward to help his sister out of the boat.

'Caerlaverock is closest,' Jennifer declared as she took her brother's hand. 'Bring the child straight to the house.' Then she paused before adding in a low tone, 'I think it might well be a boy. Please don't frighten him.'

Brendon shook his head. 'Ah would'nae m'lady. The lad'll be safe wi' me.' He stood and watched as Jennifer Sinclair climbed out of the boat, looking for all the world as though she was acceding to a dance request. He couldn't hold back a sudden grin. Then, shaking his head at the bewildering vagaries of women, he turned and stood at the door to the cabin, blocking it entirely should the child decide to run.

'Ye cannae stay there foraye, lad. Ye'll starve,' he murmured, his voice calm.

'Ye cannae stand there foraye naither,' came the impudent response. Clearly the lad wasn't yet *that* hungry.

'Ah ken. An' ah'm nae gaunnae, but ah'm nae leavin' wi'oot ye.'

'Gaun jus' bugger aff wid ye.' The response was defiant, but with an undercurrent of fear that spoke volumes.

With a sigh, Brendon ducked his head and went slowly down the steps, giving his eyes time to adjust to the gloom. In the far corner, what looked like a bundle of rags suddenly moved.

'Ah'll nae hurt ye lad,' holding his hand out in a placating gesture. 'What be yer name?'

'There was a pause and a sniff, then, 'Finn.'

'If ye come wi' me, Finn, ah'll see yer giein a hot meal. Hoo aboot some mealie puddin? That dae ye?' Brendon thought the child would probably jump on dry bread and water.

For a full minute, the lad didn't move, then slowly, the rags unfolded, and the boy stood up. Brendon had to suppress a groan at the sorry sight the lad presented. He was little more than skin and bone. 'Can ye walk, Finn?'

'Course ah can bloody walk.' The impudence was still there, but underneath, Brendon could see the lad was actually trembling. He might even collapse before they reached Caerlaverock. Swearing under his breath, Brendon retreated back to up to the cockpit and waited.

After about five minutes, Finn came slowly up the narrow stairs. In the daylight, the boy looked even worse. He was filthy, his ribs sticking out through the rags he wore. But more than that, the filth was black, covering him from head to toe. Abruptly Brendon realised where the lad had come from.

There was little doubt. Finn had somehow escaped from MacFarlane's mine.

## Chapter Eight

'I'll have to put a stop to it,' Peter declared heatedly. 'It's what my father would want me to do.'

'Aye, but not at the expense of yer own safety,' Malcolm countered.

Peter frowned. 'I'm no foolish boy, Malcolm, though you might believe me so.'

'I did'nae say that, Peter. But yer father sent me to gae ye advice, and I'll gae it whether ye want it or no.'

Peter sighed, absently noting how much stronger the stubborn Scot's accent had become since he'd come home. 'Your counsel as always is invaluable, Malcolm. But I cannot in all conscience sit here and do nothing while children are being murdered less than ten miles from our door.'

Brendon watched the exchange in silence. When he'd arrived with Finn an hour ago, he was pleased to note that the only expressions exhibited had been horror at the boy's plight. He'd been taken straight to the kitchen for some food. Once the lad had eaten his fill, only then would the housekeeper see to cleaning him up.

Brendon hadn't seen Jennifer, and he was surprised at the feeling of disappointment her absence provoked. When he'd enquired after her wellbeing, the Viscount had drily announced that his sister was fine, though the horse was still recovering. Brendon fought and failed to suppress a grin and for a second the two men were in perfect accord. But then it had been down to business.

With the unexpected arrival of Finn, the interview for the new steward had been replaced by concern for the boy. Who he was, where he'd come from and most important of all, why he'd been in such a sorry state.

Taking a deep breath, Brendon had finally voiced what he'd inadvertently seen three months ago.

'It's an evil place wi' a clan chief who's nae' the full shillin. Ah kenned aboot the gold mine, but there were tell it closed two years back.'

He grimaced and shook his head. 'The MacFarlane bade me fetch supplies frae Mosslea. It were late afore ah loaded the horse so ah thought tae take a short cut through the quarry thinkin' it were deserted.' He paused and swallowed, remembering the horror of the next hour. 'As ah were cuttin' through, ah heard shoutin' near the pit entrance. There shouldnae hae been anybody there, so ah left ma horse aback agin the trees an' gaed tae hae a look.'

'Ah gaed in the direction o' the noise and hid aback one o' the auld bothies. Front o' the mine entrance there were three wee bodies laid out on the ground. Bairns all.

I watched as the bastarts brought another three up out o' the pit, then loaded all six ontae a cart.' He gritted his teeth at the memory, then sighed. 'Ah realised the poor wee bairns haed been doon in the mine an' somehoo crushed. At first ah thought they'd been where they shouldnae, but then ah heard twa o' the bastarts speakin. The bairns had been *workin'* in the pit and frae what ah heard, there were still more doon that hell hole.

'At that moment, ah kenned if they saw me ah'd be deid, so ah crept back tae ma horse and left as quick as ah could.'

Brendon stopped and rubbed his hand wearily across his face. 'The next day ah left. Ah didnae ken what tae dae, but ah couldnae stay there wi' that monster.' He looked over at Peter before adding honestly, 'In truth, ah was hopin' the Duke'd be wi' yer.'

And now as Brendon watched the impassioned Viscount, he couldn't help feeling sympathy. It was evident that the young man had grown and matured tenfold, and he was so keen to do the right thing, it was almost painful to watch. But Brendon knew Malcolm Mackenzie was right. The Duke of Blackmore's heir apparent could not risk his own life for the sake of a few nameless foundlings. Harsh, but true, nonetheless.

The risks would have to be taken by others.

'Ah'll dae whatever ye want me tae,' he declared. 'Like ye, ma lord, ah cannae sit by whan bairns are dyin'. Ah'm ashamed I didnae act sooner, but ah'm one man an' the MacFarlane would hae seen me deid like that.' He clicked his fingers.

'Ye should hae spake ter me, lad.' Dougal's voice was subdued. Strangely enough, the old Scot hadn't been thrown out on his ear and was actually sitting next to his earlier adversary absently stroking Flossy who was curled up on his knee.

'It's a deuced evil practice to use children so,' the Reverend declared gruffly. 'Were he here, Nicholas would indeed put a stop to it. Of that I'm certain.'

'I'm here as my father's representative,' Peter insisted stiffly. 'While I don't have my father's experience, I'm not a complete...'

'...cake?' supplied a lone female voice. Brendon looked up and drew in his breath. Jennifer Sinclair had changed into a pale orange tea gown which brought out the burnished copper of her hair, currently held back with a simple ribbon. Behind her was an older woman he'd not yet met.

Malcolm indicated two unoccupied chairs around the dining table they were currently sitting at. 'How are ye feelin', lass?' he asked Jennifer as she seated herself. 'Twas a lucky encounter Brendon had wi' Flossy.'

'I'm perfectly well, thank you, Malcolm.' Jennifer cast a quick glance toward her rescuer, her lips quirking.

Climbing to his feet, Gifford went to find the housekeeper, thinking they might all benefit from a little sustenance. He'd check on the bairn while he was at it.

'Felicity, this is Brendon Galbraith. He's applyin' for the position of steward to Caerlaverock.'

Brendon stood up hastily and inclined his head. 'Pleased to meet ye,' he murmured.

'My wife, Felicity Mackenzie,' Malcolm informed him, pride evident in his voice. Mrs Mackenzie gave Brendon a warm smile before turning enquiringly towards Dougal.

'Ma father, Dougal Galbraith,' Brendon explained, hoping the lady wouldn't request any further details. He was relieved to see his da get to his feet and take off his bonnet. 'Honoured tae meet ye,' he said with a small, unexpected flourish.

After swallowing his surprise at his da's much improved manners, Brendon saw Mrs. Mackenzie cast a quick look towards her husband and gave an inward sigh. Clearly, they'd already been apprised of his father's reputation.

'How is the boy?' Jennifer asked, smiling a welcome at Dougal. As the lady of the house, she had not been introduced.

'I suspect Gifford has gone to find out,' Peter answered.

'I've already told Felicity all about my unexpected swim,' Jennifer went on, 'but from the looks on your faces there are more sobering details to come.'

Peter turned to Brendon. 'Would you tell your story to the ladies?' he requested. At Brendon's raised eyebrows, he added drily, 'If you are going to be working for the Sinclair family, you will have to get used to the fact that its female members are, in the main, forceful and dreadfully brash.'

'Eminent qualities in any personable female, as I'm sure you'll agree Mr. Galbraith.' Jennifer's quip was deliberately goading him, Brendon realised and to his surprise and discomfort he felt an instant stirring in his breeches. Bloody hell, that was all he needed.

With an uncomfortable cough, he recounted the events at the abandoned mine.

'Why that's monstrous,' Jennifer declared when he'd finished. The horror in her voice was unfeigned.

'Indeed,' Felicity added sadly, 'but not unusual I fear. Your father is a good and generous master, ensuring that everyone under his care is well looked after. However, unfortunately, he's very much in the minority. Most landowners have no concerns over those they employ, and working someone to death, whatever age they are, is more common than you think.'

'There is no school for the children?' Jennifer asked Brendon. He shook his head.

'Ah suspect most o' the bairns MacFarlane employs in his mine be orphans. Ah've asked aroond several villages hereaboot and more'an one hae told me bairns hae disappeared wi' nae warnin'. He sighed and shrugged. 'Naebodie cared. One less mouth tae feed.'

'Was Banalan one of the villages with children missing?' Peter enquired. At Brendon's nod, the Viscount looked around the table. 'Banalan is on Blackmore land. At the very least, this MacFarlane had no right to take children from there.'

'Ye didnae gie a rat's arse aboot the bairns afore milady here fell ower one,' Dougal announced with a glower.

Brendon gritted his teeth and glared at his father. He knew the old bampot's silence had been too good to last.

'We weren't aware, that's true,' Peter responded carefully. 'And I fully accept that it has been far too long since our last visit – we must indeed accept full blame for not taking sufficient care of our own. However, to say that we do not care? Well, nothing could be further from the truth, I assure you.'

'You'd do well to keep your breath to cool your deuced porridge,' Reverend Shackleford declared in outrage. 'Indeed, if I didn't have better manners,' I'd be calling you a beetle headed bumpkin and telling you to stubble it.'

'An ah'll be tellin' ye, yer all arse an' parsley an' giein ye a skelpit lug.'

'Give me back my dog.'

'Ye can ha yer wee mongrel. She's nae use fer anythin ower than catchin midges.'

The two men glared at each other while Flossy snored on oblivious. Neither attempted to move the little dog.

'Da, ye'll gie the paster an apologie noo,' Brendon grated, his tone low and furious.

'Ah'll nae be sayin' sorry tae a toom-heidit *Sassenach* God walloper.'

The Reverend narrowed his eyes. 'And I'll nae... I mean I *will not* be accepting any such apology from a lily-livered *Sawny*.'

'*Enough!*' Peter slammed his hand down on the table to emphasise his command. The two men jumped like guilty children.

'If you have nothing useful to add and are unable to be civil to one another, I will simply ask you both to leave the table. And that goes for you too, Grandfather.' Peter's voice was cold, and he sounded so much like his father that the Reverend's indignant retort died on his lips.

Fortunately at that moment, Gifford reappeared with the housekeeper, Mrs. Darroch, and two housemaids in tow. A huge plate of shortbread was placed in the middle of the table along with some other unfamiliar tid-bits. 'Ah be thinkin' ye might keep the heid wi' a bit o' sugar inside ye,' the housekeeper declared briskly. Clearly, she'd heard the altercation.

'How's the bairn?' Malcolm asked, helping himself to some shortbread.

'He's haein' a wee bath. It's takin' fower men to haud the hallion down. Any more o' his cheek an' ah'll be skelpin' his wee behind.' She handed Malcolm a dish of tea with pursed lips.

'Do you think he'll be well enough to speak with us once he's clean and dry?' Jennifer asked, helping herself to a slice of what looked a little like fudge.

The housekeeper's face softened as she shook her head in a complete about turn. 'He's fair puckled, the puir wee bairn. Ah reckon ye'll nae get any sense frae him until the morn.'

'Do you have someone who can sit with him?' asked Felicity.

'Aye, dinnae fash yersel m'lady. Ah'll sit wi' him maself.'

'That's indeed kind of you, Mrs. Darroch,' Jennifer smiled as she sipped gratefully at her tea. 'By the way, what is this exactly?' She held up the large piece of fudge she'd been nibbling on.

The housekeeper chuckled. 'Tablet, m'lady. Ye'll certainly hae more aboot yer wi' a bit o' that in yer belly.'

'It's delicious,' Jennifer enthused, taking a large bite.

'Aye, an' especially good if yer partial tae holes in yer teeth,' Malcolm interrupted drily.

'I think we may be better to delay forming a plan of action until the morning when we can possibly get some sense out of the lad.' Peter's tone made it perfectly clear that he did not intend to allow MacFarlane's evil practices to continue. Malcolm stared at the Viscount for a second then nodded his head reluctantly. 'I'll pen a letter to my father,' Peter conceded. 'If the messenger changes horses, I would expect a reply within a sennight.'

Malcolm gave a rueful chuckle. 'Ah ken yer yer father's son, ma lord, but Nicholas would ne'er forgive me if I let anythin' happen to ye.'

Peter turned to Brendon. 'Well, Galbraith, I think we've established that you're a man of character, and I'd very much like your assistance with this unpleasant matter. To that end, I'd like Gifford to begin your employment immediately...' He paused, then added, 'I know we haven't discussed what your duties will be as steward of Caerlaverock, but I trust Gifford will get to that once we've put this unsavoury problem to bed.'

Brendon felt relief swamp him, so much so that he almost sagged back into his chair. He hadn't realised quite how anxious he was. He swallowed, nodded his head, and stood up. 'Ah ken ye willnae regret yer decision, ma lord.' Then, giving a small bow, added, 'Until the morra.' He turned to his father who was busy making short work of what was left of the shortbread and tablet.

'It's time we were leavin', Da. Will ye gie yer thanks tae his lordship for not throwin' yer out on yer eejit ear?'

On hearing his name, Dougal hurriedly broke the last piece of tablet in two, shoved one half in his pocket and gave the other to Flossy who was looking up at him adoringly. Finally, he offered a muttered, 'Thank ye.' Then lifting the little dog off his lap with a sniff he added, 'Ye be a braw wee dog. I ken ye cannae help wha yer maister is,' before plonking her onto the Reverend's lap and climbing to his feet.

Augustus Shackleford hmphed and muttered, 'Aside from her having a peculiar partiality for chuckleheaded, bony kneed men in a deuced skirt.'

'What have you done with your dog?' Jennifer asked Brendon abruptly before another argument could erupt.

'What dog?' Peter frowned.

As soon as her brother spoke, Jennifer realised her mistake. There had been no dog with Brendon when he'd come to her rescue with Peter. She felt herself begin to colour up. Hot headed, she might be, but she'd never been a good liar.

To her surprise, the new steward came to her rescue. 'Did ye see Fergus frae yer bedchamber?' he asked pointedly. 'Ah thought it best tae leave him ootside. He'd hae cleared the table wi'oot breakin' a sweat.'

Jennifer nodded gratefully. 'So his name is Fergus? It suits him.'

Brendon turned back to Peter. 'He'll nae cause any bother,' he assured the Viscount.

'There have always been dogs in our family,' Peter replied nonchalantly. 'As you can see, my grandfather has Flossy and before that a foxhound called Freddy. My uncle too has a three-legged mutt he named Nelson. And that's just for starters. I can't remember all the names of my aunts' and cousins' furred companions.' He gave a smiling shrug. 'We're a large family.'

At the Viscount's words, Brendon found himself beset by an abrupt longing so acute, it nearly took him to his knees. What must it be like to be part of a large family? Turning hastily away from the table, he started towards the door. 'Are ye wi' me, Da?'

As Dougal gave one last scowl towards the Reverend, Peter

cleared his throat and said, 'Before you go, just one more thing, Mr. Galbraith. Perhaps you could tell me how you managed to gain entrance to the house without anyone seeing you?'

Clearly Peter Sinclair was speaking to his father. Brendon's heart sank as he turned back. All eyes were on Dougal enquiringly. The elderly Scot had the grace to look uncomfortable as he fidgeted with his cap.

'Ah foond a door.' He waved in the vague direction he supposed said door to be and darted a furtive glance towards Gifford who'd gone a little pale. 'Ah saw twa lasses come oot o it – ah reckon they was emptyin' the ... err... ye ken, the err... *whatever* doon the jaw-hole, if yer understan' ma meanin'.' He stopped, tapped his nose and nodded towards the ladies. 'Ah sneakt in after they'd gaun.'

Dougal felt, rather than saw Gifford's relieved stance and knew he wouldn't be using that entrance again. Still, nae matter, he had one ower the old bampot now. He looked over at the old steward and gave a brief sly wink over Peter Sinclair's head as the Viscount turned to request the door be locked at all times to prevent any further unwanted visitors.

## Chapter Nine

Finn stared incredulously up at the window. It was the first time he'd ever slept in a real bed and the only time he could *ever* remember waking up past dawn. Sitting up, he looked down at his *clean* nightshirt, then he held his hands in front of his face, spread his fingers and marvelled. Not one spec of dirt. If he was being honest, looking at them actually made him feel a bit uncomfortable – as though they weren't really his.

A tantalising smell suddenly invaded his nostrils. Putting his hands down, he leaned forward and peered at the only other piece of furniture in the room – an old trunk positioned at the end of the bed. On top of it was a hunk of bread and even a piece of cheese. It was the bread he'd smelled and the freshness of it made his mouth water.

Had they been put there for him? Climbing out of bed, he padded to the bottom and gaped at the feast in front of him. This would have been shared between ten of them. Oh not the cheese, just the bread. And it'd be so stale they'd have to dip it in water just so they could swallow it.

Reverently he put out his hand, picked up the cheese and sniffed it. He felt like weeping. Did he dare take a bite? What if it wasn't for him? Before he could decide what to do, the door abruptly opened. With a terrified gasp, he threw the cheese back onto the plate, only to watch in horror as it bounced off and landed straight at the feet of the person who'd entered the room.

Wordlessly he stared at the young woman standing in the doorway. 'Did ye nae want it?' she asked picking up the piece of cheese and wiping it on her apron. Finn stared mutely at her. 'It be fer ye,' she added encouragingly, holding the wedge out towards him. After a second's hesitation, Finn snatched it from her hand and took a huge bite, almost groaning at the harshly sweet taste flooding his mouth.

'An' the bread,' the girl added helpfully. 'Ah'm Morag, head housemaid. Mrs Darroch said ah was tae fetch ye tae the kitchen whan ye'd finisht.' Finn obligingly picked up the hunk of bread and shoved it whole into his mouth.

'Och, Mrs. Darroch willnae be happy wi' such terrible manners' Morag sniffed as she watched him swallow the last of the cheese. They looked at each other in silence for a second, then the maid sighed. 'Ye cannae gae wi'oot yer claes,' she scoffed pointing to a small pile on the floor next to the trunk. Finn made to lift up his nightshirt, as Morag hurriedly turned away. 'Have ye nae shame? Ah'll be waitin outside the door. Be sure tae bring yer empty plate.'

Regarding her bemusedly, Finn, shrugged off the nightshirt and replaced it with the britches and a coarse linen shirt that itched like the blazes. There was even a pair of shoes. Hurriedly he pushed his feet into them and sighed. They were too big, but even so, his feet had never felt so blessedly warm. He was just about to open the door, when he looked back at the bed. After a second, he went back to straighten the blanket. If he proved his worth, he might even get to sleep in it for a second night.

'Are ye meeting the Queen o' England or somethin'?' came Morag's aggravated voice. 'Ah haenae all day tae be waitin' on ye.' Seconds later, she jumped as the door was thrown open. Finn grinned as she tut-tutted and led the way down a steep winding set of stairs.

'The Maister'll be wantin' tae speak wi' ye this day, so be canny,' she told him as they entered a long narrow passageway leading to the kitchen.

'Whitfor?' Finn asked, alarm replacing his earlier euphoria.

'Dae ye think he'll nae be askin' what ye was daein hidin' in that wee boat?'

Finn fell back slightly. What would they want to know? He thought back to the day before. The lady had been kind, but the big maister had asked him questions – at least until he'd fallen asleep when the muckleheid picked him up and carried him.

Did he dare tell them about the mine? The MacFarlane had told them to keep their mouths shut lest he cut out their tongues. And Finn well knew it was no idle threat.

But if he told the truth, these people might let him stay. He'd do whatever they asked and he'd be more than happy to sleep in the kitchen or the stables. Instinctively he recognised that this family was somehow different. The lady had been *kind*. And he couldn't remember the last time anyone had shown him any care – least not without a skelpin' to follow.

Swallowing anxiously, he followed the maid into the cavernous kitchen.

∞∞∞

Jennifer woke to the sun streaming in through the window. Sleepily, she watched Jenet pull back the drapes. 'It be a braw day, ma lady,' the maid enthused, plumping up the pillows behind Jennifer's head. Delighted to see the sun after the day before, Jennifer luxuriated in the rays shining directly through the window onto the bed.

'How is the boy Mr. Galbraith brought back with him yesterday?' she asked, accepting the dish of hot chocolate.

'His name be Finn,' Jenet confided, picking out Jennifer's clothes for the day. 'Mrs. Darroch is tae bring the lad tae his lordship at ten.' She shut the wardrobe door, adding, 'His lordship askt if yer be wantin' ter speak wi' him yersell, ye've tae be quick.'

'Of course I wish to speak with him,' Jennifer answered, putting the chocolate aside and climbing out of bed. 'Will Mr. Galbraith be present, do you know?' She asked the question casually, ignoring the fluttering inside her breast at the thought of seeing the handsome Scot again.

'The Galbraith hae bin here since day-daw,' Jenet confided. 'He be verra handsome, ma lady. Ah ken he's the talk o' the steamy.' She gave a giggle and shook her head.

'The steamy?' Jennifer questioned, pulling her nightgown over her head.

'The wash-house,' Jenet clarified. 'Between me an' ye, ma lady, ah reckon more an' one o' the maids be sweet on him.'

'But not you?' Jennifer couldn't help asking as Jenet helped put on her petticoat.

'A braw man like himself be nae fer the likes o' me, ma lady. Ah'd allwis be wonderin' whose bed he be climbin' oota come morn.'

The maid's words brought a sudden blush to Jennifer's cheeks as they unexpectedly conjured up the vision of Brendon Galbraith climbing naked out of the same bed she'd just vacated. Gritting her teeth, she willed the ridiculous flush to fade, while wordlessly holding up her arms as an emerald-green morning dress was slipped over her head. Fortunately, Jenet didn't appear to notice her mistress's sudden reticence and continued chatting nineteen to the dozen until a mere ten minutes later when Jennifer was coiffured and ready to start the day.

Estimating the time to be about nine thirty, Jennifer decided she had enough time to avail herself of breakfast before they questioned this Finn. Deep in thought, she entered the breakfast room and didn't immediately notice that there was somebody already seated at the table. She almost felt as though the maid's words had conjured up Brendon Galbraith in the flesh, and as he rose to his feet, Jennifer felt a sudden perplexing sensation deep in her core that had her heart galloping uncontrollably.

'Guid mornin, ma lady,' he greeted. Had his voice been so deep yesterday? What the devil was wrong with her that even the sound of his voice set her squirming. 'Ah trust ye slept well.'

Dear God, he might as well have asked if she'd enjoyed his kiss. Face flaming, she fought the urge to slap herself. This most definitely couldn't go on. Nodding briskly, she turned towards the sideboard and took her time piling up her plate, in the hope he'd be gone by the time she took it to the table.

Unfortunately, it seemed the steward had no intention of leaving, and at length, she was forced to turn around and join him.

'Have you brought … Fergus with you this morning?' she asked for want of something to say.

'Aye,' he answered. 'The beast will nae be apart frae me fer long.'

Against her will, Jennifer found herself intrigued. 'Have you had him long?' she asked.

'Since he was whelpt,' Brendon answered, the fondness clear in his voice. 'Would hae deid otherwise.'

'He looks very fierce,' Jennifer retorted, 'though clearly Flossy wasn't afraid of him.'

'He's a big bairn,' Brendon answered with a chuckle. 'Right now he's ootside in the courtyard wi' Finn.'

'He won't run away?' Jennifer asked anxiously, half rising out of her chair.

'The dog or the boy?' Brendon asked with a devastating smile. She stared at him wordlessly. 'Ma guess is nane o the twa. Ah reckon they both like their stomach too much.' Jennifer found herself smiling back, and for the slightest second, everything aside from the two of them disappeared.

*'Flossy! If you're cavorting with that damned Casanova again, you'll spend the rest of the day in the deuced stables.'*

Her grandfather's booming voice interrupted the fleeting moment and both she and Brendon turned to watch the Reverend stomp past the window. *'Thunder an' turf, Flo, you're nought but a deuced lightskirt.'* The Reverend yelled his oft repeated admonishment as he tried to grab hold of the little dog while she continued to caper round the wolfhound's legs.

'Ah think ah'd better gie him a hand,' Brendon commented drily, as the Reverend passed the window for the second time, this time going the opposite way.

Climbing to his feet, the steward gave her a quick bow, just as her grandfather yelled, *'if you want to kick up a lark with some mongrel, you could at least choose one the same deuced size as you.'* Brendon and Jennifer stared at each other for a second, then both burst out laughing at exactly the same moment.

'Go,' Jennifer chortled as her grandfather passed the window a third time, 'I think Grandpapa might be in danger of an apoplexy.'

After a few moments, she watched through the window as Brendon ordered Fergus to *sit*. Fortunately the wolfhound didn't actually do so on top of his diminutive would-be paramour. With a gruff, 'Thank you,' the Reverend picked his errant dog up and minutes later appeared in the breakfast room.

'Having fun, Grandpapa?' Jennifer asked with a grin. She couldn't for the life of her have kept a straight face.

The Reverend narrowed his eyes but contented himself with a small grunt.

'By the way, who is this *Casanova* you mentioned?' Jennifer went on mischievously, knowing full well who her grandfather had been referring to, having secretly read the libertine's autobiography. (Another book from Aunt Pru's lending library).

The Reverend did what he always did when he didn't like the subject of the conversation – he changed it.

'Has that old cully in a skirt turned up with Galbraith this morning?'

'*Grandfather*! That really isn't very charitable of you, especially considering you're a man of God, but if you're referring to Dougal Galbraith - then no, I don't believe he's accompanied his son this morning.'

'It would take a deuced saint to be charitable to that bag of bones,' muttered the Reverend, helping himself to some breakfast.

'Well, in fairness, you did rather loom up on him unexpectedly, and Gifford mentioned there were no candles alight in that particular passageway.' She picked up her tea and took a sip. 'And anyway, how was it you came upon Dougal Galbraith? What were you doing lurking in an unlit corridor? I thought you'd decided on a nap after the journey?' Jennifer eyed her grandfather suspiciously.

'I was simply bringing succour to those less fortunate than ourselves,' Reverend Shackleford protested.

'Why on earth were you bothering the servants?' Jennifer frowned. 'Please tell me you weren't lecturing *them* on the evils of debauchery, avarice and wrath? And *surely* not sloth?'

Augustus Shackleford drew himself up. 'You may mock, child, but I'll have you know, I spent a very rewarding half an hour discussing the finer points of Proverbs, Chapter fifteen, Verse twenty seven...' The Reverend winced internally at the plumper – well, half plumper. The servant he spoke to may very well have mentioned that particular passage for all he knew, and anyhow, the fellow had certainly found their conversation very rewarding.

Jennifer bit her lip. It was easy to think of her grandfather as totty headed, but she had no wish to hurt his feelings. And his heart was in the right place – most of the time. 'Forgive me, Grandpapa,' she said earnestly. 'I spoke out of turn – a rather large failing of mine as you're obviously well aware. I have no doubt you have many insights to offer the servants – after all, think how much you taught me on our journey here?'

The Reverend gave a slightly mollified, 'hmph.' Mayhap he'd been worrying unduly and was a better advocate for the Almighty than he'd thought. And in truth, if Jennifer had received her outspokenness from anybody, it was most definitely him...

'Perhaps you will be well positioned to bring succour to the poor unfortunate children like the boy we found yesterday, who've been used so cruelly?' Jennifer went on. 'After all, we are intending to rescue them and put a stop to the MacFarlane Clan's barbaric practices are we not?'

## Chapter Ten

'So, how exactly did ye come to be working in the mine, Finn?' Malcolm asked, taking care to keep his voice as genial as possible.

The boy stared at the faces around him and gave a small cough. The bonnie lady in the green dress was the one who'd first discovered him in the boat. The big man, the one who carried him back. But those two were not in charge. The younger Maister was the one in charge, even if he wasn't the one asking the questions. Mrs. Darroch said the Maister was the son of a *Duke*. Finn could hardly imagine what a Duke might look like, but his son was very handsome. And *clean*. He had stern features, but Finn could tell he laughed easily. Would that he'd had the same insights about the MacFarlane's arse-kisser when the bastart had come sniffing around the village.

In the end, Finn shrugged. 'Naewhere tae gae. Said ah'd be gaen a hot meal wi' real meat. An we did too. Once.'

'We?' Peter interrupted. 'How many of you were there altogether?'

'More an' all ma fingers and toes.'

Brendon swore softly. 'Ower twenty bairns.'

'Why is MacFarlane using children in a mine he supposedly closed years ago? Surely, they're too small to be of much use.'

'It be too narrow fer the biguns,' Finn piped up. 'They cannae get doon small enough.' He crouched down to show them what he meant.

'There must be verra little gold left,' Brendon commented.

'Harder to get to clearly,' Peter mused. 'He must be desperate.'

'How is it the children taken weren't missed?' Jennifer asked.

'Do ye have parents, Finn?' The lad shook his head. 'Any family at all?' Another shake. Brendon sighed. 'Ye have your answer.'

'And the others, were they orphans too?' the Reverend asked, an unaccustomed lump in his throat.

'Aye, most o' em.' The lad gave another shrug. 'Some wa' sold.'

Reverend Shackleford sagged. He was well aware that child slavery was widespread, especially in the big cities. But not on land belonging to the Duke of Blackmore. Nicholas Sinclair would never turn a blind eye to such horror. He looked after his own.

'What be the name of your village, Finn?' Malcolm asked.

'Ah'm frae Banalan, but th'others frae lots o' places.'

'That gives us the excuse we need to act,' Peter declared, grim satisfaction clearly evident in his voice. 'We can be certain MacFarlane knows Banalan is ours.'

'He kens alright, but he dinnae want tae ken, if yer get ma meanin'.' Brendon shook his head. 'Forgive me ma lord, but meetin' the MacFarlane whan ye be full o' anger – ye'll be playin' intae the bastart's hands.' The steward looked over at Malcolm. 'Ye ken Alistair MacFarlane, he's be off his heid.'

Malcolm nodded. 'I was there when he killed his brother. The varmint should have been cropped then.' He turned to Peter. 'Have ye sent the missive to yer father, laddie?'

Peter shook his head. 'I thought to wait until we'd spoken with the boy. My intention is to pen it as soon as we've finished here and send it immediately.' The Viscount turned back to Finn who was staring round the table, wide eyed.

'Ye'll nae be makin' me gae back there, will ye Maister?'

Peter gave an emphatic shake of his head but softened it with a smile. 'Can you tell us where you were kept when you weren't down the mine, Finn?'

The boy bit his lip. 'Mostly we stayed doon thare.'

'You slept in the mine?' Peter queried, aghast.

Finn nodded. 'Thare's a wee chamber. Ah dinnae ken whare it be. It was ayewis dark.'

For a second there was a horrified silence, then Jennifer gave a small moan.

'Gifford, would you take Finn back to the kitchen. I'm certain Mrs. Darroch will find him something special to eat. We'll speak with him again tomorrow.'

'Aye, ah saw a bit o' tablet jus fer ye,' Gifford declared. Finn's eyes lit up, and he willingly went with the elderly steward.

'I suggest we continue the conversation when Gifford returns,' Peter declared as soon as the door closed behind them. 'Would anyone like more tea?'

Nobody wished for more refreshment, and a tense silence ensued while they waited for the elderly steward to come back. Fortunately, they didn't have to wait long.

'We cannot simply sit on our hands while we wait for Father's reply,' Jennifer declared as soon as Gifford reentered the room. 'How many more children could die while we're dithering?'

Augustus Shackleford sighed. 'We're no good to 'em if we end up decorating MacFarlane's flower beds.'

'Ah ken yer concerned, ma lady.' Gifford said, 'But like the guid Reverend said, we cannae help the bairns if we're deid. We'd be eejits tae charge in wi'oot a plan.'

'Could we send in Chapman's men?' Jennifer asked Peter.

The Viscount thought for a moment then shook his head. 'They are not an army. They are employed for our protection only. To send them against MacFarlane would be to risk outright war.'

'Can the chucklehead be reasoned with?' the Reverend asked. 'Perhaps he'll listen to a man of God.'

'A Sassenach one? Ah doot it.'

'Th'only thing we need tae ken is when the mine be empty o' MacFarlane guards so we can free the bairns,' Brendon announced. 'We cannae risk walkin' intae a fight wi' his warriors.' He paused before adding, 'Mebbe the Reverend can gie some excuse fer bein' in the area – tell the MacFarlane he be visitin' fer another purpose?'

'The MacFarlane willnae gie him the time o' day,' Gifford scoffed.

'But if he gaed wi' ma da? The MacFarlane haenae a quarrel wi' Dougal Galbraith.'

'I will not be accompanying that … that beef-witted good for nothing anywhere,' Reverend Shackleford spluttered.

'Was there bad feeling caused by your sudden departure?' Peter asked, ignoring his grandfather's dismay at being obliged to go somewhere with the elderly Scot.

'There was nae bad feelin',' Brendon clarified. 'Ah made sure tae gie a guid excu…' He trailed off before finishing the sentence and swore softly.

'I take it your excuse willnae be helpin' us now,' Malcolm sighed.

'Ah told the MacFarlane ma da haed hurt his leg.'

'How bad?' Peter demanded.

'Ah didnae say. Jus' that Da was abed.'

'How long ago was this?'

'Just ower three months back.'

'So if it was merely a sprain, it's quite possible Dougal could be up and about by now?'

'I absolutely refuse to be in the company of that bacon-brained imbecile…'

'I'm certain we can dress his leg up a little. Could he produce a convincing limp, Brendon?'

'Ma da could convince anyone he was the King o' bloody Scotland,' Brendon answered drily.

'Under no circumstances will I spend even one second with that pudding-headed pig-widgeon…'

'Do you think he would do it?'

'No, absolutely not. I will not be giving that cork-brained grubshite so much as the time of day…'

'Ah ken he'll be more an' delighted tae lie through his teeth tae the MacFarlane.'

'We'd have to come up with a convincing excuse for them both being there? An English priest and a Scottish … err… farmer?'

Brendon frowned. 'Aye, ah ken ma da might nae be so delighted tae trick the bastart wi' a Sassenach God botherer in tow.' He paused before adding, 'An' anyway, jus' visiting wi' the MacFarlane willnae get them anywhere near the mine.'

'If you think I'm telling so much as the smallest plumper to protect that lily-livered hornswoggler...'

'What if Grandfather was on some kind of pilgrimage? Perhaps searching for a relic of some description? Would that give him an excuse to get closer to the mine?'

'Ah'll hae a word wi' ma da an' see if he can come up wi' some ideas.' Brendon laughed ruefully. 'That's another thing he be good at - tellin' stories...'

'We dinnae want the MacFarlane to know the good Reverend is connected to Caerlaverock in any way,' added Malcolm. 'An' the same fer ye, Brendon. If the chieftain knows ye be workin' fer the Duke o' Blackmore, he'll likely string ye up.'

Brendon nodded with a grimace. 'Aye, the bampot hates the Sinclairs wi' a passion.'

Peter sighed. 'Why don't we reconvene here on the morrow after everyone's had a chance to think about possible reasons for Grandpapa to be visiting clan MacFarlane and how he can get close enough to the mine to see what's happening?'

Jennifer turned to the Reverend who was slowly going a dark shade of puce. 'All you need to do, Grandpapa, is find out what time the guards leave, and we'll be ready and waiting to ride to the children's rescue.'

'Someone will,' Peter interrupted her drily, 'but if you have any thought of involving yourself in the actual rescue, dear sister, be assured I will lock you in Caerlaverock's dungeon rather than risk your harm.'

'We have a dungeon?' was all Jennifer asked, intrigued. Peter shook his head and climbed to his feet.

As the rest of them rose from the table, Brendon declared his intention to go immediately to his father. 'While there's nae much likelihood o' him meeting any of the MacFarlane clan, ah'm nae aboot tae take any chances wi' his loose tongue, an we dinnae want him tae mention ma service at Caerlaverock.'

Jennifer bit her lip as she watched the handsome Scot stride from the room. She'd had no opportunity to thank him for his actions the day before. Indeed, they'd spent no time together at all. Mayhap when all this nastiness had been dealt with, there would be time for them to get to know one another a little better. As the thought popped into her head, another immediately followed it. Why on earth did she wish to get to know the steward better? She was to be in Scotland for barely a month. He was a steward and she the daughter of the house. He was an employee, nothing more.

Frowning, she pushed the ridiculous thoughts away and got to her feet. 'I shall be in the library if anybody wants me. There might be a book containing information to help us with Grandpapa's disguise.'

The Reverend threw her a sour look which naturally went straight over her head. 'If anybody needs me for any more deuced bacon-brained schemes, I'll be out with Flossy,' he declared huffily, picking the little dog up and stomping from the room.

'What's wrong with Grandfather?' Peter asked with a frown, watching the Reverend exit the room.

'I suspect he's less than happy with your choice of sleuthing companion,' Felicity commented drily. 'I really do think he's missing Percy.'

Peter sighed. 'I know how he feels. I can't help wishing Father was here.' He looked over at Malcolm and grimaced. 'I hate to admit it, old friend, but I'm out of my depth.'

The Scot gripped the Viscount's shoulder. 'It's a good man who can acknowledge such a thing. Ye're not on yer own lad. We're here tae help.'

Peter gave a rueful smile. 'Believe me, I thank God for it.' Then, laying his used napkin on the table, he added, 'I'll write the letter to my father immediately. If there's anything you wish to add, let me have it before two o'clock. I'd like the bearer to cover as much distance as possible before sunset.'

Malcolm nodded, before turning to his wife. 'Do ye have anythin' ye'd like tae say tae her grace?'

'Poor love is certain to be worried sick once she hears what's been happening,' Felicity returned. 'I'll go and pen her a few words.' She looked outside with a sigh. 'I was hoping to pay a visit to Banalan today, but I think perhaps it's better if we stay close to Caerlaverock, at least until we formulate a proper plan. Our presence will inevitably cause gossip.' She drank the last of her tea and stood up. 'Once I've finished the letter, I believe I'll go for a walk along the edge of the loch.' At her husband's sudden indrawn breath, she put her hand on his arm and added, 'Of course if you're concerned for my safety, dearest, you could always come with me.'

∞∞∞

By midafternoon, Jennifer was feeling grimy, but jubilant. She'd unearthed a tale of a rumoured hoard of treasure located near to Loch Lomand belonging to an English rector no less. According to the account she'd read, the gentleman by the name of Edward Colman hailed originally from Suffolk. His family had made a substantial amount of money from the cloth trade during the sixteenth century and rose to some prominence within the Suffolk gentry.

Colman's father had been a devout Protestant minister, but Edward himself converted to Catholicism and according to the book became a very enthusiastic preacher of his new faith. By 1673, he'd established himself as the secretary to Mary of

Modena – a fellow Catholic and wife of James, Duke of York. The Duke was the younger brother and heir apparent to the Protestant King Charles II.

When the Duke and Duchess of York moved to Edinburgh, Edward went with them after selling the family's land in Suffolk and apparently investing the money in gold jewellery – mostly small items such as rings, necklaces and bracelets that could be easily transported.

The book was very sketchy about what happened next aside from the fact that Edward Colman was embroiled in an alleged plot to assassinate King Charles and ended up being hung, drawn and quartered in 1678. Jennifer shuddered, making sure to skip most of the gorier details. Just before he was arrested, Colman seemingly made the journey from Edinburgh to Loch Lomond but there was no record of exactly where he went or why.

According to the book, since Colman died a traitor's death, all he owned was subsequently appropriated by the Crown. However, it seemed that not so much as a gold ring had been found when his lodgings were ransacked. The entire hoard of jewellery was missing.

Fearing for his life, could Edward Colman have hidden his wealth?

Sitting back, Jennifer closed the book and hugged it to her in satisfaction. This was exactly what they needed. Colman had been an English rector. Grandpapa could quite easily pretend to be a descendant of the family who'd unearthed some information about the missing jewellery. If what they were saying about MacFarlane was true, the clan chief would certainly be interested in what her grandfather had to say.

'Ye look like a wee cat who's just stolen the cream.' The deep voice of Brendon Galbraith had her jumping out of her chair in shock.

At her panicked reaction, the handsome Scot held out his hand as he came towards her. 'Och, forgive me, ma lady, ah didnae mean tae startle ye.'

With a breathless laugh, Jennifer waved his apology away. 'I was deep in thought is all,' she answered nervously. 'Have you spoken with your father?'

'Aye, an' it gaed just how ye'd imagine. His words as ah was leavin' were, *Ah'm nae takin' a baw heided Sassenach God walloper tae visit wi' the MacFarlane an' that be the end o' the matter.*

'I cannae think ye hae a problem understandin' his meanin', ma lady.'

'Perhaps they'll warm to one another eventually,' Jennifer suggested ruefully.

'Aye, when hell freezes ower accordin' tae ma da.'

Jennifer sighed. 'Do you think you'll be able to persuade him to help us?'

'Aye, he'll dae the business. Even if ah hae tae drag him there.' His grin did strange things to her stomach.

Abruptly, Jennifer realised they were actually alone in the library. 'I think I've found something that might help us,' she declared, pleased to note that her voice sounded firm and decisive.

He stared at her enquiringly as she held the book aloft. 'There's a story about an English rector who apparently hid a large cache of gold jewellery before being put to death as a traitor.'

Brendon raised his eyebrows. 'Story be the right o' it. Ah've heard tell o' treasure in the bottom o' the loch. But there also be stories aboot a monster or some such.' He shrugged. 'Ah reckon nane o' the twa be true.'

'They don't have to be,' Jennifer grinned, her shyness forgotten.

'Grandpapa is excellent at shamming it – according to my mother and all my aunts anyway – I'm entirely certain he'll be able to play the part of a treasure hunting rector with ease.'

'Can ah see the tale ye read?' Brendon asked, his interest clearly sparked. Nodding, Jennifer laid the book on the small desk she'd been using and opened it at the appropriate page. 'It says here…' she began, swivelling round to face him, only to stop with a small gasp as her nose almost touched his shirt. Swallowing, she instinctively looked upwards and stilled.

The blue of his eyes was deepened by the light streaming in through the window, but it was the intentness in them that had her heart pumping wildly. Indeed, she felt as if his eyes were about to devour her, such was their absorption. The warning signals in the back of her mind went unheeded as she felt his hand slide up between them, leaving a trail of white-hot sensation where his fingers skimmed her bodice. What seemed like a lifetime later, his fingers reached her cheek. Gently, he used two fingers to brush an errant lock of hair behind her ear while his thumb lightly rubbed against her soft skin. 'A wee bit o' dust,' he whispered hoarsely making no move to lower his hand.

The feel of his fingers set Jennifer's pulse to racing. An unnamed sensation flooded deep in her belly, so strong, she had to fight the urge to squirm. Unconsciously, she pressed herself forward, desperate to feel the length of him against her body. She felt, rather than heard his indrawn breath, then suddenly, shockingly, he stepped back – so quickly, she almost fell over. He put out his hands to steady her, and she stared up at him wordlessly.

At the feel of his strong hands on her arms, the tingling deep in her core intensified, and with an incoherent murmur, she closed the distance between them and rose onto her tiptoes, her lips wantonly seeking his.

'*Dinnae!*' Brendon's groaning rebuff just before their mouth's touched brought her crashing back to reality.

Fighting back a mortified sob, Jennifer stepped backwards as his hands dropped to his sides. For long seconds they stared at each other, chests heaving in unison. 'I'm so sorry,' Jennifer whispered. 'I…I don't know what came over me…'

Brendon shook his head violently. 'Nae, ye did naethin,' he muttered huskily. 'The fault be mine. Ah…' he stopped and threaded his hand through his hair. 'Forgive me, ma lady.' He paused again before adding, his voice so low she almost missed it. 'God help me, ye be the bonniest lass ah've e'er laid eyes on.'

Then abruptly, he turned on his heel and left.

## Chapter Eleven

Reverend Shackleford couldn't remember the last time he'd felt so aggrieved. Indeed, had Percy been here, he'd have expounded at length to the curate on the subject of his mistreatment. But since his oldest friend was unfortunately not in the vicinity to listen, that only left the Almighty. And since the reason he was so far from home in the first place, could be fairly and squarely laid at His door, Augustus Shackleford was of the opinion that the least He could do was listen.

With a sigh, the Reverend took one of the many paths down the garden, Flossy gambolling happily in front of him. It took a good twenty minutes to explain the whole problem, chapter and verse but once he'd done so, the clergyman had to admit to feeling slightly better. Perhaps he'd been using Percy a little too often as a confidant when in fact he would have done better to have taken his problems upstairs.

Seating himself on a bench, Reverend Shackleford found himself musing on what possible reason the Almighty could have had for putting such a deuced mumbling cove in his path. Abruptly, he remembered Dougal Galbraith's scathing comment about *Sassenachs*. And his own subsequent remark about *Sawnys*...

*"Ye have heard that it hath been said, Thou shalt love thy neighbour, and hate thine enemy. "But I say unto you, Love your enemies, bless them that curse you, do good to them that hate you, and pray for them which despitefully use you, and persecute you."* Matthew,

Chapter five, Verses forty-three and forty-four. The Reverend could have quoted them in his sleep.

Augustus Shackleford looked up, just as the sun poked through the clouds bathing the arbour in which he was sitting with warmth and sunlight.

'Tare an' hounds,' he muttered, giving a disgruntled shake of his head. 'Alright, alright, you've made your point. I'll give the rag-mannered, pudding headed, pig-widgeon one more chance.

'Only one more, mind…'

∞∞∞

As she climbed into bed, Jennifer found herself going over the interlude in the library with Brendon Galbraith for the hundredth time. For the life of her, she couldn't understand what had driven her to throw herself so wantonly at a man she'd only just met.

And even worse was the knowledge that if she had the time over, she'd likely do exactly the same thing again. Was there something wrong with her? No other man in her acquaintance had inspired so much as a flutter of the heart, let alone a desire to climb into his skin.

And that was it, she realised, that was exactly what she'd instinctively been trying to do. Or rather her body had. Her head hadn't appeared to have much say at all.

Groaning, Jennifer turned onto her back. Picturing the Scot in her mind, the tingling she'd felt earlier now expanded to encompass her whole body. Her nipples inexplicably hardened to points, and with a frown, she lifted the coverlet to have a look.

Was this what had driven her aunts to collectively behave so shockingly loose in the haft? Jennifer herself had never before experienced such ... stirrings. Indeed she'd wondered on occasion whether she was lacking in many of the baser emotions so prevalent on her mother's side – aside from her pigheadedness which admittedly had shown itself at a very early age.

Gritting her teeth, Jennifer determinedly turned her mind to the problem of the missing children. When she'd shared the story of Edward Colman's treasure at dinner, the response had been one of excited enthusiasm - the most surprising being that of her grandfather. She had no idea what had transpired to give him such a change of heart, but the churlish, sour-faced individual who'd stomped out of the drawing room earlier in the day was notably absent at the dinner table. Oh there had been one or two chinks in the armour of his cheerfulness – particularly when it was suggested that he and Dougal Galbraith might eventually become good friends – but overall, she had to admit that the forthright grandfather she'd grown up with appeared firmly back in charge, even if his response to the suggestion he and Dougal might warm to each other was that he doubted he'd warm to Dougal Galbraith if they were cremated together.

Brendon had not been present for dinner, but then neither had Gifford. Apparently, it wasn't usual for the steward of the house to eat with the family. Since Jennifer had grown up with Malcolm - whose official role was that of her father's valet – eating often at their dinner table, she had to admit to finding it strange. And in truth, somewhat disappointing...

Gradually Jennifer's eyes began to close until at long last she finally fell asleep.

∞∞∞

The next day again dawned fair and sunny. Without examining her reasoning, Jennifer took quite a time with her toilet, settling eventually on a day dress the colour of the wild heather that grew everywhere. Jenet pinned her hair up in a simple chignon complete with purple ribbon and she finished her ensemble with a pink and purple plaid shawl which had been a parting gift from her mother in honour of her first adult visit to Scotland.

On walking into the breakfast room, she stifled her disappointment to see it empty, taking herself to task as she did so. Really, she had to put a stop to this ridiculous infatuation with a man she could not possibly have a future with.

Unfortunately, the stern telling off didn't stop her heart from doing somersaults as she caught the sound of his deep voice calling to Fergus outside the window. Seating herself at the breakfast table, she fought to get her racing pulse under control before he came through the door.

'Guid mornin', ma lady.' His voice when it finally came was polite, but nothing more. Indeed, as she glanced up at him, she gave a small frown. His face too was closed, giving nothing away.

'Good morning, Mr. Galbraith,' she responded taking care to keep her own voice equally noncommittal. As she spoke, she busied herself shaking out her napkin and placing it on her knee.

'It's nae a guid mornin' when ah'm dragged oot o' bed tae spend time wi a turnip-heided God walloper.' Dougal Galbraith's mood had clearly not improved like that of her grandfather. Fighting a sudden urge to laugh, Jennifer bit her lip. Brendon was most definitely not amused if the tightness around his mouth was anything to go by.

'Hae ye got any o' that tablet,' the old Scot went on to ask the maid.

'Da, ye'll have what's on the sideboard and be grateful.' Dougal scowled, but didn't respond to his son's admonishment, choosing instead to help himself to a plate of ham and eggs.

The Reverend chose that moment to enter the breakfast room. He paused for a second when he saw Dougal tucking into his pile of ham, then with a small cough, offered a jovial, 'Good morning to you, Dougal. I trust you're well.'

The old Scot paused with his fork halfway to his mouth, then looked behind to see if there happened to be another Dougal behind him. Seeing nobody else answering to the same name, he frowned and turned back. 'Be ye talkin' tae me?' he muttered staring at the Reverend as though the clergyman had suddenly sprouted a second head.

Augustus Shackleford swallowed and offered a quick internal prayer before declaring gruffly that he believed they'd got off to an unfortunate start and suggesting they put the last two days behind them.'

By this time, Dougal was convinced his nemesis had been somehow replaced. 'Who be ye?' he growled, narrowing his eyes as though he might see through the imposter. 'Hae the God walloper bin taken awa by the wee folk?'

The Reverend visibly gritted his teeth, doing his best to remind himself of the sun shining down into the arbour the day before. His irritation was made worse by the fact that Flossy seemed delighted to see the old Scot, promptly jumping onto his knee and making herself comfortable. Finally managing to swallow his ire, Augustus Shackleford stomped to the sideboard and helped himself to breakfast.

'Bring me another bit o' that bread wad ye…?'

Fortunately, before all the Reverend's good intentions disappeared into the ether, Peter, Malcolm and Felicity entered the room. 'Would you ask Gifford to bring Finn to speak with us?' the Viscount asked the maid, seating himself next to Jennifer.

'Would ye like me tae bring anothor pot o' tea while ah'm there, ma lord?' Peter nodded gratefully and smiled, causing the maid to colour up and smother a slight giggle.

Jennifer regarded her brother with amusement. It was hard sometimes to understand the attention Peter was given by ladies of all persuasions. She supposed he was good looking in a very 'like their father' kind of way, but ... well, to her he was simply her sibling – and a deuced irritating one at that.

A few minutes later, Finn trailed reluctantly in behind the steward. 'How are you, Finn?' Peter asked with another warm smile. The boy gave a clumsy bow and mumbled, 'Ah be braw, thank ye, ma lord.'

'We'd like to ask you a few more questions,' the Viscount added. 'Would that be acceptable to you?' Finn stared at him for second, then nodded.

'Can ye tell us how ye escaped frae the mine, lad?' Brendon questioned, taking care not to give the impression that the boy had done anything wrong.

'Ah felled,' Finn answered hesitantly. 'Ah didnae keep up wi' th'others an' ah was locked oot the sleepin' room.' He paused and looked round. 'He would hae gien me a skelpin', so ah hid an' then followed him up tae th'entrance afore it was closed up fer the night. Ah hid 'til he gaed tae sleep.' He gave a loud imitation snore followed by a grin. 'Then ah ran.'

'How did you manage to reach the boathouse?' Jennifer asked gently.

'Ah dinnae ken,' Finn replied, shaking his head. 'Ah dae ken ah walked an' walked an' then ah saw the wee hoose...' he stopped and gave another shrug.

'Do they lock the entrance to the mine every night, Finn?' Malcolm asked. The boy shrugged, then nodded. 'Ah think so.'

'So after locking you and your companions in your ... *sleeping room*, the man would then lock the main entrance on his way out of the mine?'

'Aye.' Finn's nod was more decisive.

The question, 'Do you know the man's name?' elicited the now familiar shrug.

'We called him, *sir*.' An impish grin, 'tae his face.'

'Was he the only guard?'

Finn shook his head. 'Nae, but he were the meanest. Th'owers did as he said.'

'But he was the only one to stay overnight?'

Finn gave another shrug. 'Ah dinnae ken. He be the only one there when ah ran.'

'Thank you, Finn, you've been most helpful.' Gifford stood up to take the boy back to the kitchen, but the lad stood his ground.

'Ye're nae gaun tae send me back are ye, Maister?' It was the second time the boy had asked the same question.

Peter shook his head. 'We will not send you back, Finn. If you wish it, your home is here now, in Caerlaverock.'

'Aye, ah dae.' Finn's response was clearly heartfelt as he finally allowed himself to be led away.

'Those poor children,' Felicity murmured. 'To be locked down there in the dark. It's monstrous.'

As soon as Finn had left the room, Peter became all business. 'A perfect description, Felicity. And we *will* put a stop to it. The letter is now on its way to my father, but until we receive his reply, we must focus our attention on rescuing those unfortunates already in MacFarlane's clutches.'

He turned to his sister. 'Once Gifford is back with us, could you describe what you read in the book you found to those who weren't with us at dinner last night?'

Jennifer nodded. 'And I have some further ideas of how we can use the information,' she enthused.

As soon as the elderly steward returned, she repeated what she'd found in the book's pages. 'It's perfect I think,' she finished. 'There is enough information to make any approach to the MacFarlane Clan legitimate, but we can make up the rest of it ourselves. What do you think, Grandpapa?'

The Reverend hmphed, then, 'I think you may have more Shackleford blood in you than Sinclair. What Canterbury tale would you have me spin?'

Jennifer grinned. 'I've given it some thought. The book stated that Edward Coleman visited Loch Lomond just before his arrest. What if he was carrying the gold – mayhap in some kind of satchel – with the intention of burying it somewhere?'

'Och, why would he bother? Ah mean, he wouldnae be havin' much use fer it, an' Edinburgh tae Lomond be no small distance.' Dougal had a point. Jennifer bit her lip and frowned.

'Could he have written a letter divulging the whereabouts of the jewellery to a member of his family – perhaps someone still living back in Suffolk I would imagine the last people he'd want to see benefit from his gold would be those who would see him dead.'

'Aye an' the Reverend could be a descendant of the family...'

'...Still residing in Suffolk who somehow found the letter...'

'...and made haste up to Loch Lomond...'

'...Intendin' tae look fer the gold.'

'So where did he hide it?' Jennifer's triumphant final question was met with silence.

'It would have to be close enough to the mine for Augustus and Dougal to be able to secretly keep watch while they're *searching*,' Felicity mooted at length.

'Inveruglas,' Dougal announced suddenly. At Peter, Jennifer and Felicity's blank looks, he added, 'It be an island in the loch close tae the mine.'

'Do they still have a stronghold there?' Malcolm asked. 'I thought it long abandoned.'

'Aye it is. But the MacFarlane be still boond tae it somethin' fierce.'

'Inveruglas be the best place tae get a clear view o' the mine across the loch.' Brendon nodded slowly.

'So, what if Colman buried his gold on th'island?' Dougal looked around the table.

'Well since the gold has all but run out in his mine, I imagine it would certainly provoke MacFarlane's interest.'

'Aye, they'll welcome ye wi' open arms wi'oot too many questions.' Dougal grinned showing a mouth empty of all but a few teeth. 'The MacFarlane willnae turn awa the chance tae take the gold fer himself.'

'Likely after putting us both to bed with a mattock and tucking us up with a deuced spade,' the Reverend declared with a snort.

'You willnae be there long enough,' Brendon said. 'But ye'll be able tae keep an eye on the mine wi'oot the MacFarlane gettin' suspicious.'

'He's unlikely to leave us to our own devices,' the Reverend argued. 'Surely, he'll leave us with a guard.'

'Nae, they'll jus' take awa the boat. The MacFarlane willnae stir himself tae dae more. He be lither as well as crabbit.'

'Lazy as well as bad-tempered,' Brendon supplied.

'But if we're stranded on the deuced island...?' The Reverend trailed off, his meaning clear.

'Ye willnae be,' Brendon interjected, his manner one of rising excitement. 'We'll hide a wee boat on Inveruglas aforehand.'

'Caerlaverock's scull be swelled fer the moment,' Gifford revealed. It willnae be dried oot fer a couple o' weeks or more.' At Peter's frown, he went on to quickly explain the process of swelling - briefly sinking a boat to make it once again watertight.

'Why are we going to all this trouble?' Peter declared impatiently. 'It seems to me that we're making this rescue far more complicated than it needs to be. Can we not just simply row over to the island, watch and wait until the coast is clear, then effect a rescue without MacFarlane knowing anything about it?'

Dougal shook his head. 'The Reverend has the right o' it. If the MacFarlane catches us on his land, there'll be nae questions asked, just a sword tae yer belly an a bed on the bottom o' the loch. We cannae risk it.'

'Ye can signal to us the moment the area is empty of all but the one guard,' Malcolm declared. 'We should be able to subdue the bastard without much trouble if we have the element of surprise.'

'What if he has a gun?' Jennifer asked anxiously.

'He'll nae hae a gun tae look after a bunch o' bairns,' Dougal scoffed.

'And we will not be going in unarmed,' Malcolm stated firmly.

'It all sounds a bit deuced smoky to me,' the Reverend frowned. 'How shall we signal you that the guards have left?'

'Malcolm, Brendon and I will work on the finer points of the plan today,' Peter answered. 'I suggest you and Jennifer and Felicity work on the contents of the mythical letter written by Edward Colman.'

'An ah'll look tae be findin' us a boat,' Dougal declared with a roguish grin.

'Nae stealin', Da,' Brendon ordered. 'Ye'll be nae use tae us swingin' from a rope.'

'Dinnae fash yersel,' Dougal answered with an airy wave. 'Ah widnae dream o' breakin' the law.'

Brendon gave a disbelieving snort.

'I'm more than happy to provide you with enough money to buy a boat,' Peter stated brusquely. 'Gifford, forgive me, we've kept you far too long, and I know you have much to do. But before you get on with your daily tasks, would you please provide Dougal with sufficient coin to purchase a small rowing boat with oars.'

He stood up decisively. 'Malcolm, Brendon, perhaps we can take our discussion to the study. We'll reconvene at dinner if that's agreeable to everyone.' He looked at Brendon. 'I would be grateful if you and your father would consider joining us this evening.'

Brendon bent his head. 'We'd be honoured, ma lord.'

'As long as ye dinnae be servin any Froggy kickshaws,' Dougal added, climbing to his feet, much to Flossy's displeasure. Then helping himself to a couple of large pieces of shortbread, the old Scot declared, 'This'll dae me 'til this eenin.' Seconds later, he was gone.

# Chapter Twelve

By late afternoon, the Reverend, Jennifer and Felicity had produced a letter which both looked and sounded authentic when they read it aloud. They were satisfied it provided just enough information to intrigue, but without giving too much away. It was important that Alistair MacFarlane did not decide to simply get rid of Edward Colman's so-called descendant and search for the gold himself. They had managed to make the letter look much older by dribbling tea and water over the paper. Eventually all three had declared themselves satisfied and separated to take a well-earned rest.

As she made her way to the stairs, intending to retire to her bedchamber, Jennifer realised she no longer had her plaid shawl. She stopped and thought. No she didn't take it with her to the library which meant she had to have left it in the breakfast room.

Sighing, she turned round and retraced her steps. Where had she last seen the shawl? Likely she'd left it on the chair. She was about to push open the breakfast room door when she suddenly caught the sound of voices she didn't recognise. For some reason, the sound made her pause. She couldn't later have said what it was about the voices that stayed her hand. Likely they were servants simply clearing up, but somehow she didn't think so. The tone was all wrong.

Leaning her ear against the door, Jennifer strained to listen to the muffled voices. After a second, frustrated, she looked down at the latch. It wasn't engaged, so she gently pushed open the door, just enough to make the conversation a little clearer.

'Ah ken ye wantin' tae gae runnin' tae the MacFarlane, but we dinnae ken enough. The Laird put us here tae keep an eye on the Sinclairs. We cannae be gaun blabbin' back afore we ken if they be uptae anythin'.'

'But they hae the bairn. The one what escaped.'

'Aye an ye gae back wi'oot the wee scunner and the MacFarlane'll likely skelp ye wi'in an inch o' yer life.

'An once ye leave Caerlaverock, ye'll nae be comin' back. This be a braw place tae work. Ye cannae jus' gie that up wi'oot haein summat more tae gae the MacFarlane. Did ye hear what they gaunnae dae wi' the lad?'

'Nae. Ah cannae imagine they be takin' him back though.'

'Well, ye better find oot fer sure afore we take it back tae the MacFarlane. Ah'm nae giein up a full belly wi'oot guid reason.'

As she listened, Jennifer thought her heart was about to burst through her chest. There were spies in Caerlaverock. She felt her anger rise. How dare they? Furiously, she pushed open the door, only to stop on the threshold, biting her lip with frustration. The room was empty. The two nameless servants had gone.

Picking up her shawl which was still on the chair, Jennifer hurried towards the only other door in the room – opposite the one she'd just come through. Perhaps if she was quick, she'd catch up with them. Cautiously pulling on the latch, she stuck her head through into a dim corridor beyond. It was empty, but clearly this was a route regularly used by waiting staff coming to and from the kitchen. To her left the passageway continued on to the dining room. Gritting her teeth, she stepped through the doorway and tiptoed towards the dining room door. Once there, she took a deep breath and carefully pushed it open, just enough to peek through the crack. The room was empty.

Huffing in frustration, she closed the door and went towards what she presumed would be the kitchen. A couple of minutes later she was proved right. Hesitating on the threshold for only a second, she squared her shoulders and firmly pushed the door open, stepping into the kitchen as though she had every right to be there. Which as the lady of the house, she did.

Every eye in the cavernous kitchen turned towards her and Jennifer's bravado faltered a little. There must have been ten people in the room. There was no way of telling which two were the traitors, if any.

'Ma lady, can ah help ye wi anythin'?' A small woman as round as she was tall, stepped forward, wiping her hands on her apron. Jennifer fought the urge to turn tail and run. What would her mother have done now?

'I was wondering how Finn was doing,' she blurted in sudden inspiration, looking round to see if she could spot the boy.

'Och, bless him, he's oot wi Gifford. He be a guid lad, verra happy.'

Jennifer smiled with effort. 'Would you be so good as to introduce yourselves,' she asked after a second, another inspiration attributable to her mother – the Duchess of Blackmore always prided herself on knowing each member of the household staff by name.

The small woman drew herself up, clearly delighted to be called up to do the honours. 'As ye wish, ma lady.

'Ah be Mrs. Allen, the cook,' she went on, smoothing down her apron and giving a small curtsy. Jennifer smiled and nodded, then proceeded to watch each face carefully as Mrs. Allen went through them in turn. Unfortunately there was nothing to indicate that any of those present had been the owners of the two voices she'd overheard in the breakfast room. Indeed, they all seemed delighted to have the opportunity to meet with her.

By the time Jennifer managed to excuse herself, she was actually beginning to question her own interpretation of the conversation she'd overheard, but just as she was turning away, she intercepted a glance between the kitchen maid and the footman. Without pausing, she continued back towards the door she'd come through, fighting the urge to skip in elation. She had them. Those two were the ones she'd overheard in the breakfast room – she'd stake her life on it.

∞∞∞

Augustus Shackleford decided against resting in his bedchamber – there would plenty of opportunity for that once he'd kicked the bucket. Instead, he and Flossy did their now familiar turn around the garden, this time accompanied by Brendon Galbraith's huge wolfhound who the Reverend had discovered was as soft as a babe. In many ways, despite being much bigger, Fergus reminded him of Freddy. He was certain Flossy thought so too. Indeed, to watch the two play together, was like stepping back in time, and the clergyman found himself swallowing sudden tears, which was ridiculous since Freddy had been gone for nigh on six years. And besides, they'd likely be together again in the not-too-distant future. The Reverend chuckled. Freddy would be waiting; of that he was certain.

Sitting down in his usual seat, the clergyman closed his eyes. The events of the last few days coming so soon after such a long journey were taking their toll. He was getting far too old for this kind of tomfoolery. He found himself drifting, the noise of the gambolling dogs fading into the background.

'Be ye deid, Maister?' The Reverend's eyes flew open, and he almost jumped out of his skin. Finn was staring into his face mere inches away.

'Tare an' hounds, lad, you nearly gave me a deuced apoplexy.'

'Ah thought ye was deid,' Finn repeated, seating himself on the bench next to the Reverend. 'Be she yer dog?' He pointed to Flossy.

The Reverend gave an ill-tempered nod. 'Shouldn't you be doing something?'

Finn shrugged. 'Mrs. Allen teld me tae get some sun in ma veins.' He held out a thin white hand and pointed to the blue lines under his wrist. The Reverend frowned. They were covered over with bruises 'These be ma veins. Ah dinnae ken hoo tae get the sun in 'em.'

'You just have to sit in the sunshine, I suppose,' the Reverend answered awkwardly. 'Though if you sit in it for too long you'll end up looking like a lobster in a pot. And it'll no doubt be every bit as painful.'

'Ah niver haid lobster. What be her name?' He nodded towards Flossy.

Augustus Shackleford sighed, recognising his peace was well and truly cut up. He might not have spent much time with children, but he knew that when the questions started, they were unlikely to stop short of the Second Coming.

'Flossy.' The little dog, hearing her name, came running over and rolled onto her back, as ever playing to the crowd, even if it was only of two. Laughing, Finn got down on his knees and rubbed her belly.

'Ah reckon she likes Fergus,' he added as they watched her scamper away, back to her overlarge friend.

'I reckon she does,' the Reverend answered drily.

'Dae ye live here, Maister?'

'No, I live a long way from here in a place called Blackmore.'

'That's where the Duke lives too. Hae ye seen 'im?' The boy was clearly in awe.

Reverend Shackleford grinned and nodded, abruptly realising he was actually enjoying himself. 'He's married to my daughter, Grace.' Finn's mouth was a round O in response. He shifted a little further away.

'Dae ye hae a title, then?' he asked breathlessly. 'Other than God botherer.'

The Reverend chuckled and shook his head. 'I reckon that's the only title I need.'

'Whit it be like, Blackmore?'

'Very pretty, like here. But not the same.' The clergyman looked over at the heather clad hills in the distance. 'Not so … rugged I suppose. Do you know what that means?'

'Aye, ah'm nae stupid. Mebbe ye can tak me tae Blackmore, when ye gae.'

Just for a second, the Reverend pictured Agnes's face should he return with an urchin in tow.

'I thought this was your home now,' he answered carefully.

'Aye, but ah want tae see the Duke. Be he tall an' braw?'

The clergyman leaned back and thought. Nicholas was most definitely tall. Was he handsome? In an austere kind of way he supposed, though his son-in-law had learned to laugh over the years, which made him look less … forbidding. But then, being saddled with an entire family he hadn't bargained with, if he hadn't learned to laugh, he'd likely have been entirely dicked in the nob by now.

At Finn's, 'Wha ye laughin' at?' he realised he was chuckling to himself.

'If by braw you mean handsome, then yes, the Duke is very braw. And tall. And stern. He would make you go to school.'

'Ah dinnae need tae gae tae school, ah ken ma letters, an' ah can count tae this.' He held up both hands and stuck out his bare feet, spreading the toes.

'Twenty,' the Reverend said in an impressed voice. 'That's more than most lads of your age. How old are you anyway?' A shrug was all he got in response. 'Well, I'm certain you could count a lot higher if you went to school.'

'Could ah gae tae school in Blackmore?'

The conversation was getting decidedly uncomfortable. 'Why would you want to leave a beautiful place like this?' he asked uneasily. 'You'll be well looked after I'm certain. And you'll learn your letters and count to much higher than twenty.'

'Aye, but ye be a God botherer.' The Reverend looked at Finn's earnest face, and a wave of sadness swamped him. The lad's assumption that being a priest made one trustworthy. In truth, he knew plenty of clergymen who were anything but. For a very brief second, he considered the idea of taking Finn back with him when they returned to Blackmore.

For a *very* brief second.

Then he shook his head and scowled. 'I'm too old to be looking after a lad your age,' he declared. If he was honest – and it seemed to him that honesty was a side-effect of the aging process he'd never before considered – he'd never really done much looking after anyone but himself.

'Ah'd nae be a wee scunner,' Finn went on, oblivious to the Reverend's internal soul-searching.

'What's a scunner?' Reverend Shackleford quizzed gruffly, more to deflect the question than anything else.

The boy shrugged. 'It be jus' *scunner*. Ye ken, *bad.*'

'*Finn!*'

The timing of the shout could not have been better. With a last grin, quite clearly promising that their *discussion* was not yet finished, the boy got to his feet, gave Flossie and Fergus a quick fuss and ran back towards the house, leaving the Reverend with a lot of thinking to do.

## Chapter Thirteen

As soon as she left the kitchen, Jennifer went in search of her brother. The fact that they had two MacFarlane *spies* in the house changed everything. Though from what she'd heard neither seemed very enamoured of the idea. Mayhap they could be persuaded to change sides.

What was she thinking – changing sides? They weren't at war with the MacFarlane clan. Why on earth would the Chieftain put two of his own into Caerlaverock?

She shook her head, arriving at the study door. She gave a brisk knock, then opened it without waiting for a summons. Peter was not her father. To her surprise, Brendon Galbraith was sitting at the desk alone. 'Where is my brother?' she asked, more sharply than she intended.

The steward got to his feet; his expression impassive. 'His lordship hae gaun tae the library wi' Malcolm tae look fer another map o' the loch.'

'Oh.' Jennifer stopped, unsure what to say next. Their encounter the day before had put an end to their former easy banter.

'He shouldnae be long,' Brendon went on, his voice a study in politeness. 'De ye abide here fer him ma lady? Would ye like any tea?' Jennifer thought for a second, then nodded her head and sat down, watching furtively as his lithe form strode across the room to pull the bell. For all that he was so very large, there was also a grace about him. Like one of those panthers she'd read about in her father's library. She found herself colouring up at the direction of her thoughts. Was it hot in here?

Abruptly, the door opened to reveal Peter and Malcolm, and hard on their heels, Mrs. Darroch. 'May we have some tea?' Jennifer requested with a smile, 'And of course some of Mrs. Allen's wonderful shortbread.'

'At once, ma lady.' The housekeeper beamed at Jennifer's use of the cook's name, giving the young woman a sense of warmth and an inkling of why her mother took such care to learn the names of all of Blackmore's staff.

'How did your letter composing go?' Peter asked, laying the map in his hand onto the desk.

'Felicity has it,' Jennifer answered. 'I believe it will be just the thing. But that is not why I'm here.'

'Has something happened, lass?' Malcolm asked, sensing her unease.

Jennifer took a deep breath and told them everything that had happened since she went back to retrieve her shawl.

Peter swore softly. 'You're sure they mentioned MacFarlane?' At Jennifer's nod, he added, 'And you've seen their faces?'

'I didn't actually see their faces while I was listening to them talk, but I saw a kitchen maid and a footman exchange glances while I was in the kitchen. I am certain they were the two whose conversation I overheard.'

'Why the devil would MacFarlane put two of his clan to work at Caerlaverock? Is there already bad blood between us I'm not aware of.' Peter directed his question to Brendon.

'Nae that ah'm aware,' Brendon answered, 'but Gifford would ken more.'

'Do ye wish me tae go look fer him?' Malcolm offered. Peter nodded and the Scot disappeared through the door, just as the maid arrived with a tray of tea and shortbread.

'Please leave it on the side table,' Jennifer ordered. 'I will do the pouring.'

'Verra well, ma lady.' The maid bobbed and curtsied and went back through the door, closing it behind her. Swiftly getting to her feet, Jennifer checked there was no one lurking on the other side. Truly, this whole situation was making her most mistrustful.

'I do not think the two servants are aware of our plan to rescue the children from the mine,' she clarified, going to the tray. 'They know of course that Finn has come from the mine, and that we're likely aware there are other children being misused by Alistair MacFarlane, but more than anything, they sounded scared.' She handed Brendon a dish of tea.

'Anyone wi' a pulse be afeared o' the MacFarlane,' the steward commented drily.

'From what they were saying, neither servant has any intention of acting rashly. I believe they'll wish to know exactly what we intend to do with Finn before they act.'

'Could we turn them to our side?' Peter asked. Jennifer couldn't help but note his grimace at his choice of words, echoing her own sense of disbelief earlier.

She looked over at Brendon. There was no indication the steward thought the words strange, but then mayhap Clan wars were still common in the Highlands. She gave a slight shudder. It was a horrible thought. The last thing her father would want was for them to be embroiled in an outright war with their neighbours.

At that moment, a brief knock at the door heralded the arrival of Malcolm and Gifford. Pouring them both some tea, Jennifer repeated what she'd overheard. When she'd finished, the old steward sighed. 'It dinnae shock me, ma lady. Ye cannae trust the MacFarlane further than ye can throw the bampot.'

'Whatever happens, we dare not start a war,' Peter agonised, echoing Jennifer's concern.

'Ye'll nae be startin' anythin', ma lord. Whatever action we take, ye have tae stay oot o' it. Ye and ma lady both.'

'But we have Finn,' Peter protested. 'Those two servants are fully aware of that.'

'Aye, and they ken ah be workin' fer ye. We dinnae think they hae told the MacFarlane yet. It be likely naither can write, an it be a guid walk tae their Clan home.' He shrugged and added, 'Ah doot they wish any harm tae come tae the lad. Jus' because they be MacFarlane Clan, dinnae mean they agree wi' their Chief's actions.'

'They did seem to value their positions here,' Jennifer interrupted.

'Then perhaps we should speak with them,' Peter suggested.

'Even if they do disagree with their Clan chief, it's unlikely they'll go against him,' Malcolm argued. 'They'd be cast out. And that's a fate worse than death in the Highlands.'

'Aye, Malcom hae the right o' it. Nae matter their private opinions, they'll nae betray their clan. An it may be that the MacFarlane will send one o' his lackeys on tae Sinclair land to find oot what they ken.'

'Then we have to keep them from divulging what they know,' Peter sighed. 'We dare not simply dismiss them. That will drive them straight back to MacFarlane. And for all we know, every servant we employ could be traitors to Caerlaverock. He ran his fingers through his hair in frustration.'

Gifford shook his head. 'Ah'll stake ma life that the rest are loyal to Blackmore. The two ma lady is speakin' of came only weeks ago.'

'There be nae time tae lose,' Brendon asserted. 'Ah reckon the Reverend and ma da must be on their way tae the MacFarlane by the morra.'

'Ah'll dae ma best tae keep the two traitors busy,' Gifford added. 'By the time ah've finished wi' em, they will'nae hae time fer anythin' but sleep.'

'Once we have the children away from that dreadful place, we must secure them somewhere MacFarlane is not likely to find them.'

'Aye, somewhere away far frae Caerlaverock if the bampot comes sniffin' aroond.'

'From this moment, we say nothing that might be overheard.'

∞∞∞

By early evening, Dougal had managed to purchase a small boat which he secured out of sight near to the house. It was decided that Brendon would row the vessel up the loch into position as soon as it got dark enough to conceal it from any prying eyes.

The knowledge that they had two traitors in their midst kept the conversation at dinner stilted and anxious, and by ten p.m., those who had the luxury of retiring to their beds had done so.

After seeing his da home, Brendon headed straight towards the loch, Fergus at his heels. He knew roughly where Dougal had left the boat and knew he needed his full wits about him if he was going to get the small vessel up to Inveruglas without anyone the wiser. The midges had subsided, and the strange twilight that passed for night during the summer this far north was further darkened by the clouds. Glancing up, Brendon grimaced. While the added darkness would undoubtedly help conceal him, it would also make finding his way much more challenging.

As he strode towards the dark body of water directly in front of him, Brendon found his thoughts turning to Jennifer Sinclair. What the devil had possessed him to say he found her attractive? No good could possibly come from such an admission. She was not for the likes of him. She'd be returning to England in less than a month, and he'd likely never see her again.

Sighing, he made an effort to change the direction of his thoughts, but the image of her pressed up against him refused to be banished. Infuriatingly, he felt himself go hard which made walking particularly uncomfortable. That her ladyship was ripe and ready for him, he had no doubt. She was young and clearly not well versed in the art of flirtation, but the way she looked at him spoke volumes

At three and thirty, Brendon was fully aware that women in general found him attractive, though he rarely took up any offers of a bed and much more. It always seemed to him that his outside appearance was more important to most women than what was inside. None took the time to learn about *him*. They wanted his body but had no interest in his mind. Brendon abruptly found himself chuckling at his grandiose musings. Likely they didn't want to know because aside of his pretty face, there was nothing more worth knowing.

But deep inside, he knew that wasn't true. After just two conversations with Jennifer Sinclair, he'd sensed her interest went beyond the obviously physical. And there lay the danger.

On both occasions, he'd actually found himself wanting to share things with her. Things he could not have imagined telling anyone before she literally fell into his life. And watching her compassion for the children being ill-used by the MacFarlane and listening to her ideas of what they could do to put a stop to it, was eye opening to say the least. He would have expected a lady of her position to have little interest outside of parties and fripperies, but even her unexpected dip in the loch had not brought with it the expected histrionics. It was becoming very clear that Jennifer Sinclair was actually relishing the challenge.

The thought of her leaving Caerlaverock in mere weeks made him want to punch something. In less than a sennight, she'd somehow wormed her way into his heart. But he dared not act on it. If her father should get to hear of it, the Duke would likely do the stringing up himself.

∞∞∞

Once in her bedchamber, Jennifer was unable to settle, and as soon as Jenet had withdrawn, she climbed out of bed and went to stand at the window, pulling aside the heavy drapes. Had Brendon left yet? She peered towards the loch but was unable to discern any movement which she supposed was the whole point.

Sighing, she climbed back into bed and lay, staring at the ceiling. Although she wished with all her heart that her parents were here, Jennifer couldn't deny she'd felt so much more alive since coming to Caerlaverock. The balls and routs of the last two seasons had faded from her mind, paltry and insignificant when compared to what she'd witnessed since coming here.

She wondered if Brendon was thinking of her, then berated herself for her foolishness. The steward had more than enough to think about without adding her to the mix. He'd told her he found her attractive, but she wasn't naïve enough to believe that meant anything at all. Lots of men had told her the same in far more flowery language, though clearly most of them were thinking more of her dowry and connections than her eye colour.

Abruptly, she found herself smiling in the dark. Brendon had had no such considerations. Indeed, in the brief moments before he'd fled, he'd looked to be horrified by his admission.

What was it about the Scot that attracted her so? He was handsome, yes – possibly the most handsome man she'd ever met. But she'd never been one to be overly impressed with a pretty face. No, there was something about Brendon Galbraith – something that called to her on the deepest level. A connection she'd never experienced with anyone else – despite the fact that they'd met only days ago. And she knew he felt it too.

Jennifer was well aware that pursuing the connection to its natural conclusion would likely end in tears for both of them, nevertheless, she wouldn't, *couldn't* leave it be.

Even if it meant a broken heart.

## Chapter Fourteen

In the event, Brendon's journey to Inveruglas was uneventful. He managed to secrete the small boat against a little used section of the shore, buried amongst some reed beds.

He certainly didn't relish the swim back to the edge of the loch and appreciated the long walk back to the ramshackle tower he and his father called home even less.

By the time he finally crawled into bed, there were only a couple of hours of darkness left. The midges would soon be abroad again. He had three hours at best before Dougal would be shaking him awake.

Closing his eyes, Brendon felt Fergus jump up beside him and sleepily shifted to make room. Seconds later both the wolfhound and master were sound asleep.

∞ ∞ ∞

'You look like you didn't get to the deuced privy in time,' the Reverend scoffed as he watched Dougal hobble towards him.

'Tha's summat ye'd be familiar wi' ah'm guessin' wi all that cloth ower yer britches. 'specially when ye get the back door trots.'

Reverend Shackleford gritted his teeth but did not rise to the bait. 'If we're to make MacFarlane believe you've got a bad leg, you've got to favour it like so.'

He limped convincingly across towards the old Scot who narrowed his eyes. 'Ah cannae help it if ye Sassenach God wallopers be better at bamboozlin' than we simple folk.'

'Simple as in mutton-headed,' the Reverend muttered under his breath.

Fortunately, after a few more turns around the study. Dougal's limp looked sufficiently realistic.

'Hae ye got the letter fer us tae show the MacFarlane?'

'It's in my pocket,' Augustus Shackleford answered, patting his cassock.

'Aye, well dinnae ye lose it, else we'll be haein a dirt nap.'

Before the Reverend could respond, there was a knock on the study door, and seconds later it opened to reveal Peter and Brendon. Both men stepped inside and carefully shut the door before speaking.

'Have you gentlemen got your story straight?' Peter asked.

'Aye, enough tae fool the MacFarlane ah reckon since awbody ken's he be off his heid.'

Peter nodded. 'Dougal, Gifford has left your favourite entry point unlocked, so I suggest you leave now. If anyone sees you, the fact that you're alone should register.' He turned towards the Reverend. 'Grandfather, are you certain you wish to do this?'

'Well, now, that's the first time anyone's deuced well asked me. And just what will you do, lad, if I say no?' Peter had the grace to look a little shamefaced.

'Dinnae fash yerself,' Dougal interrupted, picking up his bag, 'yer grandda be haein a high ol' time, nae matter what he tells ye.'

The Reverend glared at the grinning Scot. 'I reckon you've a deuced maggot in your head,' he declared with a sniff.

Dougal simply winked as he headed towards the door, leaving the clergyman gritting his teeth.

'Ye hae ma thanks,' interrupted Brendon as the door shut behind his father. 'Nae only fer spendin' more an a few hours wi' ma bampot o' a da, but fer helpin' tae rescue the poor bairns.'

Reverend Shackleford hmphed before declaring gruffly, 'The Almighty's made it more than clear the children are the reason He brought me here, and in truth, I'm more than happy to be throwing a rub in the way of that varmint MacFarlane.'

He turned to his grandson. 'Dougal was right. There is no need to trouble yourself on my account. The Lord knew what he was about. Much longer with only Agnes for company and I'd likely have ended up addled.' He sighed and picked up his bag. 'I just wish Percy was here...'

Peter touched his grandfather's shoulder. 'Just think of the story you'll have to tell him when you return to Blackmore.'

The Reverend patted the Viscount's hand and chuckled. 'I reckon one of Mary's mutton pies and a night of free ale'll be waiting for me down at the Red Lion too.'

'The cart be ootside,' Brendon explained. 'Gifford hae let it be known in the kitchen that he be takin' ye tae hae a look roond the estate. Once ye meet up with ma da, Gifford'll come back wi'oot ye. It'll be dark so naebodie'll see ye be missin'.'

'Won't the servants wish to know where I am when I don't come down for dinner?' the Reverend asked.

'Och, we'll jus say ye be ill in yer bed. If they think ye be boak, they'll nae come near ye.'

'Just leave me to starve?' the clergyman asked, unaccountably miffed.

'You won't be in there,' Peter reminded him with a chuckle. 'And if you're sick, you're unlikely to want much dinner. But don't worry Grandfather, Jennifer, Felicity and I will take it in turns to bring up your gruel...'

'An by the morra, his lordship'll be tellin' the servants that me an' Malcolm'll be laid up in bed wi' it, so they'll be keepin tae the kitchen as much as they can.'

Peter grimaced. 'That's a lot of deuced gruel to get through and I can't abide the stuff.'

'Give it to Flossy,' Reverend Shackleford advised. 'She's a greedy madam and won't turn her nose up to a bit of slop.'

'Me an' Malcolm will leave here at midnight an' follow ye tae the MacFarlane Clan home,' Brendon continued. 'If the bampot haenae slung ye oot on yer ear by then, we'll abide in case ye need us. If all gaes accordin' tae the plan, we'll follow ye tae Inveruglas, stayin' as near tae the mine as we dare. Dinnae look fer us. Remember the signal.'

'Do you have the field glasses?' Peter quizzed.

Reverend Shackleford patted his bag, just as the door opened to reveal Jennifer.

'I think Gifford is getting a little anxious,' she informed them. Crossing the room, she impulsively threw her arms around her grandfather. 'Thank you for doing this, Grandpapa,' she whispered, fighting back tears. 'Please don't do anything foolish, will you. Mama will never forgive us if we bring you back in a box.'

The Reverend patted her back. 'Likely your father will increase your allowance,' he countered with a dark chuckle. 'Look after Flossy.'

∞∞∞

Those remaining did their best to indulge in light conversation during lunch, but apprehension had them itching to leave the table as soon as propriety allowed.

'I'm going to take Flossy for a walk down to the loch,' Jennifer informed the table in general, picking up the little dog and climbing to her feet. She glanced over at Felicity about to ask if the matron wished to accompany her, but before she had the chance to speak, she caught sight of the lady's white face. Clearly, Felicity was anxious about her husband's role in the rescue to come, and it suddenly dawned on Jennifer that Malcolm was no longer a young man. He'd been simply *there* for the whole of her life, strong and stalwart. Her father's rock.

Felicity would wish to be with him before he departed with Brendon after dinner.

'I'd prefer it if you did not go alone,' Peter responded. At Jennifer's glare, he held out a placating hand. 'Don't be so Friday faced, Jenny. I'm not worried about your falling into the loch again, but given the situation, I would simply prefer it if you were accompanied.'

'Ah'll go wi her ladyship, if it please yer, ma lord.'

Jennifer's eyes flew to the steward, but he was looking earnestly at her brother.

'Thank you, Brendon, but that simply gives us the added problem of a chaperone,' Peter answered tiredly. He thought for a second then pursed his lips and gave a determined shake of his head. 'Fiend seize it, this is hardly London. Yes please, Brendon, I'd be grateful if you'd accompany her ladyship.'

The steward looked towards Jennifer. 'Will ma presence be

sufficient tae put ye at ease, ma lady?' he asked carefully.

Jennifer gave a very unladylike snort. 'Don't be ridiculous. Since you've already saved me from drowning, I really think you more than qualify as adequate protection. I will meet you at the front of the house in ten minutes if that suits.'

Then, without waiting for his reply, she swept out of the room.

∞∞∞

An hour after leaving Caerlaverock, the Reverend and Gifford finally spotted Dougal waiting by the roadside. As they got closer, the clergyman frowned. Even from this distance he could tell that the horse and cart the Scot was driving was not nearly as luxurious as the one he was currently sitting on. He groaned internally. 'How long do you think it will take us to reach the MacFarlane Clan home,' he asked the elderly steward, realising he really should have asked the question much, much earlier.

'Ah reckon ye be there afore the midges eat much o' ye,' Gifford answered blithely.

Reverend Shackleford fell silent. There wasn't really much else to say.

Ten minutes later, the clergyman was seated next to Dougal on a cart that looked as though it had been put together with what leftover bits of wood happened to be lying around. He watched longingly as Gifford waved goodbye and headed back to Caerlaverock.

'Well, ma friend, it be jus ye an me. Would ye be partial tae a drop o' whisky tae ease yer arse? Dinnae fash, ye'll nae be feelin' it at all by the time we get tae the MacFarlane.'

∞∞∞

There was an oddly comfortable silence as Jennifer and Brendon picked their way down towards the loch shore. Flossy was sniffing along the trail behind Fergus, keen to keep as close as possible to her giant friend.

At first the steward had walked a respectful few paces behind, but Jennifer soon put a stop to that by turning round and ordering him to walk with her.

'Dae ye order yer servants aboot in such a manner when ye be in England?' he'd asked drily.

'Only when they're behaving like a goosecap,' Jennifer answered with a smile, 'and anyway, you're hardly a servant.'

Brendon lifted his brows and gazed at her with enigmatic blue eyes. 'Am ah nae? What be ah then … ma lady?' The intensity of his voice had her colouring up, and she had to remind herself that the Scot was no unlocked cub, happy to sit at her feet and lap up any crumbs she deigned to toss him.

Wisely, she refrained from answering. Instead, she pointed to a distant mound in the middle of the loch. 'Is that Inveruglas?' she asked, hating the now familiar breathless sound of her voice.

'Nae, that be Inchgalbraith. It were the seat o' ma clan in times bygane.'

'What happened?' Jennifer asked softly.

Brendon sighed. 'Backing the wrong side fer the most part,' he answered simply. 'First agin the Crown, then, two hundred years back, Robert Galbraith o' Culcreuch lost agin the Clan MacAulay, and fled tae Ireland. There be only a few o' us left.' He looked down at her before adding drily, 'Caerlaverock is built on what was Galbraith land.'

'Ouch.' Jennifer winced. 'Should I apologise?'

'Fer ma ancestor's foolishness? Ah dinnae think it be your fault, ma lady.' He nodded back towards the tiny island in the distance. 'Inchgalbraith – Galbraith. The island be where we come frae, but naethin' more.'

'Do you ever go there?' Jennifer asked, sensing he was making light of a sensitive subject. He shook his head, then sighed.

'Ma da gaies ower tae sit dreamin' o' days long gaun.' He stopped as they reached the edge of the loch and shrugged. 'Fer all the guid it daes him.'

Jennifer stared at the distant island, sensing it meant much more than the Scot was letting on. 'So where is Inveruglas?' she asked, going back to their original subject.

'Th'ower way,' he answered, but ye cannae see it frae here.' Unexpectedly he turned towards her and gave a small bow. 'Would ye like tae sit ma lady? Ah took the liberty o' bringin' a blanket.' With a flourish, he pulled a large tartan blanket from the bag he was carrying and laid it on the ground.

'Why, thank you kind sir,' Jennifer murmured, with a gracious bend of her head, taking his proffered hand and seating herself.

'Some lemonade an' a slab o' tablet,' the Scot added with a grin. 'Ah ken it be ma lady's favourite.'

'You ken correctly,' Jennifer retorted with a returning smile. Picking up a piece, she took a large, very unladylike bite and groaned. 'I doubt I'll ever become tired of it,' she murmured, savouring its sweetness.

'As Malcolm said, yer teeth'll be tellin' ye when enough be enough,' Brendon commented drily, sitting down next to her and handing her a glass of lemonade. 'This be Mrs. Allen's speciality accordin' tae Gifford.'

Jennifer took a small sip and nodded in approval.

They sat in silence for a few minutes, then Jennifer looked back in the direction of Inveruglas. 'Do you think any harm will come to them?' she asked in a small voice.

Brendon didn't answer immediately, then, 'Ah dinnae ken, ma lady. Ah've nae doot the MacFarlane will be thinkin' o' the jewellery fer himself. If he's resorted tae using bairns tae dig up gold from an all but deid pit, then ah ken he must be a desperate man. We're takin' a gamble he be too lazy to dae the diggin' fer the jewels himself. An' if there be anythin' we ken aboot Alistair MacFarlane, aside frae him bein' a ne'er-dae-weel, it be that he dinnae like hard work.' The Scot sighed before adding, 'Mebbe we could hae gaun tae Inveruglas wi'oot the bampot kennin' but ah doot it.'

'But if he does agree to them digging on the island, he won't allow them to leave will he?'

'Nae, lass.' Brendon answered simply.

Jennifer bit her lip. 'Thank you for telling me the truth.'

'It willnae come tae that. Malcolm and ah'll be waitin' ashore. As soon as we ken the guards hae left, we'll sneak in an' rescue the bairns. Hopefully wi'oot any bloodshed. By the time the MacFarlane awakens, we'll hae them all safe an' soond back in Caerlaverock.'

'Do you think there will be any reprisals?' Jennifer asked, trying hard to keep the fear out of her voice.

'Ah dinnae ken, but ah cannae believe he'll be wantin' tae take on the powerful Duke o' Blackmore. Everyone thinks the mine be finished. Ah cannae imagine the MacFarlane will want folks hereaboots tae ken what he's been daein. He'll sit tight in his keep 'til the dust hae settled. Then find some other way tae get coin.' Brendon paused, then added, 'If he dinnae, his Clan could be gaun foraye.'

Jennifer knew he was thinking back to the loss of his own Clan.

Impulsively, she put out her hand and laid it over his.

Brendon sucked in his breath at the feel of her small fingers against his. Their eyes met, and it was Jennifer's turn to draw in her breath as she recognised the raw desire in his. But she didn't remove her hand. They were so close, she fancied she could feel the dull thud of his heart through his shirt. As if in a dream, she lifted her other hand and cupped his cheek. She saw the very second he was lost, and triumph surged through her body as with a low groan, he leaned forward and covered her lips with his. Instinctively, she slipped the hand round his neck, and leaned into him, marvelling at the softness of his full lips.

But Jennifer knew he was still holding back. While his lips were sliding across hers, creating havoc with her senses, she sensed he was holding himself under iron control. His hands were planted firmly on the blanket either side of her. It wouldn't do. Lifting the hand that had remained on his, she slipped it too around his neck, linked her fingers and tugged.

As she'd hoped, it was enough to overbalance him. Instinctively sliding his arm around her back to break her fall, Jennifer finally found herself lying full length on the blanket, his big body half straddling hers, cocooned in his arms.

For long seconds, he stared down at her, then his glorious eyes narrowed. 'Ye did that deliberately.'

'Guilty as charged,' she whispered. This time she really could feel his heart thudding against hers though his elbow on the ground was lifting his torso slightly, keeping them apart. He'd landed with one leg thrown over her, but his knee was pressed firmly into the gap between her legs, holding that part she craved away from her. Everything about him spoke of coiled strength. He was afraid of hurting her.

Jennifer was no innocent. She was aware of what went on between a man and a woman, of the pleasure that could be given and received. But she'd never felt even the slightest inclination to experience it for herself. Until she'd met Brendon Galbraith.

Deliberately, she twisted slightly, lifting her hips, to press shamelessly into ... good God, he was huge. Even confined in his breeches.

'Ye have tae stop ... ma lady.' Satisfaction radiated through her as she heard the hoarseness in his voice. If he'd hoped the use of her title would bring her to her senses, he was mistaken. Indeed, she'd never lost them. She simply knew that she wanted this man more than any other she'd laid eyes on, and, God help her, she may never get the chance to feel this way again.

He didn't move.

Slowly, her eyes never leaving his, she slid her hands from around his neck and placed her fingertips on the neck of her dress. It took until she'd undone more than half the buttons before his eyes finally dropped. He drew in his breath at the sight of her creamy flesh covered only by the flimsiest of petticoats. Without pause, she took hold of the laces holding the delicate shift together and pulled. Mesmerised, he watched as the lace parted and she drew the fabric down until her breasts were exposed to his heated gaze. Her nipples hardened, seemingly of their own accord, and with a low groan, Brendon bent his head and took one luscious peak into his mouth.

Unable to help herself, Jennifer cried out as instant sensation slammed between her legs. Her arms fell to her side, fingers grasping and bunching at the blanket on either side of her as he transferred his attention to the other nipple. Dear God, she'd never imagined it could feel like *this*. Gasping she parted her legs and thrust her breasts towards his oh so capable lips, wanting, *needing*... He rolled the nipple between his teeth and shifted slightly, sliding his hand down her bodice to her skirt, cupping *that* part of her and rubbed. Arching her back, Jennifer opened her legs further. She was panting now. She needed to be flesh to flesh. To feel his hand slip under her skirts, to touch her *there*, between her legs. Just where she was burning up.

But instead, he … *stopped*. Her eyes flew open, and she stared confused as he gently closed her petticoat. Then he bent his head and pressed his lips against hers, a featherlight touch.

'Ah willnae take ye here, like this, where any who look can see us,' he murmured. 'Ah want ye more than life itself, Jennifer Sinclair, but ah cannae dae this.'

'You think I am a lightskirt,' Jennifer declared flatly, watching him carefully. To her surprise, he laughed.

'Nae, lass. Ah think ye be a rare jewel an' yer husband'll be the luckiest man alive.' He bent his head and kissed her softly, briefly on the lips. 'But we both ken it willnae be me.'

With that, he climbed to his feet and walked over to the edge of the loch where Flossy and Fergus were still playing.

Fighting the urge to cry, Jennifer sat up and began doing up her buttons. It was all very well to play the wanton, but she realised she wanted what came after too. What *should* come after. The touching, the teasing, the laughing. But most of all, the sense of *belonging*. She'd confused love with lust.

She wanted more than just to be bedded by Brendon Galbraith. She'd known him mere days, but despite his certainty that he would not be acceptable to her family, she knew with every fibre of her being that she wanted him for her husband.

# Chapter Fifteen

By the time the lights of the MacFarlane keep came into sight, Reverend Shackleford was convinced there remained not one inch of him that hadn't been served as either a starter, a main course or a pudding to the midges. Likely all three.

They looked like black dots, until they covered every inch of skin both outside and inside his cassock, resembling an extra black blanket. Fortunately, Dougal had shown him how to cover his nose and mouth lest the beasties start on his insides too.

When they first started to swarm, the Reverend had slapped them away, but he swiftly learned that that simply made them worse. In the end, he tucked his hands under his armpits, bent his head as close to his knees as possible and endured.

As they entered the courtyard in front of the keep, a shadow covered from head to toe in cloth, pointed them towards what looked to be a large, covered area with sheafs of hanging greenery all around the edge emitting an eye wateringly pungent smell. The horse needed no urging to get out of the writhing, biting swarm of darkness and seconds later they were through the hanging sheafs.

Once under cover, the Reverend uncurled himself and began to smack hysterically at his arms and torso until the dark blanket gradually lifted to reveal tiny red welts in its place. Clearly the beasties did not like whatever the greenery was. 'Bog myrtle,'

Dougal explained, picking a few stray midges from his teeth.

'Wha' business hae ye wi' the MacFarlane?' The voice behind them was ice. Turning round, Reverend Shackleford felt a first spasm of fear. The man standing in front of them was clearly a warrior. He'd shed his protective covering and was wearing nothing but a kilt and vest, a sword the size of Brendon's wolfhound slung over his back.

Fortunately, Dougal didn't appear particularly fazed by the fearsome sight, and climbing down from the carriage, declared in a jovial voice. 'Callum MacFarlane, ah haenae seen ye in months. Be ye well?'

The stranger, whose name was evidently Callum, narrowed his eyes and folded his arms.

'Dougal Galbraith,' he declared coldly. 'What dae ye want?'

The elderly Scot limped convincingly towards the hard-faced warrior, an ingratiating smile wreathing his face. 'Ah be lookin' fer an audience wi' the MacFarlane. Ah hae somethin' o' interest tae tell him.'

'What kind o' interest?' The mountain didn't move so much as an inch. The Reverend felt sweat begin to trickle down his cassock, inflaming the midgie bites. He fought the urge to scratch, knowing that once he started, he'd be unable to stop. Should he say something?

'Ye ken ah cannae be tellin' ye afore' the Clan Chief,' Dougal went on genially, 'he'll hae our bawbags fer breakfast if ah dae.' He chuckled at his own joke, but Reverend Shackleford could see persperation begin forming on the old Scot's forehead. Clearly the geniality was purely a façade.

The warrior stared at them for a few seconds longer, then turned on his heel. 'Abide here,' he ordered, throwing his protective covering over his shoulders and striding back out into the dusk.

'Dinnae speak 'til ah tell ye,' Dougal hissed as soon as their welcoming committee of one was out of earshot.

'Well, he didn't seem to have much faith in what came out of your mouth,' the Reverend hissed back, much more accustomed to giving orders rather than receiving them.

'Haud yer weesht,' Dougal growled. 'Yer bein' an eejit. The MacFarlane hae no love fer Sassenach God botherers, ye ken that. He willnae harm me wi'oot guid reason, but ah cannae say the same fer ye.'

Augustus Shackleford stifled a sudden flare of panic, but before he had a chance to argue, voices sounded from across the yard. Seconds later, their way out of the barn was blocked by four broad-shouldered Highlanders. The clergyman swallowed and took an instinctive step back.

'Och, it be guid tae see ye, ma lord.' For the life of him, Reverend Shackleford couldn't tell which one Dougal was speaking to. They all looked exactly the same to him.

'Save yer flattery fer them as need it. Hoo be tha' son o' yers?'

'Verra sad ma lord,' Dougal answered ingratiatingly. 'Twas ma leg pulled him frae yer employ. As ye can see, it still be painin' me.' He did a little hobble for emphasis.

Alistair MacFarlane was possibly the biggest man the Reverend had ever seen. Unlike the others, he hadn't protected himself from the midges as he'd crossed the yard and both arms were covered in black. He didn't appear to notice them at all. He walked towards them and looked in the cart. As he did so, the Reverend caught the overripe scent of freshly killed meat and had to fight a sudden urge to cast up his account.

'Whose grave be ye diggin'?' he asked nodding towards the tools lying in the bottom of the cart.

'Nae a grave, ma lord. Tha's what ah wish't tae talk tae ye aboot. Dougal gave a toothless smile. The Chieftain didn't smile back. 'Me an' ma acquaintance here be on the trail o' buried treasure...'

∞∞∞

They spoke little on the walk back up to the house. Jennifer couldn't help noticing he took care to give her a wide birth. Mayhap he was worried she would throw herself at him again if he came within grabbing distance. In truth, she was content not to force the issue, sensing that to do so would merely drive Brendon further away.

Underneath all the uncertainty, she was bubbling with a deep quiet joy. Despite the shortness of their acquaintance, she felt a deep abiding conviction that Brendon Galbraith was for her. And though he might not have admitted it to himself yet, she believed he felt the same. Currently, however, he could not imagine there was the remotest chance of a happy ending for either of them, and she could almost feel the stubborn Scot withdrawing from her, step by step.

She would simply have to bide her time until the whole dreadful business with Alistair MacFarlane was done with. As soon as the children were safe, she would write to her father.

Once they arrived back at the house, Brendon turned to her and bowed. 'Ah willnae see ye agin afore this evenin,' he said carefully. 'Please dinnae worry aboot yer grandda. Ah swear ah'll bring him back tae ye safely.'

Jennifer gazed at him silently for a second. 'I know you will,' she responded softly at length. 'Please have a care to your own safety too...' She paused then whispered, 'I could not bear it if anything should happen to you.' Then, abruptly fighting the urge to cry, she bent to pick up Flossy and almost ran towards the front door.

That evening, once she was certain Gifford had returned, Jennifer informed the housekeeper that her grandfather was feeling under the weather and would not be coming down for dinner. 'Poor man, I think perhaps he's eaten something that has disagreed with him,' she added. 'However, it might be pertinent to advise the servants to stay away from his chamber ... just in case. I will see that he has water and then tomorrow, I'll take him a little breakfast.'

Mrs Darroch nodded, not entirely able to hide her alarm and Jennifer fought the urge to grin as the housekeeper took a surreptitious step back.

Malcolm and Felicity too elected to have dinner in their room, setting the stage for the fictitious sickness to 'sweep the house', which left Peter and Jennifer as the only two at the dinner table.

At first, they sat largely in silence, until her brother suddenly put down his knife and fork and asked her if she was missing England and home.

She looked at him in surprise, unsure what had triggered the question. Mayhap he was simply worried about the responsibility that had been so unexpectedly thrust upon him.

'I love it here,' she replied simply. 'It's quite different from Blackmore – the scenery is wild and somehow calls to one, don't you think?'

'It's certainly beautiful,' he answered carefully, 'but I'm not sure I feel the same affinity as you.' There was a pause before he added, 'Are you certain your attraction is not due to the presence of a certain newly employed steward?'

Jennifer's face flamed, much to her chagrin. 'What on earth are you talking about?' she blustered at length.

'Come sister, we both know you're a terrible liar. Do you have feelings for Galbraith?'

Knowing she owed her brother the truth – if not the *whole* truth, Jennifer chose her words carefully. 'I must confess, I feel a certain kinship with him,' she said cautiously. His snort told her he wasn't at all convinced by her explanation.

'Are your feelings reciprocated? You realise that Father will have a hard time considering his suit. Especially since Caerlaverock is so far away from Blackmore.' He shook his head. 'And I have no idea what Mother will say.'

Jennifer sagged. 'He has not said whether he feels anything for me,' she confessed, 'but his manner indicates he does.' She picked up her glass of wine to give herself time to decide what to say next. 'I think he believes he's beneath my touch.'

Peter gave another snort. 'Is he aware that our mother is a vicar's daughter?'

'It hasn't actually come up,' Jennifer answered drily. 'And Mama may well be low born, but I think Papa was hoping I would make a good match.'

'A good match is one that makes you happy,' Peter countered. 'I said I thought Father would find it difficult, not that he would forbid it.' He paused before adding, 'We are in Scotland after all and strictly speaking, his consent is not actually needed.'

Jennifer stared wordlessly at her brother, her mind awhirl. 'Mayhap I should not have mentioned that,' he added ruefully when she did not speak.

'I would not wish to go against my parents' wishes,' she said finally. 'It would break both their hearts.' She sighed and took a sip of her wine. 'We are far from that point anyway. At the moment, I think Brendon is determined to stay away from me for my own good.' She said the last wryly, and Peter grinned.

'I wish him luck with it. Clearly he does not know you well enough as yet to realise such resistance is futile.' His face turned serious. 'But, once this unsavoury business is over, I am duty bound to write to Father and tell him the situation. Do not expect me to keep your secret, dearest. You are under my protection, and it would not be honourable for me to do so.'

'Though you do not balk at informing me I am able to marry in Scotland without my father's consent?' she retorted.

'I would not see you unhappy, Jenny,' he answered softly.

'I know.' Jennifer laid her hand over his. 'I will do nothing without speaking to Mama and Papa. And I do believe that even in Scotland one needs the groom's consent to marry.'

∞∞∞

The inside of the MacFarlane keep was akin to stepping back a hundred years. It had none of the luxuries of Caerlaverock and even though it was the middle of June, the hall was drafty and cold.

'Oot wi' it then.' Alistair MacFarlane wasted no time in demanding a further explanation. Though he'd allowed them inside, they were offered no refreshments, and both stood in front of the chieftain as though guilty of some heinous crime.

Dougal gave a quick glance at the Reverend before saying carefully, 'Ma guid friend here hae come intae possession o' a letter...'

'Wha' letter?' MacFarlane interrupted.

'I am a descendant of a man named Edward Colman,' Reverend Shackleford intervened before Dougal could say anything more. At this rate they'd be here til deuced Christmas. 'He died a traitor's death in 1678, but before he died, he sent a letter to his kin in Suffolk, England...'

'Yer a Sassenach,' MacFarlane declared flatly, 'An' a God walloper at that. Ye've some nerve tae come intae ma home wi' yer English bloody lies an' tricks.'

'Nae, he be tellin' the truth, ma lord,' Dougal interjected desperately, raising a conciliatory hand. Both men were sweating now.

There was silence for a second as the clan chief stared at them coldly. '*Ale!*' was all he said at length. From the corner of his eye, the Reverend could see a woman scurry to do his bidding. Once the tankard was in his hand, MacFarlane took a long swallow, then wiped his mouth on his arm. Then he nodded, once, at the Reverend.

'By all accounts Edward Colman was a wealthy man and had all his coin changed into jewellery and trinkets when he moved up to Edinburgh. Before his arrest, he came to Loch Lomond, and we know he brought the whole of his treasure with him...'

'Hoo dae ye ken?'

'The letter.' Reverend Shackleford rummaged around in his cassock for the letter they'd so painstakingly constructed. For one dreadful second he thought he'd lost it and knew his face echoed Dougal's terrified expression. Thankfully, after a full minute, his fingers brushed against the paper's edge. With a flourish, he pulled the missive out of his pocket and held out his hand.

MacFarlane looked at the letter for a second, then waved it away, indicating the clergyman should read it out loud. Clearly the clan chief couldn't read.

With trembling hands, Reverend Shackleford opened the letter and read its contents aloud. His stomach churned, and he fought to keep his voice from wavering. What had seemed so convincing when they wrote it, now sounded a pile of bunkum.

In the letter Colman purportedly wrote that a local man had rowed him over to a small island by the name of Inveruglas. He'd taken with him a large leather satchel containing all of his wealth. Once on the island, he'd asked the oarsman to return and collect him before the sun went down. During the time he spent alone, Edward Colman claimed he buried his entire wealth on the island, using only his bare hands, returning to the Lochside with nothing but an empty satchel.

'Daed he say where on the island he buried it?' MacFarlane asked, sitting forward in his chair.

'He did, but there's a splodge of... something... making the words illegible,' Reverend Shackleford answered, holding out the letter for the Chieftain to see.

'Wha's tae stop me frae takin' the letter and runnin' a sword through yer belly?'

The Reverend swallowed. 'I have studied Edward Colman extensively,' he answered. 'I have come to know the way he thought. I don't believe you will find the treasure without my help.'

'Then why come tae me? Why not gae tae th'island and dig yerelf?'

'We haed nae wish tae offend ye, ma lord. Inveruglas be MacFarlane land. We cannae dig wi'oot yer permission.'

'We'll share the treasure with you, naturally,' Augustus Shackleford added, pleased to note that his voice had lost its wobble.

'Aye, ye will.' There was no suggestion of how the non-existent jewellery would be split and the Reverend realised that Dougal was right. Alistair MacFarlane had no intention of allowing them to leave Inveruglas alive.

# Chapter Sixteen

Though Brendon did his best to put what happened with Jennifer Sinclair out of his mind, every last detail remained indelibly printed on his brain. Her softness, her curves, the way she'd responded to his touch, his *mouth*. He gritted his teeth. Just thinking about it had him hard and aching. It had taken every ounce of strength he possessed to stop when he had. He'd been so close to simply lifting her skirts and making her his completely.

But then what? The Duke of Blackmore would never consider him as a husband for his only daughter. A penniless Scotsman without even so much as a clan? It was laughable.

Except it wasn't. Sitting down on the side of the track, Brendon drew up his knees and laid his arms across them. He'd been ten ways a fool to allow himself to fall under Jennifer Sinclair's spell, but from the moment he'd laid eyes on her, he'd known she was different. Everything about her entranced him. From her impudence to her humour to her compassion. Her hair the colour of autumn chestnuts and her oh so warm brown eyes.

He'd swiftly realised she cared nothing for what people thought of her, unlike the few ladies he'd met who thought themselves so high in the instep. He laid his head on his arms with a sigh. The truth was, he'd give her the moon should she ask it of him. Just the thought of seeing her with another tore him in two.

He pictured her laughing, beautiful face again in his mind, committing it to memory. She would be gone in less than a month. And God willing, he'd never see her again.

∞∞∞

Both Felicity and Jennifer were abed when Malcolm left to meet up with Brendon. The husband and wife had said their goodbyes over dinner earlier. The Scot was exiting through the same door as Dougal, but before he stepped through, Peter clasped his hand. 'Don't do anything foolish old friend. My father would never forgive me if I allowed anything to happen to you.'

'Dinnae ye worry, lad,' Malcolm answered gruffly. 'I'll be gone no more 'an two days. And when me and Brendon return, we'll have the bairns with us.'

'If you're not back by the day after the morrow, I'll be coming to find you, Sinclair or not,' Peter vowed hoarsely.

Malcolm simply nodded and disappeared into the gloom. Peter waited to make sure they hadn't been overheard, then with a sigh, he headed upstairs to bed.

Malcolm kept to the edge of the formal gardens as he weaved his way down towards the gate in the wall. Brendon would be waiting on the track down to the loch. Despite the seriousness of the situation, the Scot was in good spirits. It had been a while since he'd been involved in any smoky business, and in truth he'd missed it, though he was certain Felicity hadn't. Stepping through the gate, he looked briefly back towards the house but could discern no movement. While he couldn't be entirely sure, Malcolm was as confident as he could be that his departure had gone unobserved.

Stepping onto the track he hefted his bag higher onto his back and strode to where Brendon and Fergus were already waiting.

∞∞∞

'Ye'll stay in here whan the MacFarlane decides what tae dae.'

The Reverend stared in trepidation at the cold austere room they were shown into. A bed and an old chest with a chair placed directly in front of it were the only three pieces of furniture in the room. A bottle of whisky stood on the chest.

Their guard threw their two bags into the room before adding, 'An' dinnae ye be touchin' that.' He pointed to the whisky bottle. 'That holds the remains o' ma lord's mother.' All three of them stared silently at the bottle in question.

'There doesn't appear to be much of her,' the Reverend commented, perhaps unwisely.

'She wa' a wee lass,' their guard retorted, glaring at the clergyman. 'A blessed saint she wa'. The MacFarlane speaks wi' her when he be troubled.' He pointed to the chair which they realised now was facing the chest.

'Ah'll see ye in the morn.' And with that, the door slammed shut, followed by the ominous sound of a key turning in the lock.

'Dae ye reckon it be really the MacFarlane's mother?' Dougal peered at the bottle. 'Ah could dae wi' a wee dram.'

'Why don't you give it a shake and see,' retorted the Reverend, picking up his bag and breathing a sigh of relief when he saw that the bread and cheese were still in there. Giving silent thanks to the Almighty, he lifted out the cloth bundle, and tearing off a hunk of bread, chewed it disconsolately.

With a sniff, Dougal left the bottle where it was and picked up his own bag.

'Do you think they believed our story?' Reverend Shackleford queried.

'Aye, else we'd be pushing up thistles by noo.' He nibbled on a piece of cheese. 'Ah wonder why they didnae put his mother in the groond?'

'You heard the guard. MacFarlane likes to talk with her.'

'Aye, but a grave be the place fer chattin' wi yer relatives.'

'Only the dead ones I hope.'

'Mebbe she haed Norse blood in her.'

The Reverend nodded, but didn't answer, instead going over to the narrow window which was set in a deep embrasure. After hesitating a second, he climbed into the aperture and pressed forward on his knees until he could see out of the opening. There was no glass in the window, and he shivered as he peered out into the night. Beyond the courtyard below he could see nothing.

'Ye dae ken we be two stories off the groond?'

'I'm fully aware of that, thank you. That's why I'm trying to get back in.'

'Dae ye hae a likin' fer climbin' oot o' windows, or intae 'em mebbe?'

'I very much doubt I have as much experience as you do since you clearly don't think twice about entering a property uninvited.'

'That be through a door, nae a window.'

'And that makes it acceptable?' The Reverend was beginning to sweat a little. He hadn't realised the aperture was quite so narrow, and the drop quite so *high*. 'Perhaps you could stop talking and give me a hand.'

'Mebbe ah'll leave ye be,' Dougal chuckled. 'Ye be blocking the draft.'

The Reverend gritted his teeth. If the mutton-head thought he'd resort to begging… He looked down and gave a small moan. He'd only thought to investigate the possibility of them escaping should they need to – and failing that, to see if he could spot either Malcolm or Brendon.

'The MacFarlane be nae aboot tae let us gae, that be why he left us all the way up here. Though should he see ye, crouchin' there like an owergrown bat, he might be tempted tae push ye oot himself.'

'Have you always been such a deuced gabster?'

'Aye. It's nae jus' th'Irish wi' the gift o' the gab.'

An almost inaudible, 'hmph,' was all the Reverend could manage while trying again to force himself backwards into the room. Unfortunately his upper arms were trapped by his side. In the end he gave up and muttered between his teeth, 'I'd be extremely obliged if you would assist me in removing myself from this deuced aperture.'

With a sigh, Dougal walked over and stared at the Reverend's back. 'Ye be stuck guid an' proper,' he muttered, adding an *eejit* under his breath. Climbing up behind the clergyman, he managed to slide his hand either side of the large man's thighs.

'Watch me baubles,' the Reverend growled.

'Hoo can ye be thinkin' o' yer baubles at a time like this?'

'I'd like 'em to remain intact if it's all the same with you,' the Reverend grated, abruptly recalling all the other times his trinkets had been put in harm's way. Truly, it was a wonder he hadn't ended up a deuced eunuch. The risks he took for the Almighty.

He held his breath as Dougal's hands slid round his hips. 'Can ye suck in ye belly so ah can slide ma hands up a wee bit more?' he muttered over the Reverend's shoulder. 'Otherwise I'll be usin' yer bloody baubles tae hang on tae. I didnae ken ye be such a jollocks.'

*Deuced cheek of the man.* Gritting his teeth, the clergyman obligingly sucked in his stomach and felt the Scot link his fingers together, fortunately just above the imperilled trinkets.

Dougal rose up slightly and lifted one knee, bracing it against the clergyman's back. 'Right then, ah'm gonnae coont tae three, then ah'm gonnae pull.'

Resisting the urge to ask if the Scot could actually count to three, since he didn't want Dougal to be tempted to push instead of pull, Reverend Shackleford nodded.

'Wan, twa, *three*.'

For a second nothing happened, then abruptly the Reverend shot free of the embrasure like a cork from a bottle, taking the smaller Dougal with him. After skidding along the stone floor they crashed headfirst into the large chest where they stared up in horror as the whisky bottle teetered perilously, before falling directly onto the Reverend's head, breaking in half and spilling the MacFarlane's saintly mother all over the pair of them.

∞∞∞

It was the early hours of the morning by the time Brendon and Malcolm arrived within hailing distance of the MacFarlane's keep. 'Do ye think yer father managed to convince them?' Malcolm asked as they crouched in the bracken to watch the keep in the predawn shadows.

'Aye. The MacFarlane'll want tae believe him,' Brendon answered. 'Ah reckon he willnae waste any time either. Wi' a bit o' luck he'll be marchin' the Reverend an' ma da oot afore daydaw tae get 'em diggin'.'

Sure enough, dawn was just touching the sky as they spied a flurry of activity outside the keep, and minutes later, the Reverend and Dougal appeared, driving the same horse and cart they'd brought with them. Behind them were half a dozen of MacFarlane's warriors.

Both men watched the procession with relief. Clearly the chief had believed the fabrication.

Climbing to their feet, the two men followed at a distance, taking care to keep out of sight.

Within minutes they could see Inveruglas, wreathed in the early morning mist. Crouching behind a large clump of heather, they watched the Reverend and Dougal unload the cart while their guards lounged about, laughing and joking. Brendon gritted his teeth. The men knew about the bairns in the mine. Truly the bastards deserved to lose their clan. They had no honour.

It took less than half an hour to load the MacFarlane boat tied up against the shore. Bigger than the boat Brendon had hidden on the island, it took two men to row it across to Inveruglas. Once there, obviously eager to be gone, they helped the Reverend and Dougal unload the supplies, then, leaving everything on the narrow shore, they pushed off and returned to the Lochside. Minutes later, all but one of them had left, taking the horse and cart with them.

∞∞∞

'De ye reckon the MacFarlane'll be wantin tae talk tae his mother afore we're awa'?' Dougal speculated, carrying the large spade towards the ruins of the tower that dominated the island.

'Does it matter?' the Reverend muttered. 'The varmint's not going to let us leave here anyway.'

'Aye it matters,' Dougal contradicted morosely. 'It could mean the difference twixt drownin' and bein' boiled alive.'

'We'd best be away before he has to decide then,' Reverend Shackleford declared, dropping the blanket he'd been carrying. 'I suggest we start *digging* round where the chucklehead watching us can't see.'

'Aye, that be perfect. The best place tae see the mine is aback the tower. The numpy cannae see what we be up tae.'

'Malcolm and Brendon should be in position by now,' the Reverend added, 'so hopefully, we'll be home and dry before MacFarlane realises his mother's had her last tot of whisky.'

The two men sat with their backs propped against the ruined fortress, well out of sight of the lone guard tasked with keeping watch on the shoreline.

The Reverend brought out his field glasses. From their position he could see the entrance to the mine and set just back, a ramshackle bothy that looked as though it might once have served as an office. The only activity he could see was around the entrance and inside the almost derelict building. He turned to Dougal. 'I count four guards. Three in that building, and one sitting near to the entrance. Have a look to see if you can spot any more of 'em.'

Dougal obligingly took the glasses and peered through them. 'There be another one jus' comin' up,' he pointed out. 'He be carryin' a lairge bag. More rocks the poor wee bairns hae dug oot ah reckon.'

They sat in silence for a while, taking it in turns to look through the field glasses, but didn't spot any additional guards. At length, the Reverend looked over at the shovel and spade lying on the ground and gave a sigh. 'I suppose we'd better do a spot of digging, just in case the blackguard comes to check on us.'

'Aye, ye'd best g'oan wi it.'

'What do you mean me?' Reverend Shackleford spluttered. 'What the deuce are you going to be doing?'

Dougal sighed and pointed to his bandaged lower limb. 'Ye ken ah cannae dae a thing wi' ma bad leg, so ah thought mebbe ah'd hae a wee nap.'

## Chapter Seventeen

Jennifer was up and seated at the window, Flossy snuggled on her lap, by the time Jenet arrived the following morning. 'Ye'll catch ye death wi'oot yer claes,' the maid admonished her, putting down the tray and hurrying over to cover her mistress with a robe.

'I couldn't sleep,' Jennifer defended, submitting to Jenet's ministrations with a smile.

'Well, that will ne'er dae,' Jenet clucked, handing the young woman a cup of hot chocolate. 'Daed the kerfuffle wake ye, ma lady?'

Jennifer frowned. 'What kerfuffle?'

The maid was busy stoking up the fire. At her mistress's question, she swivelled round and waved her hand. 'Och, it be nothin' tae bother yer heid wi, ma lady. The new footman be a surly lad an' ah kenned he wouldnae last long.'

Jennifer frowned and climbed off the window seat, much to Flossy's chagrin. 'What did he do?'

Always ready to share a bit of gossip, Jenet got to her feet. 'Well, Murray – that be the footman, ma lady – telled MacNee he be naithin but an auld woman.' Her voice dropped to a whisper. 'MacNee haes a fearsome temper, ma lady and ah've ne'er seen him so angry. They were oot in the courtyard, jus' below yer window, an' they be shoutin' lood enough tae wake the deid, so ah'd nae be surprised if it were the yellyhooin that woke ye.' She shook her head and turned back to the fire.

Jennifer felt her stomach contract with dread. 'Where is Murray now?'

'Gaun ma lady. Not half an hour back, an' guid riddance ah say.'

Jennifer placed her cup back on the tray. 'I'd like to get dressed now,' she told the maid, trying to keep the anxiety out of her voice.

'It be early yet, ma lady.'

Jennifer gritted her teeth at Jenet's obtuseness. 'I believe Flossy wishes for a walk,' she said firmly, waving towards the little dog who'd wasted no time in burrowing back under the blankets on the bed. Jenet opened her mouth to point out the fact that the animal was in fact snoring, but one look at her mistress's resolute face made her close it again. Instead she nodded and climbed back to her feet.

Twenty minutes later, Jennifer went in search of her brother, her earlier anxiety replaced by a feeling of dread. Unfortunately, it seemed her brother was also no longer abed. Biting her lip, she hurried down to the breakfast room, only to be told the Viscount had gone for an early morning ride.

Jennifer fought the urge to scream. Was Peter aware of the altercation between the footman and butler? Clearly this Murray was on his way back to MacFarlane. If he should speak with the Chieftain, their whole plan could unravel. What the deuce had happened to Gifford's vow to keep the two interlopers busy?

After conveying her wish to be informed immediately on her brother's return, Jennifer took Flossy out into the garden, her thoughts racing. Perhaps the footman had deliberately planned the argument as an excuse for him to leave. She shook her head. That made no sense. He would have been much better simply slipping away, telling no one. So, if the argument was unplanned, Murray – if that was the footman's real name – may have felt he had no choice. How long would it take him to walk to his Clan home?

After watching Flossy finish her business, Jennifer hastened back towards the house, only to be told that the Viscount had not yet returned. An enquiry about Gifford's whereabouts revealed the steward was picking up supplies from Banalan this morning. When the housekeeper asked if her ladyship would like to speak with Mr. Mackenzie, Jennifer fought the urge to laugh hysterically.

'Mr. Mackenzie is unfortunately suffering with the same sickness that has beset my grandfather,' she explained, holding out a placating hand at Mrs. Darroch's alarmed expression. 'I'm certain it's nothing to worry about, but Mrs. Mackenzie will ensure they both keep to their room as a precaution and will ring if they need anything.' When the housekeeper seemed about to ask another question, Jennifer forestalled her by asking for a pot of tea.

To her relief, Mrs. Darroch gave a quick curtsy and left without any further questions. 'Oh what a tangled web we weave,' she muttered to herself, quoting Sir Walter Scott. She stared out of the window as though watching might suddenly conjure her brother out of thin air. In truth he could be hours. She knew her sibling of old. This is exactly what he always did when a situation was beyond his control. Being forced to wait while others acted did not sit well with Peter, any more than it did their father.

She guessed that Peter had believed the steward would be in the house during his absence, while Gifford assumed the Viscount would be in residence. Jennifer grimaced. *Men*. Did they ever actually *talk* to each other?

When neither man had returned after an hour, she made a decision. She could not simply sit and twiddle her thumbs, hoping that Peter or Gifford would arrive back to save the day. She would have to take action herself.

Seating herself, she wrote a short note to her brother, then ringing the bell, asked for a horse to be brought round. Lastly, mindful of her earlier frustration, she called to Flossy and went in search of Felicity.

∞∞∞

Since Brendon and Malcolm had been up since midnight, they took it in turns to rest. Waiting was always the hardest part of any undertaking, and unless the Reverend and Dougal ran into any problems, there was nothing for either man to do until the guards had finally left the mine for the night. Fergus on the other hand seemed to have no problem with inactivity and spent most of the morning dozing happily in the watery sunlight.

At midday, they nibbled on strips of dried beef and discussed their forthcoming strategy.

'We hae tae assume at least one guard will remain after th'others leave,' Brendon mooted. 'Finn said he heard the man snoring so likely he'll hae a bed o' sorts in one o' the old bothies close tae the mine entrance. He'll nae want tae be abroad when the midges come oot.'

'We'll have to wait until the bloody beasties are gone for the night too,' Malcolm retorted. 'We'll nae get the bairns movin' if they be covered in bites.' He rolled out their map and laid it between them both. 'If we come in through here,' he suggested, pointing to a gap in the copse of trees that kept prying eyes from easily observing the mine, 'and keep tae the Lochside, we'll nae be easily spotted if there's an additional guard.'

Brendon nodded. 'Ah doot the MacFarlane will bother wi more an one though. He'll be thinkin' the bairns are safe enough locked up – an' we dinnae think he kens he's missin' one.'

'But the guard Finn described surely knows?'

'Aye and ye can bet he'll nae hae told the Chieftain. The MacFarlane uses his sword first an' his mouth after.'

It was Malcolm's turn to nod. 'So, we hope for one but keep an eye out for more.'

'What dae we dae wi' the guards once we have the key tae the mine? Dae we finish 'em?' Brendon asked matter-of-factly.

'Will it provoke a retaliation?'

Brendon shrugged. 'Who knows what the MacFarlane'll dae. But ah reckon we cannae worry aboot that. We do whatever we need tae. Better them deid than us.'

'Aye,' Malcolm agreed simply. 'And if the eejit watching over Inveruglas is daft enough to be there come sundown, we'll deal wi' him first.' He paused, then added, 'Once we've freed the youngsters, we'll need tae get 'em back to Caerlaverock as quickly as possible.'

'We could hae daen wi' Dougal's horse an' cart - the poor wee bairns are nae gaunnae want tae walk.' Brendon shook his head and sighed. 'Ah confess ah was hopin' the lazy ne'er-dae-weels'd leave the wagon thinkin' tae use it tae bring back the treasure...' he paused and chuckled. 'Truly, the MacFarlane be a bloody bampot.'

'Aye,' Malcolm conceded, 'But a dangerous one.' He shook his head. 'Ye be right though, it'll be a long walk fer wee feet back tae Caerlaverock. We'll need tae stay off the Lochside.'

'If all gaes accordin' tae plan, they'll nae be missin the bairns until the morra,' Brendon mused. 'Once they've giein the signal, the Reverend an' ma da'll use the boat ah hid tae get off Inveruglas.

'What dae ye say tae takin' the MacFarlane's boat and splittin' the bairns between the twa. We could row back to Caerlaverock wi' naebody the wiser til' the morn.'

Malcolm gave a slow grin and nodded. 'We should be able tae reach safety long before the MacFarlane discovers the bairns are gone.' Then looking over at the wolfhound curled up in the grass, his smile faded. 'What about Fergus?' he asked.

'Och, the hound could find his way back home blindfold. He'll follow the boats an' keep an eye oot fer any trouble.'

∞∞∞

Predicably Felicity hadn't been happy with Jennifer's proposal at all. 'What on earth will your mother say when she learns I allowed you to go off alone?' the matron declared.

'Well, I'm all ears if you have a better idea,' Jennifer responded tartly. 'There's no time to send a note to Chapman and his men, who are even now I suspect enjoying all the delights that Banalan has to offer. How long do you think it would take to round them up? And we both know that Peter has purposefully kept them out of what is an extremely volatile situation.

Felicity opened her mouth to speak, then closed it again with a sigh. 'Can you at least wait another hour? Likely Peter will have returned by then.'

'Murray left nearly two hours ago,' Jennifer protested. 'However, he's on foot. If I leave now, I'll reach Malcolm and Brendon before the traitor has a chance to tell MacFarlane what he knows. Hopefully, they'll be able to stop him.'

'How?' Felicity questioned sharply.

'I can't think about that,' Jennifer retorted, 'but if I don't try, then Malcolm, Brendon, my grandfather and Dougal will almost certainly be captured at the very least. All four are trespassing on MacFarlane land, and even I know that up here, no one will take the blackguard to task if he strings them up.' She paused, feeling sudden tears well up. 'I've written Peter a note. As soon as my brother and Gifford return, you can be certain they will come after me.'

In truth, the thought of her husband at the mercy of such as Alistair MacFarlane made Felicity want to cast up her account. But she had a duty towards her charge. Grace had *entrusted* Jennifer to her. How could she even consider allowing the young woman to risk her life in such a hazardous endeavour? But, in her heart, she knew Jennifer would go, with or without her consent. After a few seconds, Felicity closed her eyes in defeat. When she opened them again, Jennifer was back on her feet.

'Here's the note to Peter. I know I don't need to ask you to watch for him or for Gifford. Please look after Flossy until Grandpapa and I return.' Felicity nodded and stood up, pulling Jennifer into a brief tight embrace.

'Please don't do anything foolish, Jenny,' she whispered, feeling the answering headshake against her cheek.

Seconds later Jennifer was gone.

∞∞∞

'Do you know where Brendon hid the boat?' the Reverend asked suddenly.

'Aye, it be ower there in the reeds.'

'Shall I go and check it's there?'

Ye gaunnie nae dae that, yer numpy. We dinnae want tae draw the eejit's attention tae it.'

The Reverend bristled but was in truth too tired to do more than glower. It had taken him two hours to dig three useless holes. Naturally, he hadn't accepted Dougal's declaration that his bad leg prevented him from digging but conceded that the old Scot could only do it under the cover of the ruined tower where he could not be observed. The result was a pathetic hole that wouldn't have hidden a lady's reticule, let alone a satchel full of gold jewellery.

And after listening to Dougal's grumbling for nigh on half an hour, the Reverend had snatched the shovel from the Scot's hands, only narrowly resisting the urge to bash the addlepate over the head with it.

'How long do you think we have until sunset?' the clergyman asked, trying to ignore his recent disturbing propensity for violence.

'Ah reckon we hae aboot four hours til gloamin. The bastart'll nae be hangin' aroond tae provide a meal fer the wee beasties, and naither will the other bastarts ower at the mine.'

'Which leaves us to provide their only evening meal. Splendid.'

Dougal favoured him with a toothless grin but didn't answer. There really wasn't anything to say.

∞∞∞

Jennifer followed the Lochside, guessing that unless Murray wanted to walk the whole way back to his Clan home, he'd stick to the most used track too in the hopes of receiving a lift.

In any case, she'd doubtless get lost or worse if she attempted to find her way across the numerous trails crisscrossing the wild landscape.

She kept the horse at a sedate canter, keeping her eyes peeled for any sign of the former footman. The weather was overcast but reasonably warm, and she soon began to feel sticky and hot beneath her riding habit.

Fortunately on the insistence of both her parents, Jennifer had been taught to ride astride a horse, so she didn't have the additional difficulty of keeping her balance. She couldn't help but loose a small chuckle. The current bridle path was hardly Rotten Row.

After about an hour, another discomfort began to assail her, and she realised she'd left Caerlaverock without breaking her fast. Berating herself for her stupidity, she wondered if she'd be able to purchase anything to eat. A heel of bread and a pitcher of water would do.

As far as she was aware, there were no villages between here and the MacFarlane Keep, but surely there would be a farmhouse or croft who'd take her coin.

It was another hour before she came across a small farmhouse, nestling in a hollow to the left of the track. Surprisingly, she'd passed no traffic of any kind – neither riding nor walking, going either way. On the one hand, it meant she'd been unable to confirm whether she was on the same track as her quarry, but on the other, if he was still walking, she must be getting close to catching him up. Stopping at the croft, she could at least find out if she was heading in the same direction.

Jennifer directed her horse towards the gate and dismounted onto a large, conveniently placed boulder. Then tying her horse to the post at the side of the gate, she raised the latch and stepped through into the small yard.

On closer inspection, the croft looked deserted. Frowning, she came to a halt and stood uncertainly, staring about her. Had it been abandoned? Certainly there were no livestock noises or signs that there were any people around. There was no washing on the line, or boots lined up on the porch as was customary in Blackmore. But most telling of all, no smoke coming out of the chimney.

Feeling suddenly very alone, Jennifer backed up, staring all the while at the faceless windows. *'Hello?'* Her voice sounded loud in the stillness. She shouted again, this time frightening a small host of sparrows nesting in the dilapidated roof.

After receiving no reply for the third time, Jennifer had had enough. Plainly the croft was unoccupied, so her stomach would simply have to survive a little longer. Turning back to face the gate, she carefully picked her way towards it.

The horse's sudden bray should have alerted her, but she didn't identify the sound of footsteps until it was too late. At the last second, she felt breath hot against her neck and swung back round, briefly catching sight of Caerlaverock's former footman as he brought something large directly down onto her head. She just had time to wonder whether Felicity would ever forgive her, when whatever he was holding connected. There was a brief, blinding pain, and then, nothing.

## Chapter Eighteen

Murray MacFarlane stared in horror at the body in front of him. Had he hit her too hard? He crouched down and bent his head towards her face, sagging back in relief seconds later when he heard her soft breathing. Then he stared at her curiously again. She looked familiar. He'd decided to rest in the old croft in part because he really didn't want to arrive back at the Clan home – the thought of the upcoming interview with MacFarlane made him feel physically sick. But in truth, he had nowhere else to go since MacFee, the bampot, caught him with Ailsa.

Fortunately, he had useful information for his Chieftain, else he'd have been running in the opposite direction. Hopefully, the knowledge that the lad had escaped from the mine would be enough to stay the MacFarlane's hand, though the Chief would likely want to know why he hadn't been told sooner. Murray had an excuse for that too. He wasn't about to say he preferred the comfort of Caerlaverock to his drafty home Keep. But waiting had paid off. He now knew the Laird was thinking to rescue the other bairns working in the mine.

He didn't know when, but he'd explain he hadn't dared to stay to find out. All in all, he was confident the MacFarlane wouldn't beat him too hard.

The other reason he'd decided to rest was sheer tiredness. He'd been up since before day-daw and by the time he met with Ailsa, he'd felt as though he'd done more than a full day's work. He gave a dark chuckle. In truth, if MacNee hadn't come upon them when he had, Murray doubted he'd have had the stamina to actually do anything.

He looked back at the still figure in front of him. Bashing her on the head had been an impulse. He'd thought to take her horse and leave her, but then she'd turned round before he hit her. Had she caught sight of him? He gritted his teeth in indecision. He could strangle her now and be done with it. But murder? He would be certain to hang if he was caught – and that was if the MacFarlane didn't string him up first. She looked to be well born too.

He frowned suddenly as another thought occurred to him. What the devil was she doing out alone? The only large house in the area was Caerlaverock. Sudden terror knifed through him. Had she come from there? He leaned forward and turned her face towards him, and shock held him immobile. The woman lying unconscious on the ground in front of him was Jennifer Sinclair.

Groaning, he sat back on his heels and closed his eyes. What a bloody nightmare. He didn't dare kill her. There would be no mercy from the Duke of Blackmore if he did. But he didn't dare leave her here either. He'd have to take her with him.

Panting, he ran back towards the small croft to fetch a length of rope he'd spied earlier, his mind trying to come up with an acceptable excuse for bringing Jennifer Sinclair to his Chieftain. He could say she sought to stop him revealing their intentions. The MacFarlane might even hold her for ransom.

Gradually, his panic eased as he tied her hands and feet together and lifted her onto the horse. She was a wee slip of a thing, and it hardly took any effort. Then, climbing up behind her, he guided the horse away from the well-used track. He had no ready excuse for having an unconscious woman lying across his horse, so he'd have to find another, lesser used route.

By the time he'd directed the horse around the back of the croft and up onto the open heath, Murray had convinced himself that this had been his plan all along. In fact, the MacFarlane might even train him as one of his warriors...

∞∞∞

It wasn't often that Peter swore, but on discovering his sister had taken it into her head to go chasing after the missing servant alone, he let lose a string of expletives, some of which Felicity had never actually heard before. She hadn't the heart to berate him, and once he'd ground to a halt, she simply held out the note Jennifer had penned.

Scanning it quickly, the Viscount ran his fingers through his hair in weary frustration. Why the devil had he decided to go for a ride? Guilt swamped him. It was no good saying that if he'd stayed in the house one moment longer he'd have damaged something. That he needed to be doing *something*...

But then, anyone else would have stayed put until he'd returned, but not Jennifer. The bloody woman was a menace.

'I'll have to go after her. With luck she won't have got far. Her note stated she intended to stay on the Lochside track and would not approach her quarry. I suppose we must be thankful for small mercies.'

'I should have stopped her.' Felicity's face was white and strained, her guilt echoing his.

Peter sighed and shook his head. 'We both know that when my sister gets an idea into her head, nothing and nobody can sway her. The fault does not lie with you Felicity. You could not have stopped her. In truth she was right. Somebody needed to warn Malcolm and Brendon. I should never have left the house...' He stopped and briefly closed his eyes before adding, 'Don't worry, I'll find her. When Gifford returns, tell him to get word to Chapman. We may be forced to ask him and his men to get involved after all.'

∞∞∞

It was late afternoon when their guard hailed them. *'Hae ye foond anythin'?'*

'Should we pretend we hae nae heard him?' Dougal asked the Reverend. 'Make the bastart row ower here tae look fer himself?'

Reverend Shackleford thought for a second, then shook his head. 'We don't want to set up his bristles. Much better for us if he doesn't have the chance to view your pathetic excuse for a hole.'

Dougal merely grinned and got to his feet, walking round the ruins until he could see the guard standing on the Lochside. 'Nae, but ah reckon we be close,' he yelled back. 'Another day'll be enough.'

*'It had better be. The MacFarlane be nae a patient man.'* Dougal didn't see the point in answering that. Instead, he watched as the guard picked up his sword and began his walk back to the keep.

Dougal looked over at the Reverend as the clergyman joined him. 'The lither bastart's nae even stayin' 'til gloamin', he growled. 'He dinnae deserve tae be called a son o' Caledonia.'

'That's the old name for Scotland?' Reverend Shackleford asked, interested despite himself.

'It were the one the Romans geid us,' Dougal answered with a shrug. 'Haed tae put up a bloody great wall tae keep us oot,' he added with a chuckle. Fortunately the Reverend was too tired to rise to the bait.

They watched as the guard disappeared around a bend in the loch. 'Do you think there's a chance MacFarlane will send another guard to watch us overnight,' the Reverend asked

Dougal shook his head. 'Nae. This one didnae even finish his time.' He looked over at the tall grass bordering the loch. 'Ah reckon Bren'll hae seen 'im gae. Mebbe the guards ower at the mine be jus as bloody lither an' be gaed already.'

The two men hurried back round the ruined keep where the Reverend picked up the field glasses. 'Dae ye see anythin'?' After a second, the clergyman nodded his head.

'They're putting what looks like rocks into a cart. Likely the ore the youngens have managed to dig out today.' He paused, then began counting in a low voice. 'I can see four of 'em... ahh, there's the fifth. He's just come out of the mine entrance.' He lowered the glasses and look over at Dougal in excitement. 'It looks like they're leaving.'

'Let me see.' The old Scot snatched at the glasses and put them to his eyes. 'Aye ye be right,' he muttered. 'There be one still there. He dinnae look happy.'

The Reverend snorted. 'You can't see whether the fellow's happy or not.'

'Ye wouldnae be happy if ye were bein' left owernight there. Ah wonder if he haes any whisky? Ah'll ask Brendon tae take a look.'

'You really think your son's going to stop and check whether the mutton-head has a bottle of whisky stashed away?' Reverend Shackleford scoffed, 'Is there a signal for *get me a wee dram*?'

Dougal scowled and put the glasses back to his eyes. 'There be nae sign o' the cart, and the guard be heidin tae the wee bothy.'

'Only one?' the Reverend asked, itching to snatch the glasses back.

'Aye. Th'others hae gaed.'

'Right then, we can signal Malcolm,' the Reverend declared in satisfaction. 'What did you do with the flint and tender?'

'Ah thought ye had it?'

'It should be in your pack.'

'Nae, it be in yers, ye eejit.'

The Reverend narrowed his eyes before demanding, 'Who are you calling an idiot, you... you... buffle-headed saucebox.'

'Ye wispy haired, toom heidit, Sassanach. Gie me yer bag.' Dougal made a grab for the Reverend's satchel, snatching it out of the clergyman's hands and tipping everything onto the ground.

With an indignant, 'How dare you,' Reverend Shackleford seized the Scotsman's bag and emptied its contents directly on the top of the pile.

They both fell silent, staring at the objects littering the ground. There appeared to be everything *but* a flint and tinder.

'Thunder an' turf,' the Reverend muttered at length, 'they must have fallen into the cart. We'll have to row over.'

'There be nae time,' Dougal groaned, 'an we need tae be here tae watch in case any o' the bastarts come back. Ah cannae row there an' back that quick. Can ye?'

The Reverend shook his head despondently. 'You'll be deuced well carrying me off. Do you know how to light a fire without flint and tinder?'

Dougal shook his head. 'Dae ye?'

'Tare an' hounds, we're in the suds.'

'Tatties be ower the side an' nae mistak.'

Both men sat down on the ground, staring at nothing for the next few minutes. Then abruptly the Reverend squared his shoulders. This lily-livered chucklehead wasn't him - it was just old Nick trying to throw a rub in his way. Augustus Shackleford *always* came up with a plan.

He looked again at the items scattered on the ground in front of him. Sorting through, he found a stick of charcoal. 'Are you wearing drawers under your skirt?' he asked his dejected companion.

'Wha' dae ye mean am ah wearin'... o' course ah be wearin' drawers. Did ye not notice it be bloody drafty in th'Highlands? An' it be a kilt, nae a skirt.'

'Kilt, skirt – they all look the deuced same to me.'

Dougal drew in his breath at such sacrilege. In fact he was teetering on the verge of ordering the Sassenach bampot to name his seconds, when the Reverend's next words took the wind out of his sails.

'Right then, take 'em off.'

Dougal blinked. 'Ah willnae. What dae ye want 'em fer?'

'I'm going to write on them.' The clergyman held up the piece of charcoal triumphantly.

'Yer bum's oot the windae if yer thinkin' ah'm gaunnae get ma tackle oot jus' fer ye. An anyway, the colour o' ma drawers, ye'll nae see the markins.' He held up his kilt to reveal a pair of drawers the colour of mud. The Reverend stared in disbelief. He was no dandy, but still, he made sure to change his smalls every birthday.

'Have you never washed them?' he asked, unable to hide his distaste.

The Scot looked at him as though he was addled. 'What aboot the midges?' He asked at length.

They stared at each other for a few seconds, then Reverend Shackleford sighed. 'We'll use my drawers,' he muttered turning his back.

A couple of minutes later, he laid the largely whitish pair of undergarments down on the ground. His birthday had been a month earlier.

For once the elderly Scot refrained from commenting aside from muttering under his breath, 'Ye could scribe most o' the good book on them.'

'What are ye gaunnae write?' he asked as the Reverend took up his stick of charcoal.

'I think *"Coast clear 1 guard in hut,"* should do it. Laboriously the clergyman chalked the words across the back of his drawers in letters as large as he could fit down each leg.

'Right then. I think they should be able to see that if we stand close to the shore. Come on Dougal, there's no time to lose.'

Bemused that the English was using his given name for the second time, Dougal followed in silence, a sudden problem rearing its ugly head.

If he wasnae careful, he might actually get tae *like* the God walloper. An that wouldnae dae at all...

Five minutes later, the two of them were standing on the edge of the shore, each holding a leg high in the air, shouting and pointing at the improvised sign.

'It's nae guid, they cannae see it,' Dougal declared after five minutes. 'Ah'll hae tae climb on yer shoulders.'

'If you think I'm allowing your drawers anywhere near my person, you're very much mistaken,' the Reverend shuddered.

'Dae ah complain aboot haein tae look at yer face like a skelped arse?' the Scot answered cheerfully, stepping up onto a boulder. 'At least ah can take mine off. Right then, bend doon.'

Against his better judgement, the Reverend went over to the boulder and bent down. Oh how he was missing Percy. The curate would never have answered him back like his present unsavoury companion.

It only took Dougal a few seconds to hop up and sling his leg around the Reverend's neck. 'Jus' like auld times,' he chuckled into the clergyman's ear. Clearly the Scot was much more agile than Percy, and moments later he was sitting triumphantly on his companion's shoulders. Once the Reverend had wobbled to his feet, Dougal rose up, held up the drawers and yelled at the top of his voice.

Within minutes, Malcolm and Brendon appeared on the Lochside. 'The coast be clear, wi one guard,' Dougal yelled, flapping the drawers up and down for emphasis. Seconds later both men gave the thumbs-up sign and disappeared into the long grass.

'Well, that were easy,' the Scot crowed, throwing the drawers to the ground and sitting back down on his haunches. Unfortunately, as he sat down, the front of his kilt slid over the Reverend's face like a pungent shroud.

Reverend Shackleford gave a muffled choking sound and wobbled from side to side as Dougal tried to wrestle his kilt back over the Reverend's head, only to hook the sporran over the clergyman's ears in the process. With a panicked yell, Augustus Shackleford slowly tottered forward and despite his passenger's increasingly desperate entreaties, promptly fell headfirst into the loch, Dougal sailing like a flying fish over his head.

## Chapter Nineteen

Malcolm and Brendon wasted no time speculating why the signal had been changed – doubtless they'd find out soon enough. Their entire attention had to be on the children they were attempting to rescue.

After hiding their knapsacks near to the MacFarlane boat, Brendon ordered Fergus to stay and guard. Then after giving the wolfhound a quick fuss, he followed Malcolm towards the distant copse of trees bordering the quarry. As soon as they stepped into the trees, nearly twenty minutes later, both men drew their pistols. Once back out in the open, they used the abandoned buildings as cover as they crept towards the mine entrance. Mostly derelict, it was hard to believe any of them had housed mine workers as little as two years back.

After about five minutes, they spotted a dilapidated bothie near to the entrance with a wavering light in the window, even though it was still a couple of hours until dusk. Why the guard had picked possibly the most ramshackle of all the buildings to sleep in was anybody's guess. Perhaps he was afraid of ghosts.

The whole place was unnerving. There was no birdsong and only the distant sound of the loch slapping against the shore broke the silence. Slowly, *carefully*, they tiptoed towards the lighted window.

'It's nae yet sundoon, so he'll nae be asleep,' Brendon whispered, 'we'll hae tae finish him fast. Afore he haes the chance tae run.' Malcolm nodded, deliberately not questioning the steward's use of the word *finish*. Whatever needed to be done, they would do it.

By the time they reached the hut, both men were dripping in sweat. Pointing to the entrance, Malcolm, lifted his pistol and held up three fingers. The only thing they had was the element of surprise. That, and the fact that there were two of them.

But according to Finn, the guard left behind was a giant. And a nasty one at that.

Brendon drew his own pistol and nodded. Seconds later, Malcolm kicked in the door, and they stormed inside, only to be confronted by a man the size of Goliath sitting with his booted feet propped up on a rickety table, staring them unconcernedly.

'What took ye so long?' he questioned without moving a muscle.

∞∞∞

The first thing Jennifer was aware of was a blinding headache. And the second, that she was hanging upside down over a moving horse. Seconds later, she felt her stomach cramp as she emptied its meagre contents all over the animal's forelegs.

Slowly she managed to turn her head enough to see a man walking next to the horse. Who was he? She stared down at her hands; both were tied firmly at the wrists. She moved her ankles experimentally. The same. White hot fear swamped her, and she had to fight the urge to cast up her account again. How had she ended up here?

Trying to ignore the pain, she thought back to the last thing she remembered. The croft, returning to her horse, and then … somebody had hit her over the head. Was it the man leading her horse? Clearly he meant her ill. But surely if he'd wanted her dead, he'd have already done the deed. Slowly, she turned her head again and was able to make out the man's features. It was the footman she'd been following.

What an idiot she'd been. Why the devil hadn't she listened to Felicity? She was reasonably sure the man was taking her to MacFarlane. If nothing else, she would be a good bargaining piece. Would Brendon and Malcolm see them pass? Unlikely. It was clear the footman had taken a little-known path to avoid being seen. Pain lanced her head again, and she allowed her head to hang back down against the mare's flank. Slowly she became aware that the horse was limping. Likely she'd caught a stone, and that was the reason Murray wasn't riding. She felt a surge of hope. She had no idea what the time was, but if he'd been riding, they might very well have reached the MacFarlane Clan home by now. She couldn't see where they were but knew for certain they were no longer on the Lochside.

Forcing down the fear at the thought of being completely alone with the traitor, she agonised over what to do. Should she let her captor know she was awake? Her mouth was parched and her stomach cramping. At the very least, he might give her some water.

The decision was taken out of her hands as the horse stopped and she observed a pair of feet walk round the front of the horse, stopping in front of her. 'Are ye awake, ma lady?'

Jennifer saw no point in pretending otherwise, and managed to croak, 'Have you any water?'

'Nae, but if ye promise not tae dae anythin' stupid, Ah'll get ye doon off th'horse.' Jennifer nodded her head. Anything that would delay their journey for a little longer.

Pain lanced through her head as he dragged her forwards. For a second she thought he was going to simply allow her to fall onto the ground, but at the last minute, he took her weight and laid her on the grass. For a few seconds, she kept her eyes tightly shut, willing the agony to recede. The varmint must have hit her hard. Finally, she managed to open her eyes. Turning her head, she saw Murray sitting on the grass beside her, staring into the distance.

'Where are you taking me?' she whispered. For a second he didn't react, and she thought he hadn't heard her. She began the question again, only to stop as he turned his head to look down at her.

'Ah'm takin' ye tae the MacFarlane, but ye must know that,' he answered impassively. 'Ah'm sorry aboot yer head, but ye be an eejit tae follow me, ma lady.'

She couldn't argue with that, and ridiculously, Jennifer had to smother a sudden urge to laugh. What a deuced mess she'd made of things.

Closing her eyes again, she remembered the conversation she'd overheard. Neither servant had seemed overly keen to bring themselves to their Clan chief's attention, but once he'd had the altercation with MacNee, Murray clearly believed he had no choice.

'Will your chief kill me?' she asked, hoping to exploit his obvious reluctance. He turned his head away.

'You don't have to do this,' she continued when he didn't answer. 'My family will reward you well if you return me to Caerlaverock.'

'Wi' a rope roond ma neck,' he scoffed without looking down at her.

'They don't have to know that you hit me,' Jennifer insisted. 'I'll say I fell off the horse, that you found me and brought me back.'

For a second, she thought she'd got through to him, then he turned to her with a sneer. 'Ye'd say anythin' tae get me tae gae back tae Caerlaverock. But once yer back in the bosom o' yer precious family, ye'll toss me tae the bloody lions wi'oot a care.'

Jennifer stared at him, realising that nothing she said would sway him. He'd made up his mind. There was only one thing for it. She would have to escape.

∞∞∞

'Ah'm thinkin' naither o' ye be bampots,' the guard went on, 'so ah'll get tae the point. Ah ken ye be here fer the bairns. As soon as ah let Finn gae, ah kenned it was only a matter o' time afore ye turned up.'

'Ye let him gae?' Brendon asked incredulously.

'Aye. Dae ye think me a bloody eejit. That ah cannae coont? Ah kenned he were missin' an' ah seen him hidin'.'

Malcolm scoffed. 'According to the lad, ye treated him terrible. Him and all of the children. Why the bloody hell would you let him escape?'

'Oh ah dinnae care aboot the bairns,' the warrior assured them, 'but ah dae care aboot ma Clan.' He sighed and put his feet to the floor. In response, both Brendon and Malcolm raised their pistols, but the guard didn't get to his feet.

'The MacFarlane be off his heid. Using bairns to bring a piddlin amoont o' gold is nae worth it. The mine is finished, but he willnae hear o' it. Keeps me here to avoid listenin' tae wha' ah hae tae say.' He looked round at the shack. 'There be nae honour in this,' he bit out. 'Ah might nae care aboot the bairns but ah dinnae want tae keep buryin' em aither. Sooner or later what the MacFarlane be daein will be common knowledge an' our whole Clan'll be finished.' He shook his head. 'Ah cannae hae that.'

'So what are ye gaunnae dae aboot it?' Brendon asked.

'Ah kenned ye'd come fer the bairns, and ye can take 'em wi' ma blessin',' the guard told them. 'Dae what ye like wi 'em. Ma beef be wi' the MacFarlane himself. He's nae fit tae lead a clan an' ah intend tae take it off him.'

'What do you want from us in return for the children?' Malcolm asked astutely.

'Ah dinnae want any interference. An ah want the Laird tae recognise me as the MacFarlane. Properly.'

'I cannae speak for the Duke,' Malcolm retorted.

'Then ye'd better shoot me,' the warrior answered. 'An let the bairns die slowly while the air poisons.' He stared at them both. 'Ah've hidden the keys. An' ye'll nae find 'em afore the air turns bad.'

Brendon narrowed his eyes. 'You bastart,' he grated.

'Aye, you be right as it happens,' the warrior chuckled. 'But ah be a MacFarlane bastart.'

'How do we know you'll be a better chieftain than Alistair MacFarlane?' Malcolm asked.

'Ye don't,' the guard answered with a shrug. 'But ah cannae be any worse. An' ah swear ah'll leave ye and yours alone, if ye dae the same.'

Brendon looked over at Malcolm. He knew the decision had to be the older man's, but he had no idea what that choice would be. The steward knew that underneath his companion's affable exterior was a will of steel. Malcolm Mackenzie's loyalty first and foremost would always be to the Sinclair family. And he would never put any of them in jeopardy.

After about two minutes, Malcolm wiped his brow with the back of his gun-free hand and nodded.

'Swear,' the guard insisted.

'I swear the Laird will leave you and yours alone, if you dae the same,' Malcolm repeated. 'And you'll be recognised as the new Chieftain o' the MacFarlane Clan.' He paused before adding wryly, 'Though it might be helpful if ye told me yer name.'

The warrior nodded, satisfied. 'It be Duncan. Duncan MacFarlane. Slowly he climbed to his feet. 'Come wi' me.'

∞∞∞

'*Dougal?*' The Reverend stood shivering in his sodden cassock, peering into the murky water. He'd surfaced a minute or so ago, and so far there was no sign of the old Scot.

Augustus Shackleford felt like crying. How the deuce was he going to get off the island if old Dougal had kicked the bucket? And now there was an actual possibility the chucklehead was dead, well, the clergyman felt unaccountably wretched.

After another few seconds, he waded carefully back into the loch, shouting '*Dougal?*' Abruptly a cascade of water was tossed up into the air as the old Scot surfaced abruptly, triumphantly holding something in the air.

'Ah foond it,' Dougal spluttered. 'Ah foond the bloody treasure.'

'What the deuce are you talking about,' the Reverend answered crossly, irritation warring with unexpected relief.

Dougal waded ashore and held out his hand. Reverend Shackleford peered at the object lying in the middle of the Scot's palm. 'It looks like a ring?'

'Aye, it does. An' there be lots more where that came frae. Ah reckon they were in a satchel o' some kind, until the hide perished.'

The two men stared at each other. In the end, the Reverend said it first. 'You think this is Edward Colman's?'

'Aye, ah dae,' Dougal grinned.

'What are the odds?' Reverend Shackleford found himself grinning back. 'Who'd have thought our letter could be so close to the truth?'

'We cannae leave it,' Dougal continued.

The Reverend bit his lip. 'You really think it's Colman's?'

'Tae be honest, ah dinnae care. All ah ken is ah saw lots o' other pieces o' jewellery on the bottom o' the loch. The bag must nae hae broke long back else the gold would hae drifted doon deep long afore noo. If we wait, it'll be lost foreye.'

Right then, we'll keep looking. There's no point in keeping watch over the mine. If there's another deuced guard, we've no way of letting them know anyway. I will warn you, I swim like deuced rock, so I'll not be much help.'

Dougal grinned. 'Ye stand uptae ye knees in the loch, an hold oot yer robe, like so.' He bent his arms into a bowl-like shape. 'An' ah'll dae the hard work.'

'It's deuced cold though, Augustus Shackleford muttered. 'I'll catch an ague if I'm stood in there too long.

'It'll be bloody colder come gloamin',' Dougal answered, 'an' then the bits o' ye oot o' the water'll be a midgie banquet.'

The Reverend grimaced. 'Best get on with it then,' was all he said. 'We want to be off this damned rock before dusk.'

∞∞∞

Brendon and Malcolm watched with trepidation as Duncan

MacFarlane unlocked the entrance to the mine. Despite their bargain, neither man had lowered their pistol. Indeed, MacFarlane didn't appear to expect them to.

As the warrior stepped into the gloom, they could see the remains of rudimentary machinery that had clearly been used in the past. Ignoring it, MacFarlane picked up a lantern, lit it with a flint and tinder and led them down a set of steep stairs cut into the rock. In unspoken agreement, Brendon hung back, keeping his pistol trained down the stairs. Malcolm too gave the warrior a wide berth. The real danger would come when the children actually came out of their so called sleeping quarters. The guard could easily use the bairns as a shield.

The shadows cast grotesque shapes on the walls as MacFarlane hung the lantern onto a hook driven into the stone, revealing a small door set into the rock. Malcolm remained six feet away, his pistol pointing steadily at the warrior's head.

Seconds later, MacFarlane inserted a key into the door and pushed it open. '*Get ye here*,' he ordered, his voice loud and forbidding. For a few seconds nothing happened, then slowly Malcom heard the sound of movement, and he stared in horror as the children filed out of the pitch-black room, squinting in the meagre light of the lantern.

'Get ye up the stairs,' MacFarlane ordered, raising his hand to cuff a small girl who wasn't moving quickly enough. Malcolm raised his weapon.

'You willnae lay another hand on these bairns,' he warned his voice low and furious, 'if ye dae, bargain or nae bargain, I'll blow yer bastart head off.'

Duncan MacFarlane stared up at him impassively for a second, then he shrugged.

Malcolm stepped to one side, allowing the children to climb past him. They eyed him apprehensively as they filed upwards, but the Scot never took his eyes off the warrior below. 'They be comin' up tae ye, Bren,' he called. 'Get 'em outside.'

As the last child exited the room, Malcolm had a sudden sick premonition. 'Is that all o' 'em?' he asked. MacFarlane shrugged again.

'Go into the room.' For a second, the warrior's eyes widened in fear.

'I'm nae gaunnae lock yer sorry arse up,' Malcolm growled, 'Though, in truth, I'm sorely tempted. I want tae check nobody's been left behind.'

Hesitantly, MacFarlane stepped backwards into the doorway, just as Malcolm reached the bottom of the steps.

'Go inside.' Nostrils flaring at the commanding tone, the guard stepped into the room.

'Can ye see anybody?' Malcolm asked. He stepped to the side, better to see in the darkened chamber. To his horror, it resembled a small priest hole. He hadn't counted the children coming up the steps, but he knew they wouldn't have had enough space to sleep without curling up into small balls. He swallowed, fighting the urge to simply shoot the bastard and be done with it.

As his eyes became accustomed to the blackness inside the room, he discerned a small shape. 'Come tae me, lad,' he requested hoarsely. 'We've come tae get ye out o' here.'

Slowly the shape became a head and a body. 'Ah nae be a lad,' a small voice responded. There was a pause. 'Ah cannae walk wi ma leg.'

'Pick her up,' Malcolm ordered the warrior. 'He willnae hurt ye, sweetheart,' he added as the small figure gave a frightened gasp.

With an impatient sound, MacFarlane went into the room and

picked the girl up none too gently. 'Up the stairs wi' her,' Malcolm commanded, waving his gun towards their only exit. The little girl's nearly silent sobs were cutting him in two. He was beginning to feel as though he was down in the bowels of hell itself.

He followed MacFarlane up the stairs and out into the early evening light. All in all there were twenty-two children. All emaciated and filthy dirty.

'Dinnae forget our bargain,' MacFarlane demanded, clearly seeing murder in the other men's eyes. 'Ye might think me a bastart, but ah didnae put the bairns doon there an' it wasnae my decision to work 'em tae death. Despite what ye be thinkin' o' me, ye have ma word that the mine'll be closed. There'll be nae more.' He looked around him and shook his head before repeating, 'There be nae honour in this.' He handed the small girl into Brendon's waiting arms.

'Ah'm gaen back intae the bothie noo,' he stated. 'The MacFarlane willnae ken what happened here until the morra. An' by then, his days as Chief'll be ower.'

'Dae ye hae any support?' Brendon couldn't help asking. 'Ye cannae take on the whole Clan by yerself.'

Duncan MacFarlane gave a fierce grin. 'Dae ye think me a reckless eejit? The Clan will be mine by sundoon.' And with that, he turned his back and walked away.

# Chapter Twenty

'Ah reckon that be the last o' 'em,' Dougal gasped as he plonked a tarnished bracelet into the Reverends hands.

'There'll be enough here to see you and Brendon through a good few winters,' the clergyman commented, wading with groaning relief out of the freezing cold water. 'Tare an' hounds I've lost the feeling in me toes. If they turn black it'll be your deuced fault.'

'Ah be tae auld tae decide what tae dae wi' it. That'll be Bren.' Following the Reverend out of the water, Dougal added gruffly, 'Ah want tae thank ye fer yer help. Ye didnae hae tae.'

Reverend Shackleford hmphed. 'I could hardly have got any wetter. Thunder an' turf, it's cold. Still, at least me drawers are dry.'

The two men took the last of the jewellery back to their belongings and took refuge in the blankets they'd brought. 'Colman had good taste, I'll give him that,' the Reverend commented, taking a bite out of his cheese. 'I reckon the only way we'll be able to carry this lot is to leave all else behind. Hopefully we won't need the spade to put anybody to bed with.' He gave a small chuckle at his own joke. It was strange really. He was possibly wetter and colder than he'd ever been in his life, but he was also inexplicably happy. In truth, it was good to feel useful again.

As soon as they'd eaten, they divided the trinkets and stuffed them into the two bags, placing their essential items on the top. 'It be bloody heavy,' Dougal panted as they hefted the bags to the shore. 'It be a good thing we dinnae hae tae swim. 'Right then, let's fetch the boat an' get off this bloody island.'

∞∞∞

Their going was slow due to the horse's lameness, and Jennifer elected to walk in case her weight should make the mare worse. In truth, she had no idea where they were though she took comfort from the fact that she could still see the loch in the distance. Her captor had tied her right hand to the pommel, even thought she'd protested it wasn't necessary – she didn't think the pounding in her head would allow her to run far, despite her earlier avowal to escape. All she could do was keep her wits about her and look for an opportunity to somehow disable the footman.

Eventually, the faint track they were following turned back towards Loch Lomond and even knowing they must be nearing his Clan home, Jennifer breathed a sigh of relief. Especially as a sudden thought struck her. If they got close enough, could she jump into the loch? Despite the shock of her earlier unexpected dip, she was a proficient swimmer after spending most of her childhood summers splashing about in the lake at Blackmore.

If she jumped into the loch, would he come after her? Could he even swim?

Jennifer knew her idea was totty headed, but she could see no other way. Desperately, she watched for signs they were getting closer to the loch and minutes later was certain the body of water was getting nearer. She looked down at her riding habit. She wouldn't be able to swim wearing so many clothes. Her thoughts unexpectedly conjured up her first meeting with

Brendon Galbraith and she gave an inward chuckle as his withering comment about her weight came back to her. She wondered where he was. Whether he and Malcolm were even now going after the children.

She still had no idea of the time, but the sun was no longer high in the sky. Soon the midges would be abroad and then their progress would be truly miserable. Indeed, she realised her silent captor was increasing his pace. Pushing down her rising anxiety, she began surreptitiously easing her hand this way and that, trying to loosen the rope securing it. With her other, unbound hand, she began carefully unbuttoning her riding jacket.

She needed to buy Brendon and Malcolm enough time to rescue the children and get them away from MacFarlane land, and though the thought terrified her, she knew that jumping into the loch might do exactly that.

∞∞∞

Getting the children out of the quarry was slow going. Despite their obvious relief at being out of the underground cell, they were clearly terrified. Some were crying – silent sobs that cut both men's hearts. But neither Brendon nor Malcolm dared spend too much time reassuring them. The clock was ticking, and they needed to be away from MacFarlane land as quickly as possible. Time enough for assurance once they were back at Caerlaverock.

The little girl who'd hurt her leg was riding on Brendon's back. In truth he hardly felt her weight and the feel of her small arms around his neck, her head nestling into his shoulder prompted emotions he'd never thought to have. Silently he vowed that somehow he would take care of all these children. None of them would ever have to suffer at the hands of such evil again.

Finally, they broke free of the trees and came within sight of

Inveruglas. 'Can you see any sign of Augustus and Dougal?' Malcolm asked, his eyesight not as good as the much younger man's.

Brendon stared for a moment, then shook his head. 'Hopefully they'll be off the island by noo. Fergus'll be watching fer 'em.'

'I bloody hope so. We cannae afford to wait fer long. Can we get all the bairns in one boat dae ye think?'

Brendon grimaced. 'Ah doot it.' He gave a loud whistle before lifting his small cargo off his back and handing her over to Malcolm. Minutes later the children cried out in fear at the sight of a large animal streaking towards them. Turning towards the panicking youngsters, Dougal held up a calming hand. 'Dinnae fash yerselves,' he soothed. 'It be ma dog, Fergus. The worst he'll dae be tae lick ye tae death.'

Within seconds the wolfhound was capering around his master's ankles like a puppy. Crouching down, Brendon threw his arms around the delighted dog's neck and ruffled his fur before finally taking hold of his collar and looking into the hound's intelligent eyes. 'Find Dougal,' he instructed. Fergus wagged his tail, gave his master one last lick and took off back the way he'd come.

Following in the same direction, Brendon and Malcolm began ushering the children along as swiftly as possible. They were now in the open and in danger of being spotted by MacFarlane's men. The bairns had fallen silent, and the two men glanced at each other, fearing shock was beginning to set in.

The closer they got to the MacFarlane's boat, the more anxious both men became. What had seemed like a foolproof plan earlier, now seemed like the idea of a pair of idiots. The chances that any of the children could swim were slim at best. If either boat capsized, they would be lost.

Suddenly, when they were about fifty yards away from the

small jetty, Fergus gave an excited bark, and Brendon felt relief overwhelm him. 'He's found them,' the steward told Malcolm. A couple of seconds later they both heard a loud voice declare, 'I've already had one deuced wash. Can you not teach this mongrel some manners?'

∞∞∞

By the time Peter reached the derelict croft, he was beginning to despair of finding any sign that his sister had come this way. And truly, if she'd been bacon-brained enough to leave the track for the open moor... *No*, he wouldn't even consider it. Jennifer was headstrong but not stupid.

Dismounting, the Viscount stared up at the cottage's faceless windows with a frown. It had clearly been abandoned by whoever lived there, and if Jennifer had been here, she certainly wasn't here now.

Tying up his horse, he opened the gate and looked around – for what, he wasn't certain – but after a few seconds he spied a small log on the ground. Something about it didn't sit right. What was it doing there right in front of the gate? There were no other pieces of wood in the vicinity. Biting his lip, Peter crouched down and picked it up. As he examined it, a sick feeling of dread blossomed in his stomach. On the end of the log were strands of hair exactly the colour of his sister's. They were stuck to the wood with what he feared was dried blood.

Tossing the log into the undergrowth, Peter sat back on his heels, willing his heart to slow down. Swallowing, he scanned the area more carefully, eventually catching sight of a small scrap of satin caught on a bush. Climbing to his feet, the Viscount took hold of the fragment which revealed itself to be a length of ribbon exactly the same as the one Jennifer was wearing when he last saw her.

Fighting panic, he stepped away from the gate and looked more closely at the ground. Recent hoofprints showed a horse had been here within the last few hours. The prints led around the cottage and up onto the highland.

Someone had taken his sister.

∞∞∞

Getting the children onto the two boats proved more challenging than anything they'd done so far. Their fear that the bairns couldn't swim was borne out when, frail as they were, nearly all fought and kicked to stay on dry land, though the effort left them exhausted.

Malcolm shook his head. 'They cannae walk back. It's too far, and while it looks as though the MacFarlane is going to be busy come the morn, we cannae guarantee some of his warriors willnae come after us.'

'Why will the MacFarlane be busy?' asked Dougal narrowing his eyes. 'Ye hae nae told us what happened when ye took the bairns.'

'That's a tale fer when we're all home and safe,' Brendon insisted. 'Right noo, we have tae get these bairns onto those two boats.'

'If anythin' be getting 'em afloat it'll be their bellies,' Dougal answered. 'What food dae ye hae left?'

The four men pooled their supplies and came up with two heels of now dry bread, a lump of cheese and and some dried beef. 'It's not much between twenty-two hungry children,' the Reverend growled.

'It'll be more 'an they be used tae,' Dougal predicted. 'Here, gie us a hand.' With the clergyman's help, he divided the meagre fare into twenty-two small piles. As he was counting, Reverend

Shackleford thought back to his conversation with Finn and felt a singular sense of inevitability. *'Can ah come wi' ye tae Blackmore...'*

Hurriedly, he thrust the memory away and concentrated on the task at hand.

'There's food for all who'll get in the boat,' Malcolm promised, holding out a small piece of bread.

It was enough. Quicker than they could have imagined, the children clambered into the two boats.

The four men handed a small portion of food to each child which predictably disappeared in an instant. As soon as they'd finished, Malcolm climbed on board to ensure the weight was evenly distributed. 'Be sure ye sit tight and dinnae move a muscle,' he ordered. 'Ye'll need tae cover yer heads soon as the midges start.'

'Ye dinnae need tae teach yer granny tae suck eggs,' scoffed a small voice. There was a smattering of giggles, and Malcolm grinned in relief. Plainly, the children's fear was beginning to fade. He turned to the Reverend.

'You an' Dougal take the smaller boat. We'll follow behind. Whatever happens, dinnae stop.' He paused before adding, 'God willin' we'll nae meet any other craft. Even if it's nae the MacFarlane's we'll have a lot o' bloody explainin' tae dae.'

A few minutes later, both boats were afloat. Before climbing on board, Brendon had one last thing to do. Walking over to Fergus, he bent to stroke the dog's ears. 'Go home,' he ordered the wolfhound in his sternest voice, then, more gently, 'Home, boy. Ah'll see ye there verra soon.'

∞∞∞

It was another half an hour before Jennifer was certain the track they were following led directly onto the Lochside. Obviously, Murray was more confident that anyone who came across them would belong to the MacFarlane Clan this close to home.

Jennifer had managed to get most of her jacket buttons undone, and while her captor was seeing to his business, she succeeded in undoing the buttons on her riding boots. With her hair unkempt and her clothing dirty and unfastened, she was beginning to look more like Haymarket ware. The sloppiness of her boots also made walking more difficult, but as long as he stayed on his side of the horse, he was unlikely to spot her dishevelment or notice she was walking like she needed to use the chamber pot. Which unfortunately she did. Quite badly in fact.

Shoving thoughts of her bladder aside, Jennifer kept her eyes on the loch. As soon as they reached the main path, she would have to make her move. She was confident she'd worked the rope sufficiently to be able to free her hand easily enough, and once they were close enough to the loch, she intended to kick off her boots as quietly as possible. She would have to run in stocking feet.

The most important thing was to take him by surprise, to give her enough time to throw off her jacket. Her skirt would have to come off while she was running. That was the sketchiest part of her plan. She'd been loath to try and undo any of the buttons lest her skirt fall down around her ankles which she was fairly certain would achieve the opposite of what she wanted.

Her heart began to thud in perfect time to the throbbing in her head. Groaning internally, she swore to herself that she would never again undertake such a totty-headed errand, and what's more she would give Peter full permission to lock her up should she even look as though she was about to do anything foolish.

Five minutes later, they reached the Lochside. Unfortunately, Jennifer was on the side furthest away from the shore which gave her captor an added advantage. Determinedly swallowing her fear, she began to ease her hand through the loosened rope until it was free. Keeping it in the same position by hanging onto the horse's mane, she then began to ease off her boots, one at a time, hoping the footman wouldn't happen to look back and see them lying on the track. Finally, in her stocking feet, she dropped her left arm to allow her jacket to begin sliding off her shoulder. She was sweating now, her fear a solid lump in the middle of her chest. Once she made her move, she had only seconds to drop her jacket and run.

Muttering a quick prayer, she eased her hand down the mare's flank and stopped. Hardly daring to breathe, she slipped off the rest of her jacket and let it drop to the ground. The horse was now almost past her and still Murray hadn't noticed she was no longer beside him. It was now or never.

Taking a deep breath, she darted behind the mare and raced towards the edge of the loch, all the while fumbling with the buttons at the back of her skirt. She didn't look back on hearing his sudden shout, but inside she was screaming with fear. If he caught her now, he'd likely kill her.

She couldn't undo the bloody buttons! In desperation she yanked at the waistband and after a few seconds felt the buttons give. She could hear his breathing behind her as she let the skirt fall and kept on running – down the bank now, only feet from the water.

She felt his arm reach out, his fingers clutch her petticoat, just for one instant before the fabric tore and his hand fell away. Seconds later she jumped.

# Chapter Twenty-One

Brendon looked anxiously around them as he and Malcolm rowed in the direction of Caerlaverock. With so many in the boat, it was slow going, but still, they were making better time than if they'd walked. The Reverend and Dougal were still arguing as far as he could tell, but as long as their boat continued in the right direction...

Instinctively, he glanced behind him, but there was no sign of any pursuit, either on the shore or the loch. God willing, they'd have until the morrow as Duncan MacFarlane promised.

As he rowed, Brendon wondered what Jennifer was doing now. Would she be worried – about him? Then he grimaced. Foolish thoughts. He needed to put Jennifer Sinclair out of his mind. Otherwise he'd go daft.

Abruptly, two things happened to pull him out of his reverie. Firstly, he heard a shout coming from the shore to their right. His heart plummeted. Had they been discovered? Then, as though she'd been pulled directly from his mind, he saw Jennifer running towards the loch. He narrowed his eyes. *In just a petticoat?* He *was* going daft.

At the same time, a small girl abruptly stood up in the boat. 'Sit down, lass,' Malcolm ordered.

'Ah'm gaunnae boak,' she cried out desperately. Plainly about to be sick, the child instinctively leaned over the side of the boat. 'Sit down,' thundered Malcolm, fear clearly evident in his voice. But it was too late. The boat rocked to the side, and, with a terrified scream, the girl fell headfirst into the water.

At the same time, the woman Brendon still couldn't quite believe was Jennifer, reached the edge of the loch, a man in close pursuit. The stranger stretched out his hand to seize the edge of her petticoat, but just as he managed to grab hold, the fabric tore and with a terrified scream, she jumped into the loch, leaving him with nothing but a scrap of fabric.

'Take the oars,' Malcolm was yelling frantically. Brendon's eyes swung back to the petrified child floundering in the loch. *Shit.*

Abruptly, he became aware of two things. One, neither he nor Malcolm were going to be able to get to the child in time. They couldn't simply dive into the water for fear of capsizing the whole boat and losing all the children. Two, he realised that Jennifer was actually swimming frantically towards them, shouting, 'Leave her to me.'

Seconds later, she managed to grab hold of the child who promptly clung to her rescuer like a limpet. 'Not so tight,' Jennifer gasped, trying to keep them both afloat.

'Keep the boat steady,' Brendon yelled, as he watched the two of them go under for the second time. Without hesitation, Malcolm held the oars firmly in the water. 'Go,' he bellowed.

Brendon quickly laid his own oars on the deck, shrugged off his jacket and slid over the side, reaching Jennifer and the girl in two powerful strokes. 'Ah hae her,' he panted to Jennifer. 'Get tae the boat, sweetheart.' The endearment came out naturally, but he didn't have time to question his idiocy. Instead, he boosted her towards the side of the boat, holding the child close to him with his other hand. 'Careful,' he warned when the young woman reached out to grip the edge of the boat. 'She'll overturn if ye try and climb aboard. Hang on tae the side.' Sliding the now silent child in front of him, he pushed her next to Jennifer. 'Hold tight,' he ordered, then swam round to the other side of the boat.

With the weight more evenly spread, he was able to heave himself aboard. 'Hold on tae yer seats,' he instructed the rest of the children who were staring wide eyed at the drama unfolding in front of them. Seconds later, he carefully pulled the girl back into the boat, bundling her into a blanket, before leaning over the side again to a now shivering Jennifer.

'Are ye gaunnae be makin' a habit o' this?' he muttered, as he wrapped her in his jacket.

'Th-the man,' Jennifer stuttered. Brendon looked towards the shore.

'He be gaun.'

'Nooo,' she moaned. 'He's going to tell MacFarlane. We need to stop him.'

Without further probing,' Brendon scanned the Lochside, finally catching sight of the man running along the path towards the MacFarlane Keep. 'Ah willnae catch the bastart in time,' he grated, frustration and fear in his voice.

*'Jennifer!'* They turned towards the unexpected shout.

'It's Peter!' The young woman's voice was almost a sob and Brendon knew she was coming to the end of her tether. He looked over towards the shore where, unbelievably, Peter Sinclair was sitting astride a horse, Fergus dancing beside him.

*'We hae her,'* the steward bellowed. *'She be safe.'* He risked standing up to point towards the fleeing figure.

*'Ye need tae stop him ma lord. He be headin' fer the MacFarlane.'* For a second, he thought the Viscount hadn't heard him, but then he gave a nod and, guiding his horse away from the shore, took off

after the traitor, the wolfhound hard at the horse's heels.

Moments later, they watched as Peter reached the footman, leapt off his horse and felled the man with one blow.

'Show off,' muttered Jennifer with a sniff.

'Have ye all quite finished.' Malcolm's strained voice came from the front of the boat. 'I think my arms are about tae seize up.'

∞∞∞

'Do you think Duncan MacFarlane will succeed?' Peter asked.

Brendon nodded. 'He seemed sure o' his support. An' it's nae a secret that Alistair MacFarlane be daft in the heid. Ah doot there'll be much fightin'.

'And there will be no reprisals?' Peter Sinclair asked, relief clearly evident in his voice.

'Ah dinnae think so, ma lord. Though Duncan MacFarlane'll no doot be waitin' on his grace's public acknowledgement.'

The Viscount sighed and sagged back into his seat.

'We dare not let down our guard until we hear fer sure,' Malcolm reminded Peter.

'Be it time fer a wee dram yet?' Dougal croaked theatrically. 'Ma throat feels like it's gaunnae close up.'

'Well, that's a blessing if ever there was one,' declared the Reverend.

They were all gathered in the small sitting room. It was late, but no one could even think about retiring for bed. It was also more than a little overcrowded, especially as both Fergus and Flossy were curled up together in front of the fire.

Slowly the full sequence of events unfolded as each person added their part of the story.

The children had been put into the capable hands of MacNee and Mrs. Darroch. After a hot meal they had all been bedded down in one of the stables, though the housekeeper declared she would be organising baths first thing on the morrow. Finn had proved a capable assistant, taking time to reassure each of the children, and of course, living proof that they hadn't all come to another such as the MacFarlane.

What exactly would be done with the bairns was a decision for another day.

Malcolm was examining the pile of jewellery Dougal had gleefully tipped onto the table.

'Do you think it's genuine?' Jennifer asked.

'O' course it be genuine,' Dougal spluttered, clearly trying to keep the doubt from his voice.

'Aye, I really think it is,' Malcolm responded much to the old Scot's delight. 'But I dinnae think it belonged tae the likes o' Edward Colman. It doesnae look old enough. I reckon ye'll have tae get someone in tae tell ye true.'

'If I'm not stepping on your toes,' Peter interjected, 'I think we can get someone from London or Edinburgh to do the authentication. If you use the Blackmore name, you'll be much less likely to be taken in by an ivory tuner.'

Brendon gave a grateful nod. 'Ah wouldnae ken where tae start,' he admitted. 'In truth, the whole thing doesnae seem real.'

'You won't be wanting the job as steward any longer if the jewellery does turn out to be authentic,' Jennifer smiled. To her discomfort, the brief look Brendon gave her was expressionless, and she wondered if she'd somehow caused offence.

'What will you do with the footman?' Reverend Shackleford asked, changing the subject.

Peter grimaced. 'He kidnapped my sister after hitting her over the head hard enough to have killed her. By rights, I should simply hand him over to the magistrate.'

After rendering the traitorous footman unconscious, the Viscount had laid him non too gently over the back of his horse and returned to where Jennifer's mare was grazing unconcernedly. Tying the ex-servant's hands and feet with the same rope that was used to tie up his sister earlier, Peter had put the lame horse on a lead rein and returned to Caerlaverock, arriving much the same time as the two boats. When asked how he'd known where Jennifer was, he grinned and told them that Fergus had fetched him…

'Hoo aboot a wee dram tae celebrate fer when they string him up?' Dougal suggested.

'Be no more than the blackguard deserves,' sniffed the Reverend.

'I know you're right, Grandpapa, but I can't help feeling a little sorry for him. He was truly afraid of his Clan chief, and I cannot imagine being that terrified of someone who's supposed to be one's protector.'

'*Protector*?,' her grandfather scoffed. 'We have twenty-two bairns in a stable who can testify to that bag of moonshine.'

Jennifer nodded. 'I'm beginning to realise just how sheltered my upbringing has been. As Dougal said when we first began this endeavour, it's easy to ignore what's not put in front of one's nose.' She bit her lip before continuing softly, 'I'd like to help – with the children.'

'And I,' Felicity added, covering Jennifer's hand with hers. 'But not tonight dearest. It's been an extremely long day, and I'm surprised you haven't got a lump the size of Scotland on your head. If you'll allow me, I'll accompany you up to your room and put some salve on it.'

Jennifer laughed, then winced. 'You're right of course, Felicity. The thumping in my head is becoming harder to ignore.'

'Dae ye need tae see a doctor, ma lady?' Gifford asked, concern evident in his voice.

'Ah reckon a wee dram'll dae the trick much better than any leche,' Dougal tried again, this time rubbing his hands together for emphasis.

'Da, there'll be nae whisky this night,' Brendon finally ground out in exasperation. 'We've a long walk home.'

'Neither of you will be walking anywhere,' Peter declared firmly. 'I've had two spare rooms made up for you.' He paused and swallowed, sudden emotion gripping him. 'Do you have a favourite whisky, Dougal?'

The old Scot chuckled. 'Aye, a double,' he answered cheerfully.

∞∞∞

Whatever Felicity rubbed on her head eased the pain sufficiently that Jennifer slept like a babe, and on waking the following morning, she was relieved to find that the throbbing had lessened significantly.

Drawn by shouting coming from outside, she climbed carefully out of bed and went to the window. The children were already up and about, and Jennifer warmed to hear them laughing. Watching them play with Fergus and Flossy, she realised that some were missing, and those that were there were appreciably cleaner than when they'd arrived the day before. Likely, the rest of them were suffering the dreaded bath.

Knowing the wolfhound's presence meant Brendon wouldn't be far away, Jennifer leaned forward and finally caught sight of the handsome Scot watching the children from the periphery. The sight of him smiling brought back the enigmatic expression on his face when she spoke to him the night before, and abruptly she felt a strange sense of urgency. A need to see him as soon as possible.

Hurriedly, she turned and shrugged off her nightgown, pulling on an old woollen dress. Doubtless Jenet would be scandalised to see her dressing herself, but Jennifer didn't want to wait to be primped. Running a brush through her hair, she quickly tied it back with a ribbon and hastened out of the room.

∞∞∞

As he watched the children, Brendon abruptly found himself wondering what it would be like to have bairns of his own. He'd never had such thoughts before, mostly he suspected because his whole attention had been on ensuring he and his da managed to survive the next winter. A wife and child had always been out of the question.

But since Jennifer Sinclair had arrived and turned his heart inside out…

Brendon knew he was being a fool. No matter that she'd made her attraction abundantly clear. Ladies like her used the likes of him to warm their beds, not put bairns in their bellies.

*But what if the jewellery turned out to be genuine?*

Brendon drew in his breath sharply. He could ill afford to harbour the hope that the gold might make a difference to the Duke of Blackmore. What did his mother use to say? *Ye cannae make a purse oot o' a sow's ear*. No words had ever been truer.

Somehow, he had to put such thoughts of Jennifer Sinclair out of his mind. She might want him to bed her, but he simply couldn't do it. For him, it wasn't enough. It would *never* be enough.

As though his thoughts had conjured her up, Jennifer Sinclair suddenly appeared in the courtyard, and he drew in his breath. She was slightly dishevelled as if she'd only recently left her bed. Gone was the perfectly coiffured lady and in her place a wild sprite, perfectly at home in the woodlands and glens of the Highlands.

For the first time a glimmer of hope pierced his protective armour.

'Hoo ye be feelin' ma lady?' He asked as she came up beside him.

'Much better,' she answered, nodding towards the children with a smile. 'It's wonderful to see them so happy.'

'Aye, ma lady,' he responded a little huskily. 'This be a paradise compared tae where they hae come frae. But they cannae stay indefinitely. We'll need tae find them somewhere tae go. Ah reckon the nearest poorhouse be in Balloch.' He paused, then added, 'Ah be thinkin' tae use some' o' the jewellery Da foond tae pay fer their keep.'

Jennifer turned to the steward in dismay. 'We can't send them to the poorhouse,' she gasped. 'What on earth will happen to them?'

'There be twenty-two bairns,' Brendon sighed. 'What else dae we dae wi' 'em. At least the coin'll ensure they'll be fed and looked after.'

Jennifer gave a vehement shake of her head. 'Why can't we keep them here?' she asked. 'We could build a school, somewhere for them to live. Teach them a trade – something they'll be able to use when they're older.'

'It be a braw idea,' Brendon answered, his heart beginning to beat a little faster. 'But who'll oversee such an undertaking? There be no one at Caerlaverock wi' enough time on their hands tae dae it.'

Abruptly, all Jennifer's doubts and fears fell away. *This* was why she was here. *This* was the sense of purpose that had been missing in her life. A calmness enveloped her, but underneath it, elation was bubbling up. She gave a joyous laugh, and said simply, 'I'll do it.'

# Chapter Twenty-Two

'What do we do?' Grace whispered, trying very hard to hold back the panic. Her two oldest children were five hundred miles away and could even now be embroiled in a Clan war.'

Nicholas sighed and tossed the letters onto the table. Then he stepped towards his wife and enfolded her in his arms. 'They have Malcolm with them,' he soothed. 'His letter clearly states that he will not allow any harm to come to either Peter or Jennifer. He will give his life to protect them.'

'But what if he has to do just that?' Grace wailed into his chest. 'Child slavery, a clan chief who's dicked in the nob…' She trailed off and allowed the tears to fall.

The letters had been written three days earlier, the messenger arriving in the early hours, exhausted and white faced. Clearly, the man must have ridden almost nonstop to get to Blackmore so quickly.

'We will leave immediately,' Nicholas assured her. 'But in truth, by the time we get there, their intended rescue will have either succeeded or not and we'll be faced with the aftermath.' He stepped back and gripped Grace's arms. 'Look at me sweetheart,' he demanded gently. As she raised her tear-stained face, he said, 'Peter is a man grown. I trust him to deal with the situation. He has Malcolm, and, from what he said in the letter, Caerlaverock's new steward. He has assured me that he will not allow the situation to get out of hand. His only concern is to get the remaining children out of the mine as quickly and painlessly as possible. *He will not show his hand.*'

Grace bit her lip, then sniffed and nodded. 'Felicity said how like you Peter is.' Then she gave a watery smile and added, 'I only hope he doesn't allow Jenny to get involved.'

'Rest assured, dearest, he will lock her up if he has to – he said that in the letter too.'

∞∞∞

The rest of the day passed in a blur of activity, and Jennifer had no time to discuss her proposal to her brother. Likely that was a good thing she told herself. A decision as life changing as the one she'd just made should first be discussed with her parents – not least because Peter was liable to declare her addled.

Neither had she had the time to speak further with Brendon. No mention was made of what had happened between them, and Jennifer was beginning to wonder whether she'd imagined their connection. Oh, not on her side, but perhaps what she'd chosen to believe was love on Brendon's side, had been nothing more than the scratching of an itch. Then she remembered his endearment while they were in the loch.

He'd called her sweetheart. And she could still see the look in his eyes as he'd said it. He may not realise it yet, but Brendon Galbraith was as much in love with her as she was with him.

She just needed to convince him of it - preferably before her parents arrived...

Of course, underneath the relief that they'd been successful in rescuing all twenty-two children, they were anxiously awaiting news from the MacFarlane Clan. Had Duncan MacFarlane succeeded in his bid to take over as the Chieftain? Until they knew for sure, it was essential they remain ready for whatever revenge Alistair MacFarlane might decide to seek. If he was still in command, he was almost certainly aware by now that the children were gone.

Their six *footmen* had been rounded up in Banalan and brought back to Caerlaverock where Peter and Malcolm informed them of everything that had happened. Under their leader's watchful eyes, the men were currently cleaning their weapons and scouring the small armoury for anything that might be useful should a confrontation arise.

Then, an hour before sunset, a rider was spotted on the Lochside, another horse trailing behind him on a lead rein.

Ordering Chapman to keep his men out of sight, Peter gave instructions to allow the stranger entry through the main gate before heading outside flanked by Malcolm and Brendon.

The next ten minutes felt like hours as the three men waited for the visitor to reach the courtyard. They'd been unable to determine whether the man was wearing MacFarlane colours, though judging by the fracas taking place in the sitting room to the Viscount's left, the Reverend and Dougal were still fighting over the field glasses.

At length, the man's mount trotted underneath the archway, finally halting in the middle of the courtyard. Peter's heart slammed against his ribs as he recognised the MacFarlane colours.

'I am Viscount Holsworthy, Heir Apparent to the Duke of Blackmore. What brings you to Caerlaverock?' His voice was self-assured - aloof but not hostile - and Brendon felt a surge of admiration. Truly, Peter Sinclair would be a formidable successor to his father when the time finally came.

In answer, the rider climbed down from his horse and strode

towards them, stopping a full six feet away.

'Ah hae a message fer the Laird,' he growled.

Peter felt the sweat form in the centre of his back. 'I am the Laird's representative,' he answered. 'You may give the message to me.'

A small silence, then, 'The MacFarlane bids me tell ye it be done.' He stared pointedly at all three men, before adding, 'An' he be lookin' forrit tae speakin' wi' his grace verra soon.' Without waiting for a response, he returned to his horse and swiftly remounted – no mean feat without a mounting block.

Untying, then dropping the lead rein of the horse standing behind him, the warrior spoke directly to Brendon. 'The beast be yer da's. Ah'm tae tell ye, we used the wagon fer firewood.'

And with that, he turned his mount about and seconds later was gone

∞∞∞

That night's dinner was the most lighthearted since arriving at Caerlaverock.

Peter especially felt as though the weight of the entire world had fallen from his shoulders. As much as part of him had relished the challenge, there was another, admittedly smaller, childish part that longed to lay the burden at his father's feet. The Viscount gave a dark chuckle and took a sip of his wine. Clearly, his father had not anticipated his son and heir's first unaccompanied visit to Scotland would be quite such a baptism of fire…

Brendon, Dougal and Gifford had been invited for dinner, and despite grumbling that the wee bairns were giein her more trouble than they be worth, Mrs. Darroch had made sure that the cook produced a meal worthy of a king.

'When do you think Mama and Papa will arrive?' Jennifer asked Peter, who in turn looked at Malcolm. The Scot gave a wicked grin. 'Would ye care tae lay a bet on it ladies and gentlemen?' he demanded, using his best carnival voice. 'I say their graces will be here in exactly a sennight.'

'Who's keeping record?' laughed Peter, getting into the spirit of things.

'Being a man of the cloth, I'd better be the one laying the odds,' Reverend Shackleford declared piously, rummaging around his cassock for the piece of charcoal he and Dougal had used to such effect on Inveruglas.

With much laughter they each declared a date at which they believed the Duke and Duchess would arrive and the wager they were prepared to put on it.

Jennifer surreptitiously watched Brendon as the banter continued. He looked more relaxed and animated than she'd ever seen him. Mayhap worrying about the children had been weighing more heavily on him than she'd realised. Then she thought back to the moment she'd announced her intention to stay in Caerlaverock, to the subtle loosening of his stance as he'd listened to her ideas. Slowly, she felt a sense of rightness, of belonging, which she'd never experienced before. And she knew, without doubt, that she was the reason for his sudden ease.

Getting him to admit it though might be an uphill struggle. Nevertheless, she was up to the challenge…

∞∞∞

Something had been bothering Reverend Shackleford, ever since he'd felt that brief sense of things slotting into place. He didn't know why he should feel quite so surprised. After all, he regularly told his congregation that the Almighty moved in mysterious ways, and he himself had seen evidence of it on more occasions than he could count.

Sitting in front of the fire, his thoughts went to his oldest friend. He hated to say it, but Percy did not possess the resourcefulness of Dougal Galbraith – or the wiliness. Sometimes he thought his curate might well be too good for this world. Though he may never have actually said it, the Reverend was glad Percy had found Lizzy. They were perfect together, and in truth, she was much more a clergyman's wife than Agnes would ever be.

Then he thought back to the slight sadness he'd often noticed in her eyes when she watched the many children that seemed to be continually visiting Blackmore - too deuced many of them in the Reverend's opinion.

Percy and Lizzy had never had any children. It could have been that they'd been too old by the time they wed, but Reverend Shackleford didn't think it was by choice. In fairness, it wasn't a subject that ever came up during the times he and Percy spent at the Red Lion.

And, if he was being entirely honest, the Reverend had never really given it a second thought, until now.

What would they do if he turned up at Blackmore with Finn in tow?

Earlier, when he'd taken his customary stroll around the garden, the lad had sought him out again, specifically to be a pain in the arse as far as the Reverend could tell. But just before the boy left, he'd repeated his desire to go to Blackmore.

Was Finn's wish simply eggs in the moonshine, or could he possibly find a home with Percy and Lizzy?

∞ ∞ ∞

The next day Jennifer rose early, determination fuelling her feet.

While she'd thought to keep her own counsel until her parents arrived, she'd realised, lying awake in the early hours, that she would have to share at least some of her ideas with Peter if only to halt the process of finding the children somewhere to go. Caerlaverock certainly wasn't equipped to house so many youngsters for any length of time, but Jennifer knew that once the children went to the poorhouse, they might very well be lost. And she was determined that that wouldn't happen.

Organisation was the key.

Five hours later, Peter declared her the bossiest woman alive.

Jennifer knew her brother didn't really expect her to remain in Scotland, despite their earlier discussion about her feelings for Brendon. Neither had broached the subject since – though in truth, there hadn't really been the time – but when she sought him out to sow the seeds of her plan for the children, she could see in his eyes the gradual realisation of her intention, though neither voiced it. There was time enough for that when their parents arrived.

Next on her list was Brendon. He might be more at ease knowing she wouldn't be leaving Caerlaverock at the end of the month as planned, but that didn't mean he now believed they could be together.

It was time she put an end to his foolishness.

When she asked MacNee if he'd seen Brendon, the butler told her he understood Mr. Galbraith to be down at the old boathouse. Perfect.

Without telling anyone where she was going, Jennifer shrugged on her shawl and headed in search of her husband-to-be...

As she approached the wooden structure, she could hear someone – presumably Brendon – hammering. As she reached the door, there was a sudden pause and a muttered expletive. Thinking he might have hurt himself, Jennifer shoved the door open and promptly fell over the lengths of wood that were lying in front of it.

As she rolled over onto her back with a groan, she heard him swear again, and drop his tools. Seconds later he was crouching down next to her prone form. 'What dae ye think ye be doin'?' he quizzed her, unconsciously repeating the words from their first meeting. Only this time instead of adding the word *eejit*, he used her name. '*Jenny.*'

She made no attempt to move. Indeed, she didn't think she'd be able to – even if she tried. It wasn't because she'd been injured, but rather the realisation that he *wasn't wearing a shirt*. Speechless, she gazed up at his naked torso, her eyes travelling wonderingly from the hard planes of his stomach up to the solid muscle of his chest. The whole area was covered in a smattering of coal black curling hair that started at his belly button. She couldn't breathe.

The slightly amused look on his face turned abruptly to concern. 'Jennifer,' he barked, 'be ye injured?' He leaned down over her, his hands placed flat on the wooden floor, arms bent as he searched her face.

Without thought, Jennifer reached up and slid her arms around his neck, and this time, instead of tugging him towards her, she pulled herself upwards until her breasts were flattened against his naked chest and shamelessly, pressed her lips against his. There was the briefest of pauses, then with a low groan, his mouth opened over hers and he leaned back onto his haunches, taking her with him, his arms wrapping tightly around her back.

This time Brendon didn't hold back. His mouth plundered hers as though clinging to a life raft as their kiss finally turned into an all-consuming melding of mouths that demanded nothing less than his complete and utter surrender.

Brendon Galbraith was hers, now and always.

## Chapter Twenty-Three

The wager was eventually won by the Reverend, and as he watched the Blackmore carriage clatter into the courtyard, less than four days later, he couldn't help reflecting that mayhap he knew his daughter a little better than he'd previously thought.

As soon as Grace was helped down from the carriage, Jennifer blinked back a sudden onset of tears and ran over to embrace her mother. Indeed, by the time they stepped apart, both women were crying unashamedly.

As Peter stepped forward to greet his father, he too felt like bursting into tears. Instead, he gave a small bow and held out his hand. But Nicholas was having none of it. Without saying a word, he stepped forward and enveloped his son in an embrace that spoke volumes. 'That was the longest journey of my life,' he growled.

Grace turned towards Felicity who'd been hanging back, allowing their graces the time to reassure themselves that their offspring were not missing any limbs. The Duchess held out her hands, and with a smile, the matron stepped forward and clasped them in hers. 'Thank God you were here, Felicity,' Grace breathed.

'Err, excuse me, dearest Mama,' Jennifer objected, 'I am not entirely bacon brained you know.'

Felicity laughed and gave the young woman an arch look. 'I've taken the liberty of asking Mrs. Darroch to bring a pot of tea and some of the cook's wonderful shortbread into the sitting room,' she told Grace. 'Though I think perhaps Nicholas might wish for something a little stronger by the time he's heard the whole story...'

Grace nodded gratefully. 'I remember Mrs. Allen's shortbread,' she enthused. The three women linked arms and headed inside.

'I don't need to have the whole story now,' Nicholas was saying to Peter and Malcolm, 'but can you just tell me whether there is anything I need to be truly concerned about?'

Malcolm shook his head. 'I dinnae think so, yer grace. Yer son here did ye proud.'

'There is of course the slight problem of twenty-two children residing in the main stable,' Peter interrupted with a grin.

∞∞∞

It took them until late afternoon to relate the whole story, and at the end of it, her father was certainly paler than he had been when they started. However, all he'd said was, 'Obviously, I don't like the idea of being held to ransom, especially by someone I have no knowledge of. Is this Duncan MacFarlane likely to keep to his promise?'

Malcolm shrugged. 'I dinnae think he'll be any worse than Alistair MacFarlane.' Nicholas nodded slowly and turned to his son.

'You handled things as I would have done,' he stated simply, and for that you have my thanks.' From his father, ever a man of few words, it was high praise indeed. Peter reddened slightly and sat a little taller in his chair.

'Goodness, don't say anything further,' Jennifer laughed. 'He won't be able to get his head through the door.'

'You are equally deserving of my thanks, Jenny,' her father continued seriously. He paused before adding, 'As are you Augustus, and you Felicity.' His voice had turned a little husky, and Grace gripped his hand tightly. 'I cannot tell you what a relief it is to know that you've all come through such an ordeal unscathed and that Caerlaverock was and is in such capable hands.'

To Jennifer's relief, he said nothing about her impetuously taking off after the traitorous footman on her own, but she had no doubt the lecture would come…

'Are ye ready fer a whisky yet, Nick?' Malcolm grinned, clapping his hand on his old friend's shoulder.

The Duke gave a rueful laugh and nodded. 'So where is our new steward and his err … intriguing father?' he asked. 'I had thought they would be here.'

'I might call Dougal Galbraith many things,' the Reverend snorted, 'but intriguing is definitely not one of them. Likely he's currently helping himself to some of Mrs. Allen's tablet.'

'Brendon is down at the old boathouse I believe,' Jennifer added. Remembering the intimacy they'd shared there just two days earlier, she felt herself going pink and knew well her mother would not have missed it.

'It hasn't been used in years,' Peter explained, 'and the only reason the boat in there hasn't sunk is because it's resting on the bottom of the loch. I asked Brendon to make the whole thing safe in case any other waifs and strays should think to spend the night there.'

'Are there any foundlings left in the area?' Nicholas questioned drily.

Jennifer drew in her breath. This was it. The perfect time to bring up her plan. She gripped her hands together nervously and gave a small cough. When all eyes had turned towards her, she swallowed and managed, 'It's interesting you should say that, Papa… In truth, I… I've actually had an idea…'

∞∞∞

Both her parents had been cautiously optimistic about the idea of building a boarding school on the estate, providing someone could be found to manage such an ambitious project. Indeed, Jennifer was gratified when everyone in the room began enthusiastically contributing their opinions about the best way forward.

'Have you asked Brendon Galbraith what he thinks about the idea?' the Duchess asked suddenly.

'Naturally we have spoken about it,' Jennifer stammered, 'but like you, he thinks it will take a lot of planning…'

'Not to mention money,' her father added wryly.

'I believe it's Brendon's wish to use some of the money from the jewellery found on Inveruglas to help fund the building work,' Jennifer clarified carefully. 'But that's only if the jewels are found to be genuine, of course.'

Nicholas nodded thoughtfully. 'I think I would like to talk to our new steward – sooner rather than later.' He turned to Peter. 'Would you object if I asked him to finish his work for the day and return to the house to speak with me?'

Jennifer's heart slammed against her ribs. Peter was nodding his head. 'I think it's an excellent idea,' he answered. 'I'm certain you'll be most impressed with Brendon. Truly, Father, we could not have rescued the children without his help.'

'Aye,' added Malcolm, 'the lad's a rare one. I'd trust him wi' ma life. Indeed, I did – on several occasions. Ye'll like him, Nick.'

And though she desperately wished to be privy to the conversation, Jennifer found herself outside the room without quite knowing how she'd got there.

Damn, she'd forgotten how good her parents were at acting in unison when they wanted to be rid of someone…

Jennifer was drying her hair by the fire when there was a knock on the door. She'd been expecting it for some time. She had not seen Brendon, despite lurking upstairs on the landing while he was closeted in the sitting room with her father. She'd then spent the whole of her bath wondering what they had spoken about. Had she figured at all in the conversation? Somehow, she doubted it.

What she didn't doubt was her mother's absolute awareness of what she hadn't said – hence the knock.

Sighing, Jennifer climbed to her feet and went to the door. As she expected, her mother was standing on the other side. With a rueful smile, Jennifer stepped to one side, and her mother, every bit the Duchess, swept into the room. It was clearly going to be one of those conversations…

∞∞∞

'She wishes to remain at Caerlaverock,' Grace declared, walking back into their bedchamber.

'Why am I not surprised. I take it she also wishes to marry the steward?' Grace nodded, lying down on top of the bed next to him. In truth, she didn't know whether she wanted to laugh or cry.

'What is he like?' she asked instead.

'Honourable. In fact, if he had any more honour, he'd be unable to sit down.' Nicholas shook his head and sighed. 'I'm being unfair. The truth is, I liked him. Very much. And had I not known he had designs on my daughter, I would be ecstatically happy to leave Caerlaverock in his capable hands.'

'I think the boot is actually on the other foot,' his wife commented drily, 'and be honest dearest, if Jennifer has set her heart on him, the poor love doesn't stand a chance.'

'He's hardly what I'd hoped for,' Nicholas responded. 'He lives in a rundown tower with his father, who is, according to Augustus, a mutton-headed chawbacon.'

'Truly, it takes one to know one,' Grace answered tartly. She turned on to her side, facing her husband. 'We've always known that Jenny would never settle for someone too high on the instep, and as difficult as it is to say this, we both know that Caerlaverock suits her. She's never looked so well.

'She doesn't want the life of an indolent aristocrat, Nick. She wants to make a difference.' She gave a general wave around the room. 'Here, she can do that, and I believe Brendon Galbraith will stand right beside her.'

Nicholas was silent for a while, his eyes half closed, deep in thought. In truth, he'd long been troubled that he did not have more time to spend at Caerlaverock. The estate deserved much more attention than he was able to give it. A school for foundlings was an admirable idea. He was consumed with sudden awe for his spirited daughter. Truly, she was one of a kind.

He opened his eyes and turned his head towards Grace. 'Caerlaverock was built on what was, once upon a time, Galbraith land,' he commented mildly. 'Mayhap it's time the two families finally took possession together.'

∞∞∞

The next day, Nicholas sent for Jennifer just after breakfast. As she entered the room, seating herself gracefully opposite the desk at which he sat, Nicholas experienced a momentary pang. His daughter was a beautiful woman and would have been an asset to any drawing room in the land. Soon, he guessed, she would be attired in clothes much better suited to the lifestyle she'd chosen. Never again would she sparkle in the ballrooms of the *ton*...

Abruptly, Nicholas's thoughts screeched to a halt. What the bloody hell was he thinking? He couldn't even remember a ball where Jennifer had actually sparkled – except perhaps the one last November which had purportedly been held to remember the gunpowder plot over two hundred years earlier. As he remembered, Jennifer had set one of the drapes alight, and it had cost him a pretty penny to replace them – especially as the Baron in question was a penny-pinching, old toad-eater who'd last replaced the curtains at the coronation of King George III.

He found himself chuckling as Jennifer looked at him enquiringly. Strange how when one stopped trying to manipulate life, it very often worked out exactly as it was supposed to...

'May ah remind ye that ah've nae actually asked ye tae marry me,' was Brendon's comment an hour later.'

Jennifer waved an airy hand. 'No matter, I'm perfectly happy to do the asking,' she responded with a chuckle.

'Ye'll dae nothin o' the sort,' he retorted, glaring down at her in outrage. 'Ye tell me their graces hae given their permission, but they hae nae gaen it tae me. Ah'll speak wi' yer da this eenin…' He broke off with a whoomph as she threw herself at his chest. His lips quirked as he looked down at her, his eyes plainly revealing his happiness.

'But dinnae be thinking ah'll be sharing yer bed until we be handfasted…'

∞∞∞

The handfasting took place a mere three weeks later. It was a simple ceremony during which both Brendon and Jennifer wrapped a piece of cloth around their clasped hands and declared their wish to be husband and wife in front of two witnesses.

Unfortunately perhaps, the two witnesses they chose were Brendon's da and Jennifer's grandfather. A muttering of, 'Deuced heathen practices,' and, 'Ah dinnae ken what the world be coming tae, wedding a bloody Sassenach,' certainly didn't do much to encourage the romance of the moment. Nevertheless, both men had to concede that they'd never seen a couple look so happy.

And while the wedding breakfast was suitably formal as befitted the marriage of the Laird of Caerlaverock's daughter, the ceilidh that came afterwards was anything but. Indeed, with Dougal's instruction, the Reverend discovered a hitherto unimagined flair for Highland dancing and what's more, he vowed to teach Agnes as soon as he was back home in Blackmore…

# Chapter Twenty-Four

Naturally there also had to be a good old fashioned Anglican wedding.

Jennifer travelled home with her parents in advance of Brendon who announced he couldn't possibly have the father of the groom dressed in a kilt that last looked to have been washed not long after Culloden. Before leaving, the Reverend had quietly had a private word suggesting the groom also purchase a clean pair of drawers since the ones Dougal was wearing had clearly never been washed at all…

To Augustus Shackleford the journey back to Blackmore had been the longest of his entire life. Even Flossy had taken to curling up under the seat, her head firmly tucked underneath her paws. Dear God, he'd forgotten just how much children could talk – or mayhap he'd never actually been stuck in a carriage with one for nigh on a sennight before.

He could swear that Finn never stopped. From the moment they climbed into the carriage at Caerlaverock to the moment they stepped out of it at the vicarage. He had no idea what he'd do if Percy refused to take the lad. Agnes would likely leave him… He paused and thought for a moment. Clearly, every cloud had a silver lining.

Still, at the end of the day, he needn't have worried. He'd taken Finn to visit, and almost from the onset, both Percy and Lizzy had been captivated by the lad - although what they actually saw in him was anybody's guess. As far as the Reverend was concerned, the boy's only saving grace was his partiality to bread-and-butter pudding.

As with every other Shackleford wedding – although the villagers were quick to point out that, in actual fact, this was a *Sinclair* wedding and much more genteel – the whole of Blackmore was invited, and for one day, the high and mighty (not to mention the good and the great) mixed with the commoners – and of course the rest of the Shacklefords, who, as always, provided the entertainment.

Everyone agreed that the bride was a vision and the groom looked very handsome, even though he was wearing a skirt and had an accent that absolutely no one could understand apart from Mary Noon who had apparently courted a man from Glasgow in another life.

So, all in all, the wedding turned out to be a corker, which was no more than the Blackmore residents had come to expect from their Duke and Duchess. Indeed, as the villagers were staggering home, they were already taking bets as to who would be next.

**THE END**

The Reverend and the rest of the family will return in *Mercedes - Book Two of The Shackleford Legacies*, to be released on 19th September 2024.

# Author's Notes

Naturally I have taken some liberties with history.

Caerlaverock does exist, but in reality it's a thirteenth century castle situated near to Dumfries. The estate has been privately owned by the same family for over 800 years. If you're interested, you can learn more about it, by copying and pasting the link below into your browser:

https://caerlaverock.com

Both Clan Galbraith and Clan MacFarlane are real and were based around Loch Lomond. Both Inveraglus and Inchgalbraith do exist and were originally strongholds of the aforementioned clans, though Dougal and Brendon Galbraith and the Chieftain Alistair MacFarlane are complete figments of my imagination. You can find out more about the clans of Loch Lomond and The Trossachs by copying and pasting the link below into your browser:

https://www.seelochlomond.co.uk/discover/clans-of-loch-lomond

https://www.scotclans.com/blogs/clans-f/galbraith-clan-history

There really was an Edward Colman who was hung drawn and

quartered as a traitor, though the only item that has been found belonging to him is a gold ring. It was discovered at Balloch on the shores of Loch Lomond. The rest is entirely fiction. If you're interested, you can read more about him by copying and pasting the link below into your browser:

https://en.wikipedia.org/wiki/Edward_Colman_(martyr)

https://www.bbc.co.uk/news/uk-scotland-glasgow-west-49653771

If you're interested in visiting Loch Lomond and the Trossach National Park, I'm certain you won't be disappointed (though visiting outside of midgie season is definitely recommended). I must clarify however, that neither Banalan, nor Mosslea exist as far as I'm aware.

You can find out a little more about the area by visiting the website below:

https://www.visitscotland.com/things-to-do/landscapes-nature/national-parks/loch-lomond-trossachs

Lastly, I tried to make the Scottish accent as authentic as possible without being completely incomprehensible - no mean feat I assure you! I hope I largely succeeded and could never have done it without the following website. If you fancy taking a look, it really is fascinating.

https://stooryduster.co.uk/scottish-words-glossary/words-f.htm

# Keeping in Touch

Thank you so much for reading Jennifer I really hope you enjoyed it. For any of you who'd like to connect, I'd really love to hear from you. Feel free to contact me via my facebook page:
https://www.facebook.com/beverleywattsromanticcomedyauthor
or my website: www.beverleywatts.com

*Mercedes - Book Two of The Shackleford Legacies* will be released on 19th September 2024

And lastly, if you're enjoying the Shackleford world and don't want to wait until *Mercedes* is released you might be interested to know that I have a series of romantic comedies set in beautiful South Devon, featuring the Great, Great, Great, Great, Great Grandson of the Reverend. In this series he's an eccentric, retired Admiral who, like the Reverend would be in if he fell in…

The series is titled *The Dartmouth Diaries* and in *Book One: Claiming Victory*, the Admiral is determined to marry off his only daughter, Victory. Keep reading for a sneak peek…

## Claiming Victory

'At thirty two, Victory Shackleford is undeniably overweight, arguably frumpish and the only romance in her life is provided by her dog. She still lives at home with her father - an eccentric retired Admiral who she considers reckless, irresponsible, and totally incapable of looking after himself.
Her father on the other hand thinks Victory is a boring nagging harpy with no imagination or sense of adventure and what's more, he's determined to get her married off.
Unfortunately there's no one in the picturesque yachting town of Dartmouth that Tory is remotely interested in, despite her father's best efforts. But all that is about to change when she discovers that her madcap father has rented out their house as a location shoot for the biggest Hollywood blockbuster of the year. As cast and crew descend, Tory's humdrum orderly existence is turned completely upside down, especially as the lead actor has just been voted the sexiest man on the planet...'

## Chapter One

Retired Admiral, Charles Shackleford, entered the dimly lit interior of his favourite watering hole. Once inside, he waited a second for his eyes to adjust, and glanced around to check that his ageing Springer spaniel was already seated beside his stool at the bar. Pickles had disappeared into the undergrowth half a mile back, as they walked along the wooded trail high above the picturesque River Dart. The scent of some poor unfortunate rabbit had caught his still youthful nose. The Admiral was not unduly worried; this was a regular occurrence, and Pickles knew his way to the Ship Inn better than his master.

Satisfied that all was as it should be for a Friday lunchtime, Admiral Shackleford waved to the other regulars, and made his way to his customary seat at the bar where his long standing, and long suffering friend, Jimmy Noon, was already halfway down his first pint.

'You're a bit late today Sir,' observed Jimmy, after saluting his former commanding officer smartly.

Charles Shackleford grunted as he heaved his ample bottom onto the bar stool. 'Got bloody waylaid by that bossy daughter of mine.' He sighed dramatically before taking a long draft of his pint of real ale, which was ready and waiting for him. 'Damn bee in her bonnet since she found out about my relationship with Mabel Pomfrey. Of course, I told her to mind her own bloody business, but it has to be said that the cat's out of the bag, and no mistake.'

He stared gloomily down into his pint. 'She said it cast aspersions on her poor mother's memory. But what she doesn't understand Jimmy, is that I'm still a man in my prime. I've got needs. I mean look at me – why can't she see that I'm still a fine figure of a man, and any woman would be more than happy to shack up with me.'

Abruptly, the Admiral turned towards his friend so the light shone directly onto his face and leaned forward. 'Come on then man, tell me you agree.'

Jimmy took a deep breath as he dubiously regarded the watery eyes, thread veined cheeks, and larger than average nose no more than six inches in front of him

However, before he could come up with a suitably acceptable reply that wouldn't result in him standing to attention for the next four hours in front of the Admiral's dishwasher, the

Admiral turned away, either indicating it was purely a rhetorical question, or he genuinely couldn't comprehend that anyone could possibly regard him as less than a prime catch.

Jimmy sighed with relief. He really hadn't got time this afternoon to do dishwasher duty as he'd agreed to take his wife shopping. Although to be fair, a four hour stint in front of an electrical appliance at the Admiral's house, with Tory sneaking him tea and biscuits, was actually preferable to four hours trailing after his wife in Marks and Spencer's. He didn't think his wife would see it that way though. Emily Noon had enough trouble understanding her husband's tolerance towards 'that dinosaur's' eccentricities as it was.

Of course, Emily wasn't aware that only the quick thinking of the dinosaur in question had, early on in their naval career, saved her husband from a potentially horrible fate involving a Thai prostitute who'd actually turned out to be a man...

As far as Jimmy was concerned, Admiral Shackleford was his Commanding Officer, and always would be, and if that involved such idiosyncrasies as presenting himself in front of a dishwasher with headphones on, saluting and saying, 'Dishwasher manned and ready sir.' Then four hours later, saluting again while saying, 'Dishwasher secured,' so be it.

It was a small price to pay...

He leaned towards his morose friend and patted him on the back, showing a little manly support (acceptable, even from subordinates), while murmuring, 'Don't worry about it too much Sir. Tory's a sensible girl. She'll come round eventually – you know she wants you to be happy.' The Admiral's only response was an inelegant snort, so Jimmy ceased his patting, and went back to his pint.

Both men gazed into their drinks for a few minutes, as if all the answers would be found in the amber depths.

'What she needs is a man.' Jimmy's abrupt observation drew another rude snort, this one even louder.

'Who do you suggest? She's not interested in anyone. Says there's no one in Dartmouth she'd give house room to, and believe me I've tried. When she's not giving me grief, she spends all her time in that bloody gallery with all those airy fairy types. Can't imagine any one of them climbing her rigging. Not one set of balls between 'em.' Jimmy chuckled at the Admiral's description of Tory's testosterone challenged male friends.

'She's not ugly though,' Charles Shackleford mused, still staring into his drink. 'She might have an arse the size of an aircraft carrier, but she's got her mother's top half which balances it out nicely.'

'Aye, she's built a bit broad across the beam,' Jimmy agreed nodding his head.

'And then there's this bloody film crew. I haven't told her yet.' Jimmy frowned at the abrupt change of subject and shot a puzzled glance over to the Admiral.

'Film crew? What film crew?'

Charles Shackleford looked back irritably. 'Come on Jimmy, get a grip. I'm talking about that group of nancies coming to film at the house next month. I must have mentioned it.'

Jimmy simply shook his head in bewilderment.

Frowning at his friend's obtuseness, the Admiral went on, 'You know, what's that bloody film they're making at the moment – big blockbuster everyone's talking about?'

'What, you mean The Bridegroom?'

'That's the one. Seems like they were looking for a large house overlooking the River Dart. Think they were hoping for Greenway, you know, Agatha Christie's place, but then they spied "the Admiralty" and said it was spot on. Paying me a packet they are. Coming next week.'

Jimmy stared at his former commanding officer with something approaching pity. 'And you've arranged all this without telling Tory?'

'None of her bloody business,' the Admiral blustered, banging his now empty pint glass on the bar, and waving at the barmaid for a refill. 'She's out most of the time anyway.'

Jimmy shook his head in disbelief. 'When are you going to tell her?'

'Was going to do it this morning, but then this business with Mabel came up so I scarpered. Last I saw she was taking that bloody little mongrel of hers out for a walk. Hoping she'll walk off her temper.' His tone indicated he considered there was more likelihood of hell freezing over.

'Is Noah Westbrook coming?' said Jimmy, suddenly sensing a bit of gossip he could pass on to Emily.

'Noah who?' was the Admiral's bewildered response.

'Noah Westbrook. Come on Sir, you must know him. He's the most famous actor in the world. Women go completely gaga over him. If nothing else, that should make Tory happy.'

The Admiral stared at him thoughtfully. 'What's he look like, this Noah West... chappy?'

The barmaid, who had been unashamedly listening to the whole conversation, couldn't contain herself any longer and, thrusting a glossy magazine under the Admiral's nose, said breathlessly, 'Like this. He looks like this.'

The full colour photograph was that of a naked man lounging on a sofa, with only a towel protecting his modesty, together with the caption "Noah Westbrook, officially voted the sexiest man on the planet."

Admiral Charles Shackleford stared pensively down at the picture in front of him. 'So this Noah chap – he's in this film is he?'

'He's got the lead role.' The bar maid actually twittered causing the Admiral to look up in irritation – bloody woman must be fifty if she's a day. Shooting her a withering look, he went back to the magazine, and read the beginning of the article inside.

"Noah Westbrook is to be filming in the South West of England over the next month, causing a sudden flurry of bookings to hotels and guest houses in the South Devon area."

The Admiral continued to stare at the photo, the germination of an idea tiptoeing around the edges of his brain. Glancing up, he discovered he was the subject of scrutiny from not just the barmaid, but now the whole pub was waiting with bated breath to hear what he was going to say next.

The Admiral's eyes narrowed as the beginnings of a plan slowly began taking shape, but he needed to keep it under wraps. Looking around at his rapt audience, he feigned nonchalance. 'Don't think Noah Westbrook was mentioned at all in the correspondence. Think he must be filming somewhere else.'

Then, without saying anything further, he downed the rest of his drink, and climbed laboriously off his stool.

'Coming Jimmy, Pickles?' His tone was deceptively casual which fooled Jimmy not at all, and, sensing something momentous afoot, the smaller man swiftly finished his pint. In his haste to follow the Admiral out of the door, he only narrowly avoided falling over Pickles who, completely unappreciative of the need for urgency, was sitting in the middle of the floor, scratching unconcernedly behind his ear.

Once outside, the Admiral didn't bother waiting for his dog, secure in the knowledge that someone would let the elderly spaniel out before he got too far down the road. Instead, he took hold of Jimmy's arm, and dragged him out of earshot – just in case anyone was listening.

In complete contrast to his mood on arrival, Charles Shackleford was now grinning from ear to ear. 'That's it. I've finally got a plan,' he hissed to his bewildered friend. 'I'm going to get her married off.'

'Who to?' asked Jimmy confused.

'Don't be so bloody slow Jimmy. To him of course. The actor chappy, Noah Westbrook. According to that magazine, women everywhere fall over themselves for him. Even Victory won't be able to resist him.'

Jimmy opened his mouth but nothing came out. He stared in complete disbelief as the Admiral went on. 'Then she'll move out, and Mabel can move in. Simple.'

Pickles came ambling up as Jimmy finally found his voice. 'So, let me get this straight Sir. Your plan is to somehow get Noah Westbrook, the most famous actor on the entire planet to fall in love with your daughter Victory, who we both love dearly, but - and please don't take offence Sir - who you yourself admit is built generously across the aft, and whose face is unlikely to launch the Dartmouth ferry, let alone a thousand ships.'

The Admiral frowned. 'Well admittedly, I've not worked out the finer details, but that's about the sum of it. What do you think…?'

*Claiming Victory* is available from Amazon.

# Books available on Amazon

## The Shackleford Sisters

*Book 1 - Grace*

*Book 2 - Temperance*

*Book 3 - Faith*

*Book 4 - Hope*

*Book 5 - Patience*

*Book 6 - Charity*

*Book 7 - Chastity*

*Book 8 - Prudence*

*Book 9 - Anthony*

## The Shackleford Legacies

*Book 1 - Jennifer*

*Book 2 - Mercedes will be released on 19th September 2024*

## The Dartmouth Diaries:

*Book 1 - Claiming Victory*

Book 2 - Sweet Victory

Book 3 - All for Victory

Book 4 - Chasing Victory

Book 5 - Lasting Victory

Book 6 - A Shackleford Victory

Book 7 - Final Victory will be released on 13th December 2024

## The Admiral Shackleford Mysteries

Book 1 - A Murderous Valentine

Book 2 - A Murderous Marriage

Book 3 - A Murderous Season

## Standalone Titles

An Officer and a Gentleman Wanted

# About The Author

## Beverley Watts

Beverley spent 8 years teaching English as a Foreign Language to International Military Students in Britannia Royal Naval College, the Royal Navy's premier officer training establishment in the UK. She says that in the whole 8 years there was never a dull moment and many of her wonderful experiences at the College were not only memorable but were most definitely 'the stuff of fiction.' Her debut novel An Officer And A Gentleman Wanted is very loosely based on her adventures at the College.

Beverley particularly enjoys writing books that make people laugh and currently she has three series of Romantic Comedies, both contemporary and historical, as well as a humorous cosy mystery series under her belt.

She lives with her husband in an apartment overlooking the sea on the beautiful English Riviera. Between them they have 3 adult children and two gorgeous grandchildren plus a menagerie of animals including 4 dogs - 3 Romanian rescues of indeterminate breed called Florence, Trixie, and Lizzie, and a 'Chichon" named Dotty who was the inspiration for Dotty in The Dartmouth Diaries.

You can find out more about Beverley's books at www.beverleywatts.com

Printed in Great Britain
by Amazon